Dedication

Writing a book is quite an undertaking. In fact, the process is a long and tedious journey. Throughout this expedition, my wife, Colette, has been my constant companion and friend. Faithfully and tirelessly over the past year, she has read and edited my manuscript more times than I can count. Equally important, she encouraged me to persevere at times when I was weary. Chances are you might not be reading this book without her ongoing support. With that said, I dedicate this book to her, and despite my name being on the cover, this was a beautiful collaboration.

STRANDED
IN
THE WILD

Book One

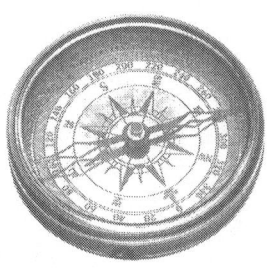

Gary Rodriguez

Published by LeaderMetrix Inc.

ISBN: 978-1-7325236-1-6 (paperback)
ISBN: 978-1-7325236-0-9 (hardcover)
ISBN: 978-1-7325236-2-3 (e-book)
ISBN: 978-1-7325236-3-0 (audio book)
Library of Congress Control Number: 2018907803

Editor – Colette Rodriguez
Final Editor – Lisa Rojany
Cover Designer – Hope Nixon
Interior Design – Deana Riddle

Published in the United States of America

Chapter One

Saturday, 8:14 P.M.

Good evening, this is Channel 7 Breaking News, and I'm Valerie Parker. Four teenagers are missing tonight from an adventure camp in Northern Idaho. Early reports say the teens and their river guide were in a rafting accident sometime this afternoon. The names of those involved are being withheld pending notification of their parents. According to local authorities, rescue teams are already searching the river area. Up until now, this camp had earned the title "The safest adventure camp in Idaho." Tragically, after today, all that is changed. Stay tuned to Channel 7 for more details as they develop.

Earlier that afternoon . . .

"Alright, listen up! The last set of rapids is about a quarter of a mile ahead. Don't be frightened by the uproar. As we get close, it'll sound like a tornado. So you'll have to listen carefully for my commands over the roar of the river," Doug warned.

As soon as he finished speaking everyone heard the clamor of doom, though it was still a quarter mile away. Just as their river guide had predicted, the noise of the upcoming torrent was daunting. The closer they got, the thunderous pounding intensified. The tornado analogy Doug had used to describe the sound of the Class III rapids could not have been more accurate.

"Here we go! Paddle forward! Keep us straight!" the guide commanded loudly.

The river turned hard to the right, and then they saw the nightmare ahead. The level of turbulence was like nothing they had seen thus far. The water appeared entirely white and rushed forward at a furious pace, breaking over and against large rocks on both sides. The only safe way through was a narrow slot between a set of boulders, which they needed to navigate just right.

"Watch for rocks!" Doug cautioned with a shout. "And hold on!"

The terrified teens and their skilled guide flew into the tight gap between the boulders. Suddenly, the craft was encircled by high white water. They shot through the first surge and then saw the river bend slightly right again to reveal a new set of obstacles.

"Paddle left!" Doug yelled over the roar. "Hard left!" he shouted again.

"Rock!" Savi screamed.

Water drenched them from all directions. And just for a moment, Conner removed his right hand from his paddle to wipe off his glasses.

"Rocks left!" Savi shouted.

Suddenly, the bottom of Conner's paddle struck a rock and flew into the air. The paddle spun and hit their guide, Doug, in the face with such force that it knocked him unconscious. He fell bleeding on the back of the raft.

"Doug's down!" Rico shouted. "Doug's down!"

"Rocks right!" Jade yelled.

"Paddle right! Hard right!" Rico shouted.

The raft careened out of control down the river. With Savi on the left side and being the only paddler, Conner did his best to hang on to Doug.

"Rock left!" Jade screamed.

Now sideways, the raft hurled itself into a rock so hard that Conner lost his grip on Doug, and their guide flew out of the raft and into the raging river.

"Doug's in the water!" Conner yelled frantically. "Oh my God! Our guide is gone."

Thursday, two days earlier . . .

It was a warm August afternoon, and Camp Arrowhead buzzed with activity. Since midmorning, new teenage thrill seekers had been streaming into the adventure camp.

Savannah Evans, who had arrived earlier in the day, was on her way to the message board to check out the day's schedule when she noticed another car pulling into the drop-off zone.

Curious, she stood at a distance and waited to catch a glimpse of the new camper. But before she saw the passenger, a commotion erupted in the vehicle.

An agitated woman, who Savannah assumed was the girl's mother, began yelling inside of the car. "Come on, Jade! Get out—we've got a plane to catch!"

Savannah watched in shock as a tall, slim girl with a pained look on her face scurried out of the back seat. A backpack and two suitcases tumbled out after her, while a purse slowly wound itself around her arm. There were no hugs or attempts at a goodbye, only a slamming door and the vehicle peeling off with a shower of gravel. The girl left standing in the dust cloud fell to the ground next to her luggage, sobbing.

Stunned, Savi waited to see if anyone would come to the girl's rescue—but everyone else stood frozen in place gaping, just like her. Knowing how embarrassed the girl must feel, Savi hurried over to her and bent down on one knee.

"How about I help you with some of this stuff? It looks like a lot for one person to carry."

Startled, the girl tried to shake her off. "What do you want? Just leave me alone—I don't need any help!"

Savi hesitated for a second, then leaned forward and spoke calmly, "I don't want anything. I just thought you could use a hand."

"I told you, I've got this. Leave me alone."

Savi held her ground and leaned even closer. "I'm Savannah, but my friends call me Savi."

She waited while the girl collected herself, slowly lifting her tear-stained face to see who was speaking to her so kindly. As Savi looked into the girl's face for the first time, she inhaled sharply.

What a beautiful face.

"What? I look stupid, right?" the girl snapped. "I already know that. Now leave me alone!"

Savi hesitated then shook her head and frowned.

"No, I don't think you look stupid. I wasn't thinking that at all."

In her sixteen years of living in Oxford, Mississippi, she'd never seen a girl as striking as this one. Despite the tear tracks on her cheeks and a pair of puffy eyes, she still looked like a model from the pages of a magazine. Her milky complexion contrasted by her long shiny black hair and dark brown eyes could make any girl envious. She appeared flawless. As close to perfect as a girl her age could look.

Slowly, the girl started to realize that Savi was trying to be friendly and helpful.

"I feel like an idiot."

"Who wouldn't feel lousy? Come on, let me help you."

"Savi, I'm really sorry I snapped at you. My name's Jade. Do you mind if I call you Savi?"

Savi smiled. "Sure, I'd like that."

"I'm so mad at my mom for doing that to me."

"Well—you won't have to deal with her for a while. Come on. Let's see what cabin you're in. Maybe we're in the same one."

Jade stood up and with Savi's help gathered up her belongings and headed for the camp office. Savi looked down at Jade's Coach purse, Tumi suitcases, and North Face backpack.

All this great stuff but she seems so unhappy.

Savi glanced at Jade and saw tears in her eyes and a look of sadness written across her face. Carrying Jade's suitcase, Savi reached out and patted her shoulder, as if to say, it'll be okay. Jade appreciated the gesture and flashed a friendly grin. Savi smiled back and hoped she had found a new friend at camp.

"I notice you're limping, Savi. Did you hurt your ankle?"

"I injured it a few years ago."

"Sorry—I didn't mean to . . ."

"That's okay. It's no big deal."

"I'm way too nosy," Jade apologized.

"No worries. It's not like you asked me how much I weigh."

Savi laughed and nudged Jade with her elbow. Both girls smiled and continued walking toward the camp office.

"How about I tell you about my ankle later?"

Jade nodded in agreement.

Upon reaching the office, they found the cabin assignments posted outside the main door. Jade seemed more relaxed now that she had time to recover from her rough landing at Camp Arrowhead.

"Jade, we're over here! Those are the boys' cabins, not the girls'. But I'm sure they'd be thrilled to see you."

Jade blushed and flipped back her hair. Then she made her way over to where Savi stood in front of the girls' cabin assignments.

Savi ran her finger down the list of names, "What's your last name?"

"Chang," Jade answered.

"Here you are. Oh, that sucks! We're in different cabins. Let's go inside and see if they'll put us together."

Jade smiled broadly at Savi's boldness.

"Why not? Let's give it a try."

The girls did their best to persuade the camp director to put them in the same cabin. Unfortunately, he wouldn't budge. But he told them he'd keep in mind their desire to be together when planning future events. After leaving the office, they dropped off Jade's gear at her cabin and picked up a cold drink. Outside the snack shack, they found a shady spot to sit on a carved log bench.

"Well, I promised I'd tell you about my ankle. Now is as good a time as any."

"You know you don't have to," Jade assured her.

"I know, but I don't mind."

"I won't lie, I'd like to hear."

"So here goes. I was eight when the U.S. National Gymnastics Team came to Mississippi to put on an exhibition at Ole Miss."

"Ole Miss?"

"Oh sorry, that's short for the University of Mississippi. It's in Oxford. That's where I live. Anyhow, my dad took me to see the competition, and it changed my life."

"How?"

"We watched the different gymnastic routines, and they inspired me. I fell in love with the sport right away, especially the balance beam. The girls were so graceful and powerful. Right away I started dreaming of becoming a world-class gymnast. For the next three years, I trained on the beam and competed in a bunch of events. I really believed I was going to make the U.S. National Team." Savi got quiet and looked at Jade.

"I'm not boring you, am I?"

"No way! I'm into it. Go on."

"Okay, but tell me if I'm boring you or talking too much."

"You're not at all. Tell me what happened."

"Well, in just three years, I was ranked fourth in the nation in my age group. My family and friends were so excited for me. But only the top three girls qualified for nationals. The final cuts were in Nashville. I ended up tied for second place with this girl named Julie. With only one routine to go, I was freaking out! My only hope of beating her and getting into nationals was to do a perfect routine and stick my landing. I was killing it until my final element, an aerial summersault. It had always been the most difficult part of my routine. I had trained for this one moment for three years, and I knew I could pull it off. The summersault was flawless, but unfortunately as I landed on the beam . . ." Savi paused and looked at her ankle. "My left foot hit the beam wrong, and my ankle snapped like a dry branch."

"Oh Savi, that's awful! I'm so sorry."

"Yeah, me, too. Because that ended my career in gymnastics and my dream of going to the Olympics."

"They couldn't fix it?"

"No, they tried, but it never healed quite right. I've learned to live with it. Now I get around just fine."

"Wow, what a story!"

"Well, now you know a lot about me, but I know nothing about you. Next time, it's your turn. Okay?"

"For sure."

They sat quietly for a few moments and finished their drinks. Then they stood up to go.

"I can't believe how tall you are. You must be at least five seven."

"Actually, I'm five eight."

"I knew you were up there, but five eight! I wish . . . I've always been on the short side. I'm only five two. But you know what they say: Good things come in small packages."

Jade smiled and nodded in agreement.

"I need to go to my cabin and unpack, Savi. It won't take me long. I'll be back in a while."

"I should do that, too."

Savi glanced back at Jade and hollered over her shoulder, "I'll look for you later!"

"Okay, later!"

On the way back to her cabin, Savi passed three boys leaning against a big tree and joking around. She caught their attention as she walked toward them. One of the boys noticed her limp and nudged the others.

"Look at her. I didn't know this camp had special needs kids!" he said with a raised voice hoping she would hear him. "They better not pair me up with gimpy girl in some activity."

Savi heard the insult but kept walking as if she hadn't. Then she overheard one of the other kids say, "Good one, Conner!"

By the time Savi got back to her cabin, she was seething and red-faced. She gazed at herself in the mirror hanging on the wall by the bed. Medium length auburn hair framed her lightly freckled face and a turned up nose. But it was her hazel eyes that exposed the hurt and anger she felt.

Still furious over the incident, she turned away from the mirror to consider what to do next. She sat on the edge of her bed and stared out the window at Conner. For the next few minutes, she watched as unsuspecting passersby suffered similar abuse from the taunting trio. Conner and his friends seemed all too satisfied to entertain themselves at the expense of others.

"I'm not letting that coward get away with that!"

Abruptly, she stood and headed outside onto the front porch. The mean boys were still joking around by the same tree. Savi yelled as loudly as she could in their direction, "Hey, Conner! You're nothing but a bully. Your mom's on the phone and says you forgot to pack your blankie and your stuffed animals!"

Instantly, a roar of laughter erupted from those within earshot. Conner glared in shock at Savi. Now it was his turn to feel the sting of humiliation. He slinked away to his cabin and wasn't seen again until after the dinner bell.

Savi felt good about putting Conner in his place. But finding the taste of revenge so sweet made her feel kind of ashamed.

Just then Jade shouted from across the campground, "Savi, come check this out! We're in the same raft tomorrow!"

Savi quickly joined Jade at the message board for an enthusiastic high five.

"And guess what? We've got boys in our raft," Jade said eagerly. "Two of them."

"Two?"

"Yeah, one's named Rico Cruz, and the other is some guy named Conner Swift."

"What?" Savi shouted. "Conner Swift? I just met that jerk! I'm not getting on a raft with him. No way!"

"Oh, yes you are, young lady!" Camp Director Anderson said behind her. "All raft assignments are final. There will be *no* changes!" the director repeated as he walked away.

Savi stood furious, staring blankly at the message board.

What could be worse than being on a raft with Conner Swift? Savi was about to find out.

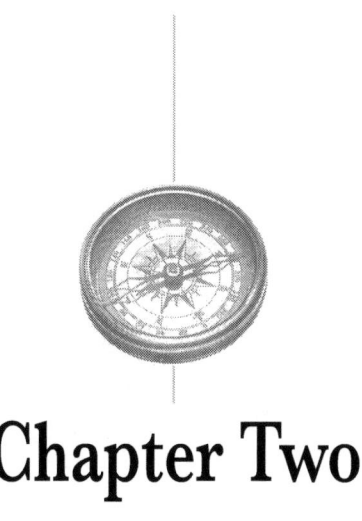

Chapter Two

The smell of barbecued burgers mixed with the scent of pine and a crackling fire wafted through the evening air as dusk ushered in a starlit night. Chirping crickets added to the magical atmosphere.

The bonfire cast a bright glow on the faces of those standing around it. Campers circled the brick fire pit hoping to stay warm and get close enough to hear the Fright Night stories that were about to begin.

Opening night at the adventure camp was famous for hair-raising tales told around the campfire. Some girls brought blankets not only to keep warm but also to muffle their screams during the really scary stories.

"Jade, over here!" Savi motioned.

Jade spotted Savi, and moments later the two of them sat together near the fire on a big warm blanket. Across the way, the girls noticed Conner showing off his glitzy watch to some interested onlookers.

"Who wears a watch anymore?" Jade asked in a mocking tone.

"I guess rich boys from Chicago do," Savi replied.

"How do you know he's from Chicago?"

"I overheard some girls talking about him in the bathroom. Apparently, his dad's a big shot and owns half the city. I hear he's seventeen and thinks he's God's gift to all girls on planet Earth!"

"I've got to admit—he is cute. But his cocky attitude and the mean things he said to you today turn me off."

"How'd you hear about what happened to me?"

"A girl in my cabin said she overheard him insulting you this afternoon."

"Did she tell you what I did to him?"

"No, what?"

"I did something I'm not totally proud of."

"Well, what did you do?"

"Let's just say I tried to get revenge. That's what I'm not proud of."

"Whatever you did, he deserved it!"

"Maybe. But that doesn't make it right."

"Who cares what's right?"

"I do. And that's not the kind of person I want to be."

"Huh! I wish I was a little more like that."

Unknown to the girls, Rico Cruz stood alone on the other side of the fire pit. He scanned the unfamiliar faces glowing in the firelight. Suddenly, he spotted Jade. He had never seen her before, and he didn't know her name. But from the moment he saw her face he could hardly look away. Her beauty surprised and captivated him.

Are you kidding? She's so beautiful!

Quickly he looked around to see if he had accidently said that out loud. He hadn't; his secret was still safe for now.

Rico had become the "hot topic" with girls throughout the camp. Apparently, he was accustomed to lots of female attention, not only because of his dark complexion and good looks but also because of his "bad boy" persona. He had a reputation as one of those tough, nice guys, the tender-warrior type.

Gradually, like dominoes falling one by one, an anxious hush fell over the crowd. Moments later, a collective gasp interrupted the stunned silence. Rico looked over his shoulder and saw a solitary hooded figure dressed in a black robe approaching the fire. When the mysterious stranger's face became visible in the firelight, several girls screamed. Startled campers cowered in fear when they saw the hooded stranger's horrifying mask. Even Rico seemed a bit unnerved.

Jade and Savi were so scared they quickly hid their faces in a blanket. Now only their eyes were visible through a small slit in their covering. "Now I see why they call it 'Fright Night'!" Savi said in a shaky voice.

Jade was too frightened to talk.

Then the cloaked figure told the first of his three scary tales. As the stories continued, tensions mounted because everyone knew the spooky narrator would save the worst for the last.

Visible fear descended slowly over the spellbound campers like a mist covering the streets of San Francisco on a foggy summer night. Any hopes of a good night's sleep abruptly vanished for most of them. Some teens were so terrified they froze in place. Several others sprang to their feet, and pretending to be tired, scampered back to their cabins. Meanwhile, the sinister figure became quiet and just looked around at the crowd for what seemed like forever.

By this time, Jade decided she'd had enough and quickly tried to free herself from the blanket clutched tightly by Savi.

"Savi, let's go!" she blurted out. "I don't care what anyone says. I'm not sleeping in some strange cabin alone tonight."

Before Savi could answer, the creepy storyteller started speaking again in a disturbingly deep and raspy voice.

"Before my last story, I am required to warn you about the disembodied spirits that lurk about at night here at Camp Arrowhead. They live to torment new campers, especially on Fright Night!"

"Okay, we are for sure staying in the same cabin tonight!" Savi gasped.

"Do you believe in spirits?" Jade asked nervously.

"Tonight, I do!" Savi responded while pulling the blanket back over her head.

Then the hooded man started his final story.

"For those of you new to this area, Camp Arrowhead is located just twenty-five miles from the legendary feeding grounds of a flesh eating beast known as Vexel."

"OMG, Savi, who the heck is Vexel?"

"I don't know, and I don't want to know!" she replied, her tone deadly serious.

Just then, a girl yelled from the back of the crowd, "What does Vexel look like?"

The cloaked man pondered the question a moment and then replied, "Unfortunately, no one knows what it is or what it looks like."

After another pause, he went on to say, "Because nobody who has seen it has ever survived the encounter! Of course, there are many opinions about who or what it might be. But no one really knows for sure. Ten years ago there was an accident at a zoo about forty miles from here. Several dangerous animals escaped, and they have never found any of them."

"What kind of animals?" a girl asked anxiously from the front row.

The hooded man turned toward her and paused. Instinctively, she leaned back away from the storyteller and grabbed the arm of a boy next to her whom she didn't even know.

"A lion, a black panther, and a giant gorilla went missing, and they were never found. Many people believe that Vexel is one of those animals. Whatever it is, it prowls relentlessly and hunts in the nearby wilderness. Other people say it may be a huge grizzly bear that survived a forest fire several years ago. But again, no one is certain."

All at once, Conner Swift jumped up from across the fire pit and shouted, "If I see Vexel, I'll kick his butt and eat him for lunch!" His boast raised a smattering of nervous laughter.

Rico shook his head in disgust at Conner's arrogant attitude and instantly disliked him.

Conner continued to brag to those around him about carving up Vexel for his next meal. Little did he know that by this time the next day, Vexel would be thinking the same thing about him.

Chapter Three

A restless night's sleep finally came to an end for the new group of adventurers. And despite the warning the evening before, no dismembered spirits were seen at Camp Arrowhead during the night.

A golden sunrise ushered in the morning accompanied by a symphony of birds singing their favorite songs. The birds' breathtaking harmonies served as a wake-up call for those still sleeping, including Savi and Jade.

Gradually, Camp Arrowhead started to stir. One by one, sleepy teens emerged from their cabins and meandered over to the message board to check out the day's activities. Soon eager voices and laughter were heard everywhere, and a sense of anticipation filled the air.

Rico woke at the crack of dawn when what sounded like a squirrel scurried across the roof above him. He tiptoed out of bed in order not to wake the others sleeping in the cabin. After brushing his teeth, Rico put on jeans and a T-shirt. He slipped out the door and made his way to a grass field across the camp where others had assembled for a pre-breakfast football game.

On his way, Rico stopped at the message board to check the pairings for the rafting trip later that day. He saw that Conner Swift and he were in the same raft.

Give me a break! How'd I end up with that guy?

After his initial dismay, he noticed that two girls, Jade Chang and Savi Evans, were also assigned to the raft. Though he had seen Jade the night before, he didn't have a chance to talk with her. But by the end of the day, all that would change.

In the meantime, Conner also heard about the football game and was heading to the field. A competitive person by nature and a superior athlete, he thought the game would give him a prime opportunity to show off his ball-handling skills. When he got to the field, the players were choosing teams. Several kids wanted Rico to be a team captain because of his muscular physique and the strong arm he showed during warm-ups.

Rico noticed that Conner was looking for a team. He made sure it wouldn't be his team. Rico skipped over Conner every time it was his turn to pick a player. After both captains had finished choosing their team, Rico secretly celebrated that he and Conner were on opposing sides.

Because of the limited number of participants, each player had to play both offense and defense. When his team had the ball, Rico was the quarterback. On defense, he lined up as a pass defender. On the other side, Conner was a receiver on offense and a pass rusher on defense. The boys were eager to impress each other with their athletic talents from the opening kickoff. But no one was more committed to showing off than Conner.

"I'll race down the right sideline. Hit me deep," Conner told his quarterback.

"If you get open, I'll get you the ball," the quarterback replied.

The teams faced each other on the line of scrimmage ready for the first play. Rico stood on the other end of the line from Conner guarding a different receiver. "Hut-one, hut-two, go, go!" the quarterback yelled. When the center snapped the ball, Conner sprinted down the sideline as promised. The quarterback delivered a perfect strike right into Conner's waiting arms.

He caught the ball in full stride and took it in for the game's first touchdown.

"That's what I'm talking about!" he shouted as he spiked the ball into the ground and followed that with a victory dance. Several of his teammates ran to congratulate him.

"See how the pros do it?" he bragged to Rico as he passed him to line up for the kickoff.

"Oh yeah? Let's see how you do when I'm guarding you, Hot Dog!" Rico fired back.

"How 'bout you eat my dust like the other guy did!" Conner shouted back as he walked away.

Rico's team took the ball on the next series and drove it to the twenty-yard line. Despite their best efforts, they failed to score because of some good defense and a dropped pass. Following two scoreless drives by each team, the moment Rico had waited for finally came.

Conner's team had the ball. Again, he urged the quarterback to throw his way.

"Listen, this time I'm going down the opposite sideline. I'll do a stop and go. Hit me deep again. I can't wait to show this Rico guy who the captain of our raft is."

At the line of scrimmage, Rico crouched low directly across from Conner. The way they glared at each other, even a casual onlooker would see the tension between them.

"You're going to work up an appetite trying to chase me down," Conner bragged. "Maybe after I beat you, you can mow my lawn, huh, chico?"

Rico flushed red with anger but said nothing. His furious glare revealed the rage he felt.

Conner planned to fake out Rico with a quick move and then fly past him for another score.

"Hut-one, hut-two, hut-three, go, go!" the quarterback yelled right before the center snapped the ball.

Conner was ready to use his fake-out move when Rico heard the signal caller shout, "Go, go!"

In the blink of an eye, Rico charged across the line and smashed into Conner. He hit him so hard that his feet flew out from under him and he landed on his butt. Conner tried to talk but lacked the air to do so. Rico stood quietly over him as he fought to catch his breath and figure out what happened.

Suddenly, the breakfast bell rang across the camp. Looking down, Rico put on his best Hispanic accent and mocked his vanquished opponent, "Hey, señor, Chico is looking forward to seeing you later today in the raft. Enjoy your breakfast, amigo." Then Rico turned around and headed for the dining hall.

Conner lay groaning on the ground for the next few minutes before concerned teammates helped him to his feet. They escorted him back to his cabin where he spent the breakfast hour eating his pride and recovering his senses.

The largest building in Camp Arrowhead housed the dining hall. It served both as a place for meals and where campers hung out in the evening and played games. Savi and Jade were on their way to breakfast when they saw a few boys were helping Conner back to his cabin.

"What happened to him?" Jade asked a kid nearby.

"Rico, that's what happened."

"What does that mean?" Savi asked.

"He knocked Conner on his butt!"

"Who's this Rico guy?" Jade asked.

"He's right there!"

"Right where?"

"He's the one in the black shirt and jeans going into the dining hall."

"Thanks," the girls echoed as they turned and walked toward breakfast together.

"I didn't see his face, did you, Savi?"

"No." Her faced showed her disappointment.

"Well, I guess it's time to meet this guy and see if he's worthy of our attention," Jade said with a smile.

"Sounds good to me. But I hope Conner is okay."

"Really? After what he said to you yesterday?"

"Don't get me wrong. I hated what he said to me. I just hope he's okay."

"You're a lot different than me, Savi. If he said that stuff to me, I'd enjoy seeing him suffer a little."

"I need him healthy," Savi joked. "We need someone to row for us later, don't we?"

Both girls laughed as they opened the door to the dining hall. Inside, Jade looked to her left and Savi to her right. They wanted to get a look at the mystery man.

"Hey, girls!" a voice came from behind them. Jade turned around, and suddenly she was face to face with Rico for the first time. Neither of them spoke at first. Rico finally broke the awkward silence.

"I saw you last night by the fire. I just wanted to say hi. I'm Rico."

Savi saw that Jade was a bit embarrassed and at a loss for words. So as good friends do, she came to her rescue. "Hi, Rico. I'm Savi. I noticed we're all in the same raft."

"Hey, Savi. I saw that, too. It's great to meet you."

"Where are you guys from?"

"I live in Oxford, Mississippi. How 'bout you?"

"San Antonio. Where are you from, Jade?" he asked.

"I'm from San Francisco."

"Cool. I've never been to the west coast."

"Have you done a lot of white water rafting?" Jade asked him.

"Not on this level of rapids. It sounds wild!"

"Yeah, I know. I'm a little nervous. Well, actually a lot nervous," Jade confessed. "But I'm really looking forward to it."

"Me, too," Rico agreed. "Don't worry. It'll be awesome!"

"Well, I guess I'll see you later." He glanced at Jade before turning and walking away.

He hadn't gone very far when he heard a gentle voice behind him, "Hey Rico, thanks for saying hi."

He turned around at the sound of her voice, and once again was captivated by Jade's beauty.

"I hope I see you later," she added.

All at once, the camp director burst into the dining hall and shouted, "Is Rico Cruz in here?"

Rico stepped forward. "That's me, Mr. Anderson. What's up?"

"I hear you were involved in an incident on the football field earlier?" he said with a scowl on his face.

"It depends on what you call an incident."

"Follow me, young man, you've got some explaining to do." With those parting words, Rico accompanied Director Anderson to his office.

Savi and Jade were concerned for Rico and wondered what might happen to him. They grabbed a couple of apples and granola bars and hurried off to the office to find out.

Chapter Four

Director Anderson sat behind his desk while Rico waited patiently on a metal folding chair across from him. The director advised him that he had learned about the disturbance on the field from the camp nurse. She told him that a few teammates had asked her to check on Conner's condition. An hour after the punishing blow on the field, he was still hurting.

After interviewing several participants from the game, the director was ready to talk with Rico.

"Well, young man, after speaking with different witnesses, I now have a better understanding of what motivated your aggressive behavior on the field. The boys I spoke with claim that it was Conner Swift who initiated the conflict by insulting you with a racial slur. Is that correct?"

"Yeah, but it's nothing I haven't heard before," Rico replied.

"Well, that kind of behavior is not tolerated at Camp Arrowhead. And neither is the physical retaliation you displayed on the field earlier today."

Rico quickly decided that it was better to agree with the director than argue with him. So he sat quietly and took his medicine while resisting the temptation to talk back.

"I've got a guy down in his cabin who's seeing stars, and it's the middle of the day. That's not good, Rico, not good at all! A hard hit is one thing, but knocking someone silly is way over the top. I need assurance there will be no more altercations between the two of you. Have I made myself clear?"

"Yes, sir," Rico said respectfully.

"Before you go, there's another thing you need to know. I'll be talking with Conner later to inform him that if I hear one more racial comment, he'll be spending the summer in the kitchen on cleanup detail. There's no tolerance of that kind of behavior at Camp Arrowhead."

"Is that it, Mr. Anderson?"

The director nodded. "That's it."

"Then I'll go and get ready for the raft trip."

Once outside, he noticed Jade and Savi sitting on a nearby bench. It looked like they had been there a while. As soon as they saw Rico exit the office, they hurried over to him, eager to hear the details of his encounter with Mr. Anderson.

"What happened in there?" Jade asked curiously.

"Oh, nothing much. Director Anderson just told me he's thinking about retiring and wondered if I'd be interested in applying for his job," he said straight-faced.

The girls looked at each other, and then back at Rico. Then everyone burst into laughter.

After a few minutes of laughing, Rico decided it was time to pack for the raft trip, only a few hours away. Savi and Jade knew they had better do the same.

As Jade started to walk away, she looked over her shoulder at Rico. Just then, he turned to look at her also. Equally embarrassed, they both spun around quickly and continued to their cabins grateful they were in the same raft.

Twenty excited campers spent the rest of the morning preparing their backpacks for the white water adventure. They also took the time to review their rafting safety manual.

These rafters were the first of five groups to participate in the white water adventure.

Savi's dad, a former army sergeant, had inserted a "Crisis Only" water-tight pouch in her backpack to use in the unlikely event of an emergency. Though initially objecting to the extra weight, she now carried the bag without complaint. She recalled her dad telling her about mishaps he had experienced in the field during his days in the military. He challenged her to always hope for the best but prepare for the worst.

Savi's mom also made a thoughtful contribution. She gave her a stash of Fig Newton cookies and a big pack of Red Vines that she gladly tucked into her bulging pack.

Conner was also getting ready for the raft trip following a morning spent recovering from Rico's bone-jarring hit. However, a mandatory meeting with the director interrupted his preparations. On his way to the office, he plotted out his strategy to minimize the tongue-lashing he knew he was about to receive.

"Hi, Mr. Anderson," he said, sporting a fake smile when he entered the office. "I heard you wanted to see me."

"Take a seat," the director said as he pointed to the chair in front of his desk.

"First, I want to know how you're feeling," he asked with concern. "I heard you took a hard hit on the field this morning."

"I'm fine. I just got the wind knocked out of me, that's all. Thanks for asking."

"Well, that's good to hear. Now let's talk about the issue I brought you here to discuss," the director added. "I understand you used a racial slur on the football field this morning. Is that true?"

Conner knew this was his moment. He anticipated the director might ask this question, and he had a rehearsed answer all ready. It was show time.

"I'm embarrassed to say yes, Mr. Anderson, I did use a racial slur," he said apologetically. "And I can't begin to tell you how ashamed I am of myself. I've never said anything like that before. I don't know what came over me. It just slipped out. I'm really mad at myself for saying something like that." His head dropped for effect. "I was just getting ready to apologize to Rico when he knocked me to the ground so hard I couldn't see straight. I can't remember for sure, but he may have hit me as I was coming up to tell him how sorry I was." The director studied Conner carefully, trying to determine if he was sincere or just pretending to act repentant.

"I realize that what I did was wrong," he said convincingly. "Mr. Anderson, I give you my word. It won't happen again."

Once again the director examined Conner carefully to ensure he wasn't playing a game of deception. After thinking for a few moments, he decided to take the apology at face value, despite his doubts.

"Alright, I'll take you at your word. But I need to be crystal clear about the punishment for any future slip-ups."

Then, to Conner's relief, Mr. Anderson moved on to a new subject.

He notified him that he was reassigning him to another raft. His plan was to separate the two of them and avoid future confrontations. Conner winced and thought if he changed rafts everyone would assume he was afraid of Rico. So he pleaded with Mr. Anderson and promised there would be no more confrontations if he were allowed to remain in the raft with Savi, Jade, and Rico. The director relented and agreed not to make the change.

Conner thanked Mr. Anderson and shook his hand vigorously.

"You won't regret your decision, sir. I'll be on my best behavior."

As he left the office, Conner whispered to himself, "Now that was an Oscar-winning performance."

Chapter Five

An annoying mosquito buzzed passed Jade's ear as she prepared for the impending white water adventure. She sorted through her suitcases trying to narrow down what to bring.

For seventeen years, Jade had lived in San Francisco. She was much more familiar with the inside of a cable car than the inside of a raft. Her idea of an adventure was finding a new clothing store. Though she'd been on plenty of free floating vessels she had never floated down a river in a raft. Jade worked hard to get her white water certification, but it was in a simulation class, not on a river. This was her first venture into the wild. Now, way out of her comfort zone, she secretly feared for her safety.

Jade's family traveled on vacation often, but they never visited nature settings. Instead, they spent their free time exploring cities in the U.S. and around the world. Name a major city, and Jade had probably visited there. Growing up, she'd been to Broadway shows, the world's most famous museums, and the finest restaurants both in the U.S. and abroad. Though admittedly fearful and anxious, she looked forward to the rafting trip, along with the other adventures Camp Arrowhead had to offer. And with Rico in the raft, there was added incentive to take the risk.

Across the way, Rico did a final check of his gear. Though he'd done very little white water rafting, he was an experienced backpacker and hunter.

Rico spent several summers camping, hiking, and hunting with his family. That is before his mother died of breast cancer when he was only thirteen. After that, the camping trips stopped abruptly. Rico's dad lost all interest in visiting places he'd been with his wife and family before her death. This trip was Rico's first time back in the woods since losing his mother four years earlier.

Suddenly, Mr. Anderson's voice blared over the camp speakers, "Lunch service begins in thirty minutes. All those going on the rafting trip, your safety orientation will begin sharply at one o'clock on the football field. Bring all your gear because you'll be leaving for the river immediately after the orientation. All campers please bring your cell phones, mobile devices, and laptop computers to the storage area to the left of the office before lunch. They will be secured there during your stay and returned to you on the last day of camp. All such devices are strictly prohibited at Camp Arrowhead, starting at noon today."

Murmurs of protest went up throughout the camp. But they quickly died down once everyone realized there was virtually no Internet or cell service available within miles of Camp Arrowhead anyway.

After reluctantly handing in their tech devices and eating lunch, the rafters returned to their cabins and retrieved their gear. Then, as instructed, they descended onto the football field for the mandatory safety orientation.

Approaching the area, they saw several rafts sitting on the grass. Each one had a different number on it, and standing beside it, an experienced guide designated to lead that team on the adventure.

Savi and Jade were among the first to arrive at the field and found their raft marked with a red number nine. Both girls were lugging overstuffed backpacks and were relieved to set them down near the float.

"Hi! I'm Doug Walker," their guide announced. "One of you must be Jade and the other Savi. Who's who?"

"Hi, Mr. Walker, I'm Savi." She reached out to shake his hand.

"Nice to meet you, Savi, but please call me Doug. And you must be Jade?"

"That's right. Mr.—I mean, Doug. Great to meet you."

In the meantime, Conner discovered that Jade and Savi were friends. Similar to most boys in the camp, he found Jade fascinating, and he wanted to get to know her. But to get close to Jade, Conner first needed to make up with Savi. And he committed to do it before the trip started. So on his way to the field, he devised a plan.

When he arrived, the girls were standing with one of the guides near the raft. He decided this was his opportunity.

"Hey Savi!" he called out a few feet behind her. When she heard her name, she immediately turned around. Seeing Conner approach made her uncomfortable and angry. As fast as she had turned around to see who had called her name, she turned her back on him.

"Savi, please, I need to say something."

"Don't do it," Jade interrupted.

"Please, Savi, I just need a minute."

"What is it, Conner? If you can't tell me in front of Jade, I don't want to hear it."

"Okay . . . I want to apologize for my stupid comments earlier. I was hanging out with some guys I just met and tried to impress them. Unfortunately, it was at your expense. I'm very sorry for anything I said that hurt you."

"It sounds like you've been saying a lot of stupid things since you got here."

"Come on, Savi, let's wait over here!" encouraged Jade.

"No! Please don't go. Just listen a second."

"Then talk fast."

"You're one-hundred percent right. I've acted like a loser. I know it's asking a lot, but will you . . . will you forgive me? I know I don't deserve it, but I'd like a chance to make it up to you."

Savi felt conflicted. Her upbringing had taught her the importance of forgiveness, and now she was being challenged to live out what she professed to believe.

"Okay, Conner. I'm going to give you another chance. But don't ever talk to me like that again. Got it?"

"You've got my word on it," he responded convincingly.

Just then, Rico approached the group. Conner stepped aside while the girls greeted him warmly. Rico and Conner barely acknowledged each other, and neither of them wanted to talk.

Now that his team had arrived, Doug introduced himself to the boys and began his safety orientation.

"Alright, before we board the bus for the river and head for the launch site, you need to hear some basic instructions. Then I have to give you a few serious warnings. The Salmon River has another name. It's called the 'River of No Return' because of its swift current. It flows four hundred twenty-five miles through central Idaho and drops more than seven thousand feet before it comes together with the Snake River. In other words, this is serious stuff," Doug cautioned.

The girls gulped and looked at each other anxiously, then Doug continued.

"Many people have lost their lives on this river, though I'm happy to say no one from Camp Arrowhead is on that list. We take pride in our commitment to safety and our spotless record. I've been rafting this river for fifteen years, and I've only had a couple of close calls. In both cases, it was because a rafter failed to listen to my instructions. So you need to remember, there's only one leader and guide on this trip, and that's me. If you do what I tell you, and when I tell you, you'll be just fine. Any questions?"

"No!" they responded in unison.

"Okay, each of you has read the safety manual and passed the safety test earlier. So there's no need to go over that again. But there are some things I need to warn you about, and you must take this seriously. This river boasts some of the highest class of rapids in the country. Now here's the good news," he paused momentarily, "we won't be going on that part of the river. Our journey will only take us to Class I, II, and III level rapids. Though you'll find these rapids quite challenging, they are nothing like the Class IV, V, and VI rapids farther down the river."

Doug looked at the four rafters and saw they were nervous. He realized that before his final warning, it might be a good time to relieve some tension. So he decided to tell them one of his notoriously corny jokes.

"Knock, knock!"

The group looked at each other confused. Again, Doug repeated more emphatically, "Knock, knock!"

Finally, Savi took the bait, "Who's there?"

"Fish."

"Fish, who?" Savi asked rolling her eyes.

"Fish *you* out of the river, if you don't do everything I say."

None of them would usually laugh at a joke this bad, but their anxiety was peaked, and they all did. Doug seemed humored that he had made them chuckle despite the stress they were feeling. Nevertheless, he needed to give them one last piece of instruction and a final warning.

"Tomorrow the bus will pick us up after rafting about five miles downstream. That's the only pickup point for forty miles. Beyond that spot, the wilderness has no roads, and the river is treacherous with high walls and virtually no way out again for about twenty-five miles. And that far south, you'd be in Vexel's territory. You've all heard about Vexel, haven't you?"

"The last thing I want to think about is Vexel right now," Jade said nervously. "I'm freaking over this river already."

"Okay," Doug replied. "But listen carefully. If anything happens to me, you must remember to get out of the river ahead of the extraction point colored in red and named rightly 'Last Chance.' For the last quarter mile leading up to the final take out point, there are warning signs posted every few hundred yards. I know you're all good swimmers, but I'm hoping you don't need to prove it," Doug said with concern.

Jade and Savi looked at one another anxiously.

"If, God forbid, for any reason you miss the takeout spot at 'Last Chance,' you'll be in serious trouble. And I'm not kidding."

He took out his map, unfolded it, and began tracing the river's course. "Look, almost immediately after Last Chance, you'll find yourselves in Class III rapids. About a quarter mile later, you'll come to a fork in the river. It will come up fast so watch for it," he cautioned. "Whatever you do, you have to stay away from the left side of that fork. The right side is treacherous, but if you can hold on, you've got a chance to get to the shore down the river. But if you do go left, you guys will be in serious trouble. Before you know it, you'll be in Class III and IV rapids and soon after a long Class V that even experts have a tough time navigating. Those rapids will propel the raft about six miles down the river before you even know it."

"Doug, this is a ton of information. Should we be writing it down or something?" Savi asked.

"No, I just want to point out the dangers connected with this river."

He found his place on the map again and continued.

"After that, you're immediately caught up in Class IV and V rapids for about thirteen miles, and that's the worst part. If you're still alive, you'll be twenty-five miles down the river, where there is a takeout point. Unfortunately, it's in the dense wilderness and a long way from camp. Worst of all, you'll find yourselves stranded in the middle of Vexel's hunting grounds."

"You're not telling me that you believe Vexel is real, are you, Doug?" Jade asked nervously.

"Well, there's something in those woods. It is anyone's guess, but some vicious man-eating beast has killed three people over the past six years. And that doesn't count all the animal carcasses found, including a large black bear that something tore apart and ate. I'm not making this stuff up. We call him Vexel because he has 'vexed' the wilderness to the south of us for the last six years. Even experienced trackers haven't been able to locate him. And one of them was his latest victim," the guide lamented.

"But if you pay attention to me and do what I say, you shouldn't have to worry about any of this stuff."

Savi had listened carefully to Doug's instructions. Though she was somewhat apprehensive along with everyone else, she had spent plenty of time in the Mississippi backwoods with her dad and didn't fear the water or the wild. Nor was she overly concerned about the guide's warning about the lower river or Vexel because Doug appeared to be a competent and highly experienced guide. Therefore, it seemed unlikely that they would have to deal with any of the potential issues their guide had pointed out.

After the forty-five minute talk and a short demonstration, Doug quizzed them on what they had learned. The group passed the test with flying colors. Next he assigned each person a "safety buddy." He paired up Rico with Savi, leaving Conner and Jade as partners. The match-ups left Rico disappointed. The opposite was true for Conner. He was thrilled to be partnered with Jade and hoped it might provide him an opportunity to divert her attention from Rico.

Despite the setback, Rico hid his feelings, not wanting to show Jade his disappointment, or even worse, tip his hand to Conner.

"Well, here's the bus, right on time," Doug said and pointed toward the approaching vehicle. "Don't worry about the raft. They'll deliver it directly to the launch point. Just bring all your gear and put it in the luggage compartments on the side of the bus."

"The fun is about to begin," Doug said with excitement. "This trip will be the most exciting rafting adventure of your lives!" Soon they would all discover just how right Doug was.

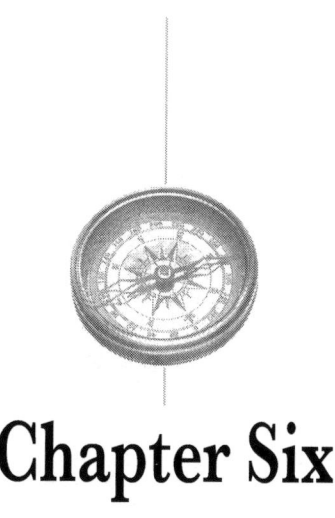

Chapter Six

The bus trip to the river took about thirty minutes. Savi and Jade sat together up front, while Rico found a back seat next to a teammate from the morning's football game. Conner chose to sit alone a few rows behind the girls, not wanting to let on that he was still hurting from the collision with Rico.

Following Doug's safety orientation, Savi and Jade were quiet and somewhat pensive. They used the time on the bus to reflect on safety procedures and pointers they learned about rafting. Both of them now realized the value and importance of their preparation and training.

"It's easy to see why we had to go through white water certification before the trip," Jade sighed, breaking the silence.

"Yeah, can you imagine getting on this river if you never learned how to use a paddle? It would be suicide!" Savi responded.

"I hope the training I did pays off," Jade said. "I trained inside in a simulator mimicking white water conditions. That's how I learned about paddling, built up my strength, and eventually got my certification."

"You . . . you mean you've never been on a real river? You trained inside?"

"Yep, that's what I'm saying. I've never even been on a real river," Jade confessed.

"I sure hope it was a good simulator!"

Just then, the bus turned down a narrow dirt road, and for the first time, they could see the Salmon River. The water flow seemed peaceful enough at first sight, but they knew that looks could be deceiving. Based on what Doug said, the stretch of water in front of the launch point was an unusually calm part of the river. Within a couple of minutes, the bus arrived at its destination.

Twenty rafters were on the bus. Each team of four had a highly trained guide in the raft with them. The watercrafts were scheduled to launch separately at twenty-minute intervals.

The raft assigned to Savi, Jade, Rico, Conner, and their guide Doug was marked with a big red 9 and slated to be the first one to be launched. The schedule indicated that raft would enter the water at 2:00 P.M., which was just fifteen minutes away. So when the bus arrived, they gathered up their gear and promptly headed down to their raft for a final safety check. The long awaited adventure was about to begin following one last inspection.

The rafters hurried to grab their gear once the driver unloaded it. Doug took a moment to talk with the bus driver and confirm details about the pickup slated for the next day. By 1:55 P.M. the team was fully equipped and standing by the raft. Doug told the teens to put on their life jackets, sunglasses, and red safety helmets and then performed his final safety inspection.

Rico and Conner hadn't spoken since the football field, and nothing changed at the river's edge. Doug got in the raft first and seated himself at the back end. Then, to their regret, he instructed Rico and Conner to sit next to each other on different ends of the middle inflatable seat. Savi and Jade were the last ones to board and sat side by side in the front. Once they strapped all their gear securely to the vessel, Doug gave each of them a paddle.

"Can you hear my heart beating?" Jade asked Savi.

"Nope. All I can hear is mine," she admitted.

Then Savi bowed her head and said what most certainly was a short and silent prayer.

"Rico! Conner! You guys ready?" Doug yelled.

"I'm good to go," Rico acknowledged.

"Me, too!" Conner added.

"Girls, you okay up there?"

"Let's go for it!" Savi yelled.

Jade didn't answer.

"Jade? What about you?"

"I think so," she said tentatively.

"Okay, I'm untying us. Right forward!" Doug shouted.

Jade sitting right front bow, and Rico sitting middle right, knew this was their cue to paddle and move the vessel left. Savi sat, front left of the bow, and Conner, center left. They both waited patiently and listened to the guide's instructions.

Everyone knew from their training that if they wanted to turn right, they'd have to paddle on the left side of the raft. Conversely, when moving to the left, the opposite was true. Also, everybody learned a series of important commands that were needed to navigate through the rapids and to steer safely around dangerous obstacles. These commands included "all forward," which meant everyone paddles in unison; "all rest;" "left back;" and "right forward."

"All forward," Doug commanded. Then for the first time, everyone's paddle was in the river, and the raft surged ahead.

"Listen up! Light rapids are ahead. Savi and Jade watch for rocks," Doug cautioned.

"We will!" the girls yelled back.

Before they saw the upcoming rapids, the thunderous roar of rushing water increased in volume. Turning the vessel slightly to the left, they got their first glimpse of a short stretch of rapids.

"Steady forward," Doug hollered. "Here we go!"

Moments later, the raft sailed smoothly through the light rapids. Apprehension mixed with exhilaration showed on their faces.

"Rock left!" Savi shouted.

"Left forward, stop right!" Doug yelled back in response.

Savi and Rico paddled hard, but Jade and Conner stopped rowing and withdrew their paddles from the swift waters. The raft veered to the right and shot past a large rock on the left.

"All forward!"

After going around the big rock, Savi glanced over at Jade and couldn't help but laugh. Jade, so engaged with the intensity of the moment, didn't realize her sunglasses were half-cocked to one side of her drenched face. It looked like several buckets of water had been thrown on her, or that she'd been swimming in her outfit. Savi wished she had a phone so she could take a picture of her new friend's comical look.

"Rock right!" Jade suddenly yelled.

"Right forward, left stop!" Doug commanded. This time it was Jade and Rico's turn to paddle furiously while Savi and Conner lifted up their paddles.

Once again, the raft shot safely by a rock jutting out of the river.

"All rest! Good job."

The relieved rafters raised their paddles from the cool water and breathed a collective sigh of relief. They could see the turbulent waters were starting to calm down. Excited about their success, they proudly turned to congratulate one another, knowing they had each paddled well.

For a time, they floated on a comparatively light current until they heard the sound of upcoming rapids.

The same routine played out during the half hour as they sailed through different stretches of challenging white water.

But for the moment, they relished the calm. To Doug's delight, the team performed flawlessly during their initial test on the river. They were also relieved to discover they were approaching their first planned rest stop.

Once on shore, the girls congratulated each other and then sat on the beach for some much-needed rest. Conner plopped down next to Jade and Savi, and the trio took turns trading stories about their first encounter on the river. Rico decided to use the break to talk with Doug; he hoped to learn more from the guide's many years of experience.

Savi and Jade treated Conner graciously, despite how he had behaved just the day before. Either Savi had indeed forgiven him, or she was putting on a good show. Whatever the case, Conner took full advantage of his opportunity. He was extra friendly to Savi while subtly starting to make his move on Jade.

"I can't believe how great you both paddled out there, especially you, Jade," he said. "When I didn't have to paddle, I was watching you. You really did well."

"Thanks, Conner, I tried my best," she said proudly. Savi glanced at Rico and noticed that although he was listening to Doug, he was also keeping an eye on Conner and Jade.

For the next few minutes, Conner poured compliments on Jade, hoping to win her favor. By the look on her face, and the way she was looking at him, he seemed to be making progress.

"Okay, gather up, everyone."

Once they did, Doug informed them that the next set of rapids were two of the most difficult of the adventure. He also reminded them of the importance of working as a team, calling out obstacles, and listening to his every command. Everyone nodded and realized that they were about to face the most dangerous waters on this final leg of the first day's journey. Once over the treacherous rapids, it was only a short float to the overnight campsite.

Now that the break was over, they made their way to the raft.

Following a quick safety check, Doug led the way, and they all climbed back into the raft.

"Everyone set?"

Each rafter declared they were ready. Before Doug untied the rope holding the raft, Jade turned to Savi.

"Could the rapids be as bad as he said?"

"I don't know, but we're about to find out!"

Chapter Seven

For a time the river was calm and the paddling easy, but everyone realized dangerous waters were just ahead. The tension in the raft was palpable. They knew from experience that the current could change radically in a matter of seconds.

"Okay, in about a quarter mile we're going to hit the first set of Class II rapids," Doug cautioned. "They come one after another, without much of a break between them. Then we'll hit the Class III, that's the rough one. If we get into any trouble, try to keep the raft balanced and stay low."

"You ready to rock?" Conner shouted.

"Just paddle when Doug says to, Hot Dog!"

"Listen!" Savi shouted.

A roar echoed in the distance, but this time it was even more thunderous than before. Everyone knew the raft was rapidly approaching the first set of Class II waters that Doug had forewarned the team about.

The intensity of the river changed quickly, and so did the volume of the roaring waters up ahead. The rumble grew louder with each passing second.

"Around the next bend I need a strong paddle right. There's a big rock as soon as we enter the first rapid. Jade and Rico, you're up first!" Doug shouted over the noise.

Both teens nodded, indicating they understood. A few moments later the river turned slightly left. As they made the turn the violent uproar was so overwhelming that Savi and Jade glanced at each other like friends about to meet their maker. Sadly, they knew that there was no turning back at this point.

"Here we go!" Doug yelled. "Now, paddle hard right!"

At his command, Jade and Rico started to paddle with all their might. Within seconds, the raft was caught up in the first rapid and racing down the turbulent waters.

"Paddle hard right!" the guide yelled again.

Moments later, they flew past a large rock and were swept into a powerful current. Fully engaged, the team obeyed every command instantly.

"Rock left!" Savi shouted.

"Paddle left!" Doug yelled in reply.

Savi and Conner tried to steer clear of the large rock ahead, but the backside of the raft struck it. Out of control they held on and braced for impact.

"Paddles up, hold on!" Doug shouted.

The collision momentarily lifted Savi and Jade off their seats. Both girls screamed as the raft bounced off the rock and turned a bit sideways.

"Hard right! Hard right!" Doug commanded. Jade and Rico fought to straighten out the vessel. Eventually, they succeeded, and once again they were in the middle of the river moving swiftly down the torrent.

Within minutes, they hit the end of the first set of rapids and now had a moment of desperately needed rest.

"Okay, one down and one to go," Doug said. "Everybody good?"

Still shaken by the collision, the girls could only lift one hand and nod.

The roar of the second rapid sounded as frightening as the first. But this time they sailed through it without much difficulty and without getting sideways. The team skillfully avoided every obstacle and paddled flawlessly through the raging current. Doug commended them for their efforts and informed them that they had about a half mile of calm water before they'd encounter the most severe Class III white water. The turbulent waters ahead were the last rapids between the group and the campsite.

"Savi, are you okay up there?" Rico asked.

"Yeah, I'm good. But this river is so intense."

"Jade, what about you?"

She turned toward Rico and immediately burst into tears. He quickly leaned forward and grabbed her hand.

"Hey, you're doing great! It's almost over. Just one more to go."

"I know, but it's the worst one," she sobbed.

"Hey, look at me," he said as he slid toward her and took off his sunglasses so she could see his eyes. "I know this is tough. It's tough for me, too. But you can do this."

Jade appreciated Rico's encouragement and wished she could hug him. But the grip of his hand on hers had to be enough for now.

"Thanks, I'll be okay," she replied with a sense of renewed confidence.

Rico let her hand go and slid back onto the inflatable bench.

Conner watched Rico comfort Jade and was frustrated with himself that he hadn't thought to console her first.

"Conner, you doing alright?" Doug asked.

"Yeah, I'm cool." But he didn't do a particularly good job of masking his irritation.

"Alright, listen up! The last set of rapids is about a quarter of a mile ahead. Don't be frightened by the uproar. As we get close, it will sound like a tornado. You'll have to listen carefully for my commands over the noise of the river," he warned.

As soon as he finished speaking, from a quarter mile away, everyone heard the clamor of doom. Just as Doug had predicted, the noise of the upcoming torrent was daunting. The closer they came to the rapids the thunderous roar intensified. The howling of a tornado that Doug had used to describe the sound of the Class III rapids could not have been more accurate.

"Here we go! Paddle forward! Keep us straight!" the guide commanded loudly. The river turned hard to the right, and then they saw the nightmare ahead. The level of turbulence was like nothing they had seen so far. The water appeared entirely white and rushed forward at a furious pace, breaking over and against rocks on both sides. The only way through it was a narrow slot between a set of boulders, which they had to hit just right to make it through safely.

"Watch for rocks!" Doug warned with a shout. "And hold on!"

As they flew into the tight gap between the boulders, white water rose above the raft on both sides. They shot through the first surge and then saw the river bend slightly right to reveal a new set of obstacles.

"Paddle left!" Doug yelled over the roar. "Hard left!" he shouted again.

"Rock!" Savi screamed.

Water drenched them from all directions. Foolishly, Conner took his right hand off his paddle to wipe off his glasses.

"Rocks left!" Savi shouted.

Just then, the bottom of Conner's paddle struck a rock and flew into the air at Doug. The paddle spun and hit him in the face with such force it knocked him unconscious. He fell bleeding onto the back of the raft.

"Doug's down!" Rico shouted. "Doug's down!"

"Rocks right!" Jade yelled.

"Paddle right! Hard right!" Rico shouted.

The raft careened out of control down the river. With Savi on the left side and being the only paddler, Conner did his best to hang on to Doug.

"Rock left!" Jade screamed.

Now sideways, the raft hurled itself into a rock so hard that Conner lost his grip on Doug and their guide flew out of the raft and into the raging river.

"Doug's in the water!" Conner yelled frantically. "Oh my God! Our guide is gone."

The fork in the river that the guide had warned them about earlier suddenly appeared. Both sides looked equally treacherous, but they remembered their guide's instructions to do everything possible to stay to the right. Realizing they had two paddlers on the right and only one on the left, Rico shouted over the roar, "Jade, switch sides! You and Savi paddle hard left!"

"Where's Doug?" Savi screamed.

"Hard left, or we're going down the left fork," he yelled.

"There's Doug!" Jade cried out.

Doug, now conscious, was being propelled down the river to the right of the raft twenty feet away and slightly behind them. He was facing up with his feet pointing down the river, which his experience had taught him was the only chance to survive the raging waters.

The raft quickly floated by the final two warning signs before the Last Chance takeout. A few seconds later, to their horror, they zipped past the Last Chance takeout spot.

"Doug!" Savi shrieked.

As hard as they tried, they could not maneuver the raft to the right side of the river's fork. Seconds later, the vessel shot through the left fork while Doug was swept down the right fork still fighting for his life.

"Doug! Doug!"

Jade and Savi kept screaming Doug's name but to no avail. He was gone. The weary group quickly realized that they were on their own, trapped on the most dangerous side of the river, and speeding toward even more turbulent waters.

"Conner, look for Doug's paddle!" Rico shouted.

"No way! I'm staying down!"

"Rocks left!" Savi screamed. "We're going to hit them!"

"Get low and hold on!" Rico hollered.

Chapter Eight

The raft smashed against the rocks and would have flipped over except that all the rafters stayed down and held on to their safety straps. Moments later, they hit another large boulder and again came perilously close to capsizing. Fortunately, they shifted their weight and balanced out the raft, averting disaster for the time being.

The terrified teens were now at the mercy of the turbulent waters as everyone hung on for their lives. The raft felt like a bucking bronco, tossing them up and down and side to side. Throughout the ordeal, they had to shift their positions and balance the weight to keep the raft from flipping over.

Eventually, the power of the current started to ease, and they found themselves in a section of the river surrounded by steep walls. Just as Doug had warned, there was no place to land because of the sheer rock walls that encased the river.

"What are we going to do?" Jade cried out.

"Try to find your paddle," Savi replied.

Rico quickly scanned the surroundings. "We've got to get off this river, but I don't see any place to land."

"My paddle, it's gone!" Jade screamed hysterically.

"Jade, come on! We'll figure this out. We still have two paddles," Rico said.

"Savi, I need you back here with me. Conner, look for Doug's paddle now, or I'll beat the crap out of you when we get to shore!"

"Just try it!" he shot back. "I've already looked for it, and it's gone. And who made you the boss? You don't know any more than the rest of us. I don't have to listen to you!"

"I'm your new babysitter. Now shut your mouth, or I'll throw you off this raft! Got it?"

Conner could see that Rico was deadly serious. And after watching Doug fight for his life in the turbulent waters, Conner had no interest in joining him. Though still mad, he decided he had better quiet down.

Suddenly, they started to hear the now familiar roar of rapids ahead. Savi and Rico now sat opposite one another in the middle seat clinging to the only paddles left aboard. Savi sat on the left side of the inflatable bench and Rico on the right.

"Jade, keep an eye out for rocks. Savi, give your paddle to Conner. And Conner, get up here and help me."

"No way I'm giving him my paddle," Savi fired back. "I'll help you, and I'm keeping my paddle, thank you."

"Seriously! You think you can do this?"

"If not, I'll die trying," she said.

"Okay then, it's you and me. Don't let me down."

Savi got quiet and focused.

The thunderous rapids ahead grew louder by the second. By this time, they had traveled over twelve miles down the river with no foreseeable way off.

"Okay, Savi. Listen to my commands and try to keep the nose pointed down the river."

"Got it."

"You're pretty brave for a girl."

"What's that supposed to mean? Apparently, you've never met a Mississippi girl!"

"You ready?"

"Let's do it."

"Lord, help me!" Savi whispered.

"Here we go!"

"Rocks right!" Jade yelled.

The next series of rapids were daunting, with plenty of threatening big rocks along the way. But to everyone's relief, the rapids were not as daunting or challenging as the Class III surge that had ejected their guide from the raft. Sadly, the incident had not only cost them Doug but two of the four paddles as well.

Rico and Savi were skillful navigating the raft over the next several miles of intermittent rapids. And Jade courageously held on up front and pointed out rocks the paddlers needed to avoid.

Suddenly they began to hear a horrific roar in the distance. A sound like nothing they had heard before. If Class III rapids sounded like a tornado, the torrent of water they were quickly approaching roared like three tornadoes. They knew it had to be at least a Class IV—or even worse.

Doug had warned them that in the unlikely event they missed the Last Chance take out point, they had to go down the right fork of the river. Unfortunately, they had sailed down the left side instead. Now they faced the worst rapids the Salmon River had to offer. The very ones their guide had warned them about. Frightened and by themselves, they now moved swiftly down the most perilous fork of the river.

The roaring ahead was already deafening and getting louder by the minute. Savi and Rico knew they had to muster all their remaining strength if they were all going to survive this next series of rapids.

"Savi, just like last time we've got to keep the nose in the middle. That's our only chance. If you see we're going to hit rocks, pull your paddle up so we don't lose it."

"Okay."

"Jade, are you ready? You'll have to hold on!"

"We're not gonna make it!" she yelled after looking at the white water and glancing back at Rico with a look of terror.

"Yes, we will! Now hold on and call out the rocks!" he shouted back.

The first rapid they hit propelled them at a speed that went beyond anything they had experienced before.

They shot down the river like a roller coaster with no seat belts and no track. Miraculously, they kept the nose of the raft downstream and averted disaster.

Following the first set of rapids, Savi and Rico were able to take a short break. Then, without warning, the river turned to the right and on the left was a landing spot about ten feet long. Unfortunately, they saw it just seconds too late, and the current carried them right past it.

Rico was becoming more and more frustrated by Conner's lack of effort. So he yelled back to him in a mocking tone, "How's the ride back there, Hot Dog? Can we get you anything? Maybe some lunch, you must be hungry from all your hard work."

"Shut up, Rico! I don't have a paddle. What do you want me to do?"

"You really wanna know?" Rico snarled back.

"That's enough, you two! We don't have time for this," Savi scolded. "Put on your big boy pants and let's figure out how to get out of this alive."

By this time, the raft had gone about twenty miles down the river, and the terrain had changed significantly. A rugged wilderness now surrounded the watercourse. It was so thick that it looked like nighttime beneath the canopy of trees and dense foliage.

The water was still fast, but Savi and Rico were quickly learning to paddle and steer their way down the treacherous river. But the strenuous work of paddling through the powerful rapids had taken its toll on them, and they were both thoroughly exhausted.

"Savi, we've got to figure out how to get off this river. I don't think I can paddle much longer."

"I agree. My arms are burning like they're about ready to fall off."

"Let's paddle to the right and see if we can toss the anchor into the trees and stop the raft. I mean, what do we have to lose?"

She quickly agreed with Rico's plan. So the weary rafters paddled as hard as they could and moved the raft to the right edge of the river. The tree line came right up to the water's edge, with hardly any riverbank. Despite their efforts to get out of the swift current, the raft was still moving fast alongside the right tree line. Just then the current started to pick up again. In the distance, they could hear they were approaching another powerful rapid. Unless they tossed the anchor into the trees in a hurry, they might not get another chance.

"Savi, hard left, and I'll throw the anchor."

"Hey, useless!" Rico snapped at Conner. "Here's my paddle. Get up here and help Savi paddle. Make sure you keep the raft as close to the right shore as possible. Got it?"

"Just give me the paddle, and I'll help her."

On Rico's command, Savi paddled with all her remaining strength and with Conner's help. All at once, the current grew stronger. The deafening roar of new rapids ahead convinced Rico it was now or never. So with a mighty heave and all of his strength, he tossed the anchor toward the tree-lined shore.

"Big rock on the right!" Jade cried out.

The anchor landed between two trees just as the raft was about to pass a large rock. As soon as the mooring got caught up in the trees, the raft instantly swung hard to the right. The vessel struck the rock so forcefully that Rico, Savi, and Conner were immediately knocked to floor of the raft. But Jade got the worst of it because she had been sitting in the front. The collision propelled her from the raft into the water, and to make matters worse, she smashed her shoulder against a large boulder. Wincing in pain, she found herself wedged between the vessel and the huge rock. She did her best to cling to the lifeline, which was the rope threaded through the top of the raft.

"Jade's in the water! She's pinned against the raft!" Savi screamed.

"Push your paddles against the rock and see if you can move the raft off of her so she can breathe!" Rico yelled.

"Hurry, Conner, help me push!" Savi pleaded.

"I am!" he grunted.

"Hold on, Jade!" he shouted.

"It's pulling me under!"

"Okay, I've got you. Now let go of the rope."

"No way, I'll drown!"

"Jade, let go of the rope now!"

Jade felt the strong current dragging her gradually deeper even with her life jacket securely on. Injured and with her strength almost gone, she knew she had no choice. Finally, Jade let go of the safety line with her left hand and reached up as far as she could. Rico quickly grabbed her outstretched hand. Now he had a vise grip on both her wrists and even though it was painful, she knew he wouldn't let go.

After much difficulty, and many painful screams, he managed to get her back into the raft. She was hurt badly, soaking wet, and traumatized. Her shoulder was bleeding, and her back ached from the brutal beating she had taken while pinned against the huge boulder.

"Untie your backpacks. Get me the safety kit, and bring Jade's pack with you ashore. We've got to get away from this raft and onto those rocks," Rico said in desperation.

"How?" Savi asked.

"Right over there. See that little ledge on the side of the rock? Once we get there, we can get to shore."

"What about Jade?" Savi whispered to Rico. "She can't do that."

"You let me worry about Jade. You and Conner get your packs and don't forget hers. Take everything we need and come to me one at a time. In the meantime, keep the raft balanced. I don't want to move her till I have to."

Rico helped tie a rope around Savi's waist and led her to the right side of the vessel. He held the line as she made her way to the small rock ledge.

"Great job, Savi. Now move over to that big flat rock and Conner will toss you the backpacks. Conner, throw her the packs and do your best to keep everything as dry as you can."

Savi not only made it to the flat rock, but she managed to catch all four backpacks Conner threw to her without them getting any wetter than they already were.

Then Rico untied the rope from his waist that connected him to Savi. She quickly reeled the line back to shore and coiled it to use later. Conner went next. He got to the rock ledge without much trouble. Now it was time to move Jade.

"My shoulder is killing me," she moaned through tears. "I can't make it to the ledge. I'm too scared. I don't want to fall into the water again."

Rico convinced her that there were no other options. She grimaced in pain as he helped her up. The side of the vessel from which they were exiting was jammed tightly against a large rock. If Jade somehow ended up in the water, Rico saw she'd still be within reach between the raft and the rock. But he worried that if she fell, she might drown because of her injuries and her lack of strength.

"Savi, I've got a line tied around my waist. I'll throw the rest of it to you. Once you catch it, tie it as tightly as you can around a sturdy tree."

Then he turned to Conner. "Make sure you help her secure the line."

Savi and Conner did exactly what was asked of them. Now Rico was ready to assist Jade to the ledge.

"Okay, you need to sit up a minute so I can tie a rope around your waist." Rico had a sharp hunting knife strapped to the outside of his right leg that he used to cut another piece of line. Then he tied one end of the rope around Jade's waist and the other end to his waist. Finally, he attached both of them to the line anchored by the tree on the shore.

"Now, Jade, get up carefully and give me your hand. You've got one long step to the ledge, but you can do it. I'll be right behind you."

"I'm scared. I don't know if I can do it!" She was trembling now.

"You've got to do it. It's our only hope. I've got you. Just lean forward, and I'll hold you with the rope until you're ready to go."

Wavering, she was reluctant to take the necessary step.

"Come on, Jade! It's just one long step."

Jade leaned forward and placed her left foot on the ledge. She was just about to put her right foot down when, suddenly, she heard Savi gasp. Out of the corner of her eye, Savi saw something coming down the river. Once she realized what was happening, she thought, *Oh God no!* Then she screamed, "Watch out!" pointing at the log hurtling in their direction. "Rico, it's going to hit the raft!"

Chapter Nine

Rico spun around to see a log barreling down the river toward them. Jade looked over her right shoulder to see what was happening and slipped off the rock; she fell feet first into the water between the rock and the raft. The current immediately swept her into the V between the rock and the vessel. Again she was pinned and suffering. Although tethered to Rico by the rope around both of their waists, she struggled to keep her head above the water.

"I can't breathe!" she gasped. "The raft—it's crushing—"

Rico whirled around just in time to see Jade fall.

Savi yelled a desperate last second warning.

WHAM! The log smashed into the back of the raft with violent force. The jolt caught Rico somewhat off guard because he had redirected his attention to Jade. The sudden impact knocked him backward and into the water. Instinctively, he grabbed the lifeline as he tumbled over the left side of the raft and clung to it with all his strength. Jade and Rico let out simultaneous moans when they felt the rope around their waists tighten.

"Rico, try to work your way back around the raft!" Savi shouted. "That will take the pressure off the line. I'll come help her!"

Rico nodded and yelled back, "I'm trying, but the current's strong!"

"Conner, hold on to my rope and pull it when I tell you to!" Savi commanded.

Earlier she had tied a rope to a nearby tree and knotted it to her waist clip.

"Keep it tight," she ordered Conner as she stepped carefully onto the ledge. After reaching it, she knelt down as close to her friend as she could get. Jade was screaming and clinging to the lifeline, now with only one hand because of her shoulder injury. Savi quickly grabbed the strap on the back of Jade's life jacket in case she lost her grip on the lifeline. Now the more urgent task was keeping Jade's head above water. Eventually, Savi helped Jade put her other hand back on the lifeline. The weight of the raft still pressed up against her chest, reducing her ability to breath.

"I can't . . . hold on . . . any longer," Jade groaned.

"She can't breathe, and she's going under!" Savi screamed. "I've got to cut the anchor line! The raft is crushing her."

"Conner, forget about my rope and come here and hold on to Jade. I'll cut the raft loose."

Conner moved as quickly as he could on the slippery ledge. Savi knew there wasn't a moment to spare. When Conner was close enough to grab the strap on Jade's life jacket, Savi took her pocketknife out of her vest pocket and without warning or hesitation, jumped into the water between the rock and the raft. She tried to snag the lifeline at the back of the raft, but she missed it. Instantly, the swift current carried Savi to the front side of the vessel where she was finally able to grasp the lifeline.

Similar to what Rico was doing on the other side of the raft, she began the laborious task of working her way against the current to the rear of the vessel.

"Rico, are you alright?"

"Yeah. I'm getting there. But it's tough against the current."

Rico had worked his way almost to the back of the raft by using the lifeline and putting one hand over the other. Every inch he moved the rope's pressure lessened on Jade. Finally, Rico made it to the back of the raft and carefully went around Savi, who was now also at the rear of the vessel. Then he let go of the lifeline. The current immediately swept him into V where Conner had hold of Jade.

Right away, Rico could see that Jade was in bad shape. "Savi, we have to get the raft off of her now!" Conner shouted.

"Listen, Rico! When Savi cuts the anchor line, lift Jade out of the water as far as you can. I'll pull her onto the ledge," Conner instructed.

"Savi, hurry! Cut halfway through the anchor line and then on the count of three finish the cut!" Rico shouted.

"Okay, but check my line to make sure it's secure."

"It's good!" Conner assured her.

"I hope you're right!"

"Okay, I'm cutting it halfway. Ready? One—two—three!"

The final cuts caused the line to pop right before it snapped. Instantly, the current swept the empty raft down the river and out of sight.

When Savi let go of the lifeline, the force of the river swept her into the big rock near the ledge. Fortunately, she had anticipated this happening and hit the boulder squarely, feet first. Quickly, she reeled in the slack on her rope and knotted it. Dangling in the river at the end of the line, she realized the only thing between her and death was a rope tied to a tree. Gradually, she worked her way over to the widest part of the ledge. Then she took a moment to catch her breath and regain some strength. Eventually, she pulled herself out of the water and rolled onto the ledge. Exhausted, she watched as Rico and Conner worked to help Jade.

It took awhile, but finally, they were able to pull Jade out of the water. Conner and Rico hoisted her onto the same rock ledge as Savi. Jade was bleeding and laboring to breathe, but she was fully conscious. Savi crawled along the ledge until she got to Jade. She sensed it was Savi but didn't have the strength to turn her head.

Rico was the last one to make it to the ledge. He had watched Savi climb the rock and inch her way to the wider part of the edge. Following her lead, he hoisted himself out of the water and worked his way across the flat part of the rock until he reached the others.

After everyone had moved safely to dry ground, the priority was dealing with Jade's wounds. Savi first treated the injuries on her hands, back, and shoulder and then carefully put some ointment on the rope burn around her waistline. Though battered and hurt, Jade was already breathing better and starting to look like herself again.

Confident that Jade would be okay, the weary trio collapsed inside the tree line and took the next hour to revive themselves.

After a while, Jade was able to sit up, though not without severe discomfort.

"This is so messed up! I'm not sure I can hardly walk, let alone hike."

"Don't worry about that now," Savi reassured her. "We're not going anywhere for a while. Here, just lay back down. Get some rest while we figure out what to do next." Savi stayed by Jade's side until she drifted off to sleep.

Once Jade was asleep, Rico, Savi, and Conner moved several feet away from her so that they wouldn't disturb her. But they stayed close enough to keep her in full view.

"We're so screwed!" Conner grumbled.

"Oh great, just what we need from you, more negativity," Rico fired back frustrated. "Can't you ever be positive?"

"Okay then, let me rephrase what I said. We are so positively screwed! Is that better?" He glared at Rico.

"You two have to stop this bickering now!" Savi demanded. "If we want to get out of this alive, we need to work together as a team. You both need to quit acting like two year olds. And I mean it."

Savi sat with arms folded and glared at both of them. "I don't care how much you don't like each other. You need to shake hands and get over it. The two of you have said and done enough cruel things to each other. Look at Jade! She needs all of our help, or she's not going to make it. You two have to get this fixed right now. Otherwise, we're all going to die out here."

It was apparent that Rico hated the thought of shaking Conner's hand, but he knew Savi was right. Summoning all the courage he could muster, he lifted his hand and extended it to Conner.

Conner froze and stared at Rico's hand. Instantly, Savi interjected. "Conner!"

Hesitantly, Conner raised his hand, and he and Rico shook hands for the first time, though not very convincingly.

"That's better. Now let's go check on Jade. Then we'll figure out what to do."

At six-thirty that night, Camp Arrowhead verified that Raft 9 was missing. Rescue crews were assembled and dispatched down the river. When rescuers reached the river fork just past the Last Chance takeout, the team decided to search the right side, knowing that the guide would have told them to stay away from the left.

By nightfall, the rescuers feared a bleak outcome. After an evening of searching, they found no raft, wreckage, or sign of the teens. A new and violent weather system had shifted direction, complicating matters further, and was now heading their way. This development meant a more extensive search could not begin until morning.

Savi reached into her pack and pulled out the sealed package marked "Crisis Only" that her dad had insisted she carry. Now more than ever she was grateful for his wise forethought. With keen interest, she surveyed the package's contents. She found it contained a small box of wooden matches, butane lighter, and a compass that she clipped to a metal ring on her vest. Also in the pack were ten energy bars, four of which she put in her pocket; a thin plastic tarp; and a miniature flashlight.

Almost miraculously, Jade was now on her feet and testing her ability to walk. She was still very sore and shaken, but three hours of sleep had helped her feel a little bit better.

The boys were busy gathering broken branches for a fire that Savi was about to start. After sunset, the temperature dropped steadily; now there was a chill in the air. Unfortunately, their clothes were still damp, adding to their discomfort.

The tired foursome gathered around the welcoming fire, hoping it might thaw them. Stranded at least twenty-five miles from Camp Arrowhead, the group was overwhelmed by the realization that they were in grave danger. Unsure of what to do next, they sat silently in front of the flames, each one hoping for a miracle.

After a few minutes, Rico decided to use his time near the fire to carve a point on a fallen tree branch. It was evident to everyone that he was making a spear.

Meanwhile, Savi decided to open up the Fig Newton cookies in her pack. When she did, the scent of sugar and shortening filled the night air. She gave a couple of cookies to each of them, and for the next few minutes, they savored each tiny bite.

Suddenly, they heard a loud rustling of bushes and branches snapping downriver not very far from where they had set up their makeshift camp.

"What was that?" Jade whispered anxiously. "It couldn't be Vexel, could it?"

"Quiet." Rico rebuked her with a hush. He raised the tip of his nearly finished spear.

Again they heard more noise in the woods. This time they could tell, whatever was out there, it was getting closer.

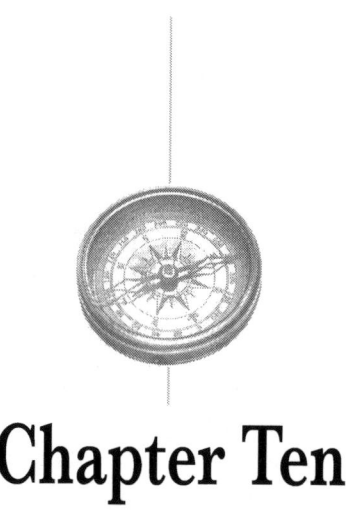

Chapter Ten

Rico and Savi's backpacks were sitting just a few feet away from them. However, Jade and Conner had propped their packs against a tree about thirty feet away. The only way to retrieve their backpacks was to go toward the terrifying sounds coming from the woods.

Rico leaned forward and spoke in a whisper. "Savi, you and Conner help Jade. Take my backpack and go straight upriver about three hundred yards. That's about the length of three football fields. Then make a hard left and go straight inland about two hundred yards. When you get there, wait for me. I'll grab the other two packs and catch up with you. No matter what happens, just keep going. I'll find you in the area I told you to wait. Leave the fire, and go now."

"Forget those packs and come with us," Savi whispered back emphatically.

"No, just go!"

Savi grabbed his hand. "Be careful. Those packs aren't worth your life."

"Do what I said. Now!"

Rico jumped up and tiptoed over to get Jade's and Conner's backpacks.

Meanwhile, Conner helped Jade to her feet and assisted her up the left side of the river. She could only move at a moderate pace and suffered with every step. Savi trailed close behind, guarding the rear and keeping an eye out for Rico.

Back by the fire, Rico, spear in hand, continued to move stealthily toward the backpacks. He heard menacing sounds coming from the woods and feared that whatever was out there was big and getting a lot closer. Grabbing the packs, he turned and moved quietly away.

Suddenly in the trees behind him, about fifty yards away, he heard a deep growl followed by a huge belted roar that stopped him dead in his tracks. Startled, he was sure he had just heard the sound of a bear.

He remembered reading about Camp Arrowhead and the hundreds of known grizzly bears that lived in northeastern Idaho. He stood and listened a moment for any additional movement. Again he heard branches breaking followed by a mighty roar.

Disregarding his advice to the others about being quiet, Rico scurried past the smoldering fire and headed upriver as fast as he could. Once he was a safe distance from the campsite, he stopped and crouched down before glancing back from behind a small group of trees.

The sight of the bear unnerved him. As terrifying as the beast looked, he knew it wasn't a grizzly. Instead, Rico saw a medium size black bear snooping around the camp in the fading firelight.

The bear slowly and carefully sniffed his way through the camp. Rico waited for a few moments to see if the beast had spotted him. Then he quietly slipped away. When he decided it was safe to pick up the pace, he did. Now the goal was to catch up with the others and warn them about the prowling black bear.

After he had hiked about three hundred yards, he turned left and headed away from the river. Suddenly, he heard a branch snap no more than ten yards ahead of him. Instantly, he froze in place. Slowly he bent down on one knee and looked in the direction of the noise. Another branch snapped, then he caught a glimpse of Savi's backpack.

"Savi!" he shouted in a whisper.

She turned and was surprised and relieved to see Rico a few yards behind her. For the first time, without even thinking about it, they hugged.

"Listen. There's a good size black bear behind us. I saw it sniffing around our camp. We've got to get away from the river as fast as we can. This area must be a passageway where bears come down from the mountains to feed in the river."

"Or he sniffed out my cookies," Savi countered.

"You're right. Maybe the scent of the cookies did it. Is the package sealed?"

"I think so. Let me check."

"Hurry, we've got to keep moving," he said impatiently.

Savi put down her backpack, opened the flap, and ensured the package was sealed tight. Without warning, the bear roared again, and he wasn't very far away. Savi grabbed her pack just as Rico grabbed her arm, then the two of them started running in the direction of the agreed meeting place.

"Rico, we left Conner's pack!"

"Leave it for now. We've got to get out of here. The bear must be tracking us."

In just a couple of minutes, they caught up with Jade and Conner. As happy as they all were to see each other, this was no time to celebrate.

"Where's my backpack?" Conner asked.

"We had to leave it," Rico told him.

"How come you have yours?"

"Because I was wearing it when we heard the bear. Now let's go! He's not far behind us."

While hurrying to find cover, Rico told Jade about the black bear, adding to their already high level of anxiety. Pausing for a minute to catch their breath, Rico changed places with Conner so he could help Jade. She was bleeding again and so exhausted that Rico nearly had to carry her. Ever conscious of the danger shadowing them, they plodded forward, looking for some place to hide from the predator. Any place.

The pace decreased because of Jade's condition, the darkness, and their unfamiliarity with the terrain. After the bear roared again in the distance, there was no longer any doubt that the beast was stalking them.

Rico possessed the only weapon that might be able to protect them from an animal as big as a bear.

If they hoped to survive, they had to stay close together and find a place to shelter quickly. The moonlit night provided just enough light for them to see where they were going. All of a sudden, they entered a clearing about a hundred feet around. On the other side of the open area was a large cluster of rocks. They were all physically spent, especially Jade. She was in severe pain and needed treatment. Unable to go on any longer, the group decided to head to the rocky area and try to hide. Seconds later, the bear roared again from less than a couple hundred yards away.

Conner spotted an indentation that looked like a cave within the rock formation. When they got closer, they saw that it was indeed a cave. The little grotto was about four feet wide and ten feet deep and was covered by a large boulder that served as a roof. For better or worse, there was only one way in and one way out.

"Give me the backpacks," Rico demanded. "Hurry! We've got to get the food out of here."

"Let's just take the food out and keep the packs with us," Conner proposed.

"We don't have time for that," Rico decided. "Give me the backpacks now!" he ordered again.

Rico traded his spear for the backpacks. Then he took off running and deposited the packs on the right side of the clearing, though they were still visible from the cave. Then he hurried back to the rock shelter.

Savi did her best to comfort and treat Jade while Rico and Conner waited and watched at the entrance. For about five minutes, it was quiet. Then the loudest roar they had heard broke the silence. Suddenly the medium size black bear emerged from across the clearing. Conner had to hold back a gasp when he saw the scary silhouette of the animal. All at once the beast stopped and stood fully erect on its hind legs. Peeking from the cave, they saw the scary creature was at least seven feet tall. Both boys' hearts raced wildly. They were glad that the girls were deeper in the cave and could not see the bear.

All at once, the creature bent back down and began sniffing his way around the clearing. After a few minutes, he worked his way over to Savi's backpack. He ripped and clawed at it until the bag's contents were scattered everywhere. It was apparent the hungry bear was searching for food. Savi's cookies were his first find. He ripped open the package without difficulty and lowered his head to munch on the tasty treats. Then he focused his attention on the "Crisis Only" pack and the energy bars still tucked inside of it.

"Well, there goes your backpack, Savi," Conner whispered. "Two down, two to go," he added with a smirk. Rico turned and looked at him with a stare that Conner had seen only once before, back on the football field. Conner quickly looked away and decided it was best to drop the subject.

After the bear was satisfied that he had stripped Savi's pack of food, he looked up and surveyed the clearing. Again, he returned to the backpacks, clawing at the remaining two bags. Meanwhile, Savi helped Jade sit up and take a drink. As she did, Jade let out a painful gasp. The bear heard the sound and instantly turned his head in the direction of the cave. He watched for a moment and then stood up, sniffing the air. After a few seconds, he started to walk with purpose toward the cave.

Rico took a couple of steps back and raised his spear.

"Conner, get behind me," he whispered. "Here's my knife. If anything happens to me, you've got to protect the girls."

The bear moved across the clearing. All at once, the beast picked up a scent that told him he was not alone. Determined to find the origin of the strange smell his nose had detected, he continued to snoop around the rocks until he was just a few feet away from the enclosure.

As it neared the opening, the dark creature stood up once again. Then the bear turned and peered into the grotto. As soon as it did, its eyes locked on Rico, standing alone at the entrance. The bear snarled and then roared ferociously. He opened his jaws wide and lunged forward.

Chapter Eleven

Knowing the bear was about to charge him, Rico gripped his spear firmly with both hands. He took a step back and assumed a defensive position. Terrified by the ferocity of his adversary, he raised the tip of the spear upward toward the bear. Instead of charging at Rico, the beast first swung his mighty paw and attempted to claw him.

The bear let out a growl when he missed his target. He swung again furiously. This time, he hit Rico's spear and nearly knocked it out of his hands. Hoping to scare the creature away, Rico yelled loudly and jabbed at the bear several times with the tip of the spear. For a moment, his tactics worked, and the animal backed away and let out a vicious snarl.

Rico knew that if the bear got into the cave, everyone was dead. He also knew that he couldn't fight off this wild beast for long. So in the act of desperation, he pulled back his spear as far as possible hoping to lure the bear toward him. As Rico had expected, the beast took the bait and moved closer. Then it lunged at him violently. Taking the creature by surprise, he thrust the spear forward forcefully and plunged it into the side of the bear's stomach, then retracted it. The sound of the wounded animal's loud cries chilled Rico to the bone.

The bear backed away momentarily, and then it became even more aggressive.

"Conner, if he gets in here keep stabbing him!" Rico shouted. "Don't stop till he's dead."

During the battle at the entrance, the petrified girls were curled up together in the rear of the cave. In their wildest dreams, Savi and Jade could never have imagined that they might die from a bear mauling. But now that was a real possibility only moments away.

They could hear the horrible commotion at the entrance, but they weren't able to see the bear from their position, nor did they want to. About the only thing Savi and Jade could do was hope Rico and Conner were winning the fight for all of their lives.

Conner stood directly behind Rico as his terrified backup. He was the last line of defense if the bear fought and clawed his way past Rico.

In the bright moonlight, Rico was able to see that the predator was bleeding heavily. Now they realized that any hope of survival relied on severely wounding or killing the ruthless predator.

Again Rico pulled the spear back, tempting the bear to rush him. He didn't have to wait long. A moment later the snarling beast surged forward, its claws waving wildly. When he got close enough, Rico lunged at him and drove the spear deep into the center of the bear's gut. The creature's response was instinctual. It howled in agony and swung its claw ferociously. The cruel blow cut into Rico's left arm and knocked him onto the floor of the cave.

Seeing Rico down and writhing in pain, Conner vaulted forward with a hunting knife and stabbed the bear three times in the leg. As he stabbed the beast, it clawed him on the left side of his face, and he too crumpled to the ground screaming. Now both boys were wounded and bleeding near the entrance.

With Rico and Conner injured, Savi knew she had to act without hesitation. Terrified, she pulled out her knife with trembling hands and began making her way toward the entrance expecting to encounter the bear. When she got to the opening, she was relieved to see the severely wounded creature hobbling away. It wailed with every step as it made its way toward the edge of the clearing.

Rico had lodged his spear in the bear's stomach, and the three knife wounds Conner inflicted seriously damaged the creature's left leg. As it limped away, leaving a trail of blood behind, the bear pawed at the spear hoping to dislodge it from its midsection. Finally, after several swats, the beast succeeded, and the bloody spear fell to the ground. Howling and growling, the wounded bear continued across the clearing until it finally disappeared into the woods.

Now that the bear was out of sight, Savi knew her first order of business was to find one of the medical kits quickly so that she could treat her wounded comrades. She peered out of the entrance and surveyed the clearing. Darting toward the mangled packs, she discovered that the bear had done quite a job on them. Her backpack sustained the most damage and was beyond repair. Its contents were scattered everywhere.

Conversely, Rico and Jade's packs were mauled but still usable. After sifting through the debris, Savi found two medical kits. She stuffed them into backpacks and headed back to the grotto. On the way, she picked up Rico's bloody spear that the bear had discarded and brought it back with her.

By then, Conner's face was bleeding profusely. With a deep gash three inches long on the left side of his face, Savi was glad he couldn't see himself in a mirror. Otherwise, he'd know that his wound would leave a permanent facial scar. Her hands shook as she dabbed the disinfectant over the nasty gash. He winced and pulled away, but understood the treatment was necessary to prevent infection. After she had finished tending to Conner, she put her arms around him and whispered in his ear, "You were brave tonight. Thanks for protecting us."

Rico had also suffered a traumatic injury, and the wounds on his arm were still bleeding. However, after careful inspection, the claw marks weren't nearly as bad as it first appeared. Despite the painful slashes, once the wound was cleaned and dressed, Rico discovered he had full use of his left arm.

"Hey, man, you were solid tonight," Rico turned and told Conner as they fist bumped for the first time.

"You, too. You think that was Vexel?"

"I don't know. But if Vexel is any fiercer than that, I don't want any part of him."

"What should we do now?" Conner asked, following Rico back into the cave while pressing his hand against the blood-soaked bandage on his face.

"I think we should stay here for the night. We're all hurting and too exhausted to travel."

"What if the bear comes back?" Conner asked.

"Grab the spear and follow me. We'll go and salvage what we can from the mess of backpacks."

The two of them left the cave and headed for where the bear had trashed the packs. From across the clearing, they could see their belongings strewn everywhere.

After leaving the cave, they looked back periodically to ensure no unwelcome predators advanced on the girls. Quietly and deliberately, they picked up what they could and returned to the shelter and safety of the grotto.

Once they settled in, the guys agreed to take two-hour shifts guarding the entrance. They elected to exclude Savi from the rotation knowing that she was completely exhausted. After treating both Rico and Conner's injuries, Savi had unintentionally fallen asleep while sitting against the wall inside the cave. She slept so soundly that the guys didn't have the heart to wake her up.

Jade had fallen asleep on the floor of the grotto next to Savi. She still needed time to recover from her injuries and near-death experience on the river.

The first two hours passed by surprisingly fast. Other than the chirping of crickets and the occasional hooting of owls, all was quiet. Conner looked down at his watch and decided it was time to wake up Rico for his shift. He quietly nudged him, and after he had made sure he was awake, he laid down near the entrance and quickly drifted off to sleep.

An hour into his watch, Rico was startled by troubling noises. In the distance, the harsh sound of animals fighting shattered a fragile calm that had finally settled over the cave. The horrific noise frightened everyone awake. The fierce battle waged on for a couple of minutes before one last awful howl pierced the night air. Then came a deafening silence.

Jade sat up terrified. "What was that?"

"I'm not sure," Rico replied, "but it sounded like it was a good distance away. I don't think we've got anything to worry about for now."

"Go ahead and sleep. I'll keep watch. The morning will be here before we know it."

Savi got up and stepped passed Rico. She held a knife firmly in her hand.

"What are you doing?" he whispered in an annoyed tone.

Savi stopped and turned back. "I've got to get some things."

"What things?"

Savi didn't answer. Instead, she quietly darted across the clearing until she came upon her shredded backpack. Bending down and sifting through the debris field, she picked up a few items and put them in her vest pocket and then hurried back to the cave.

"What was that for?" Rico asked.

"I told you, I needed to get some things."

"What kind of stuff would prompt you to risk your life?"

"Well, look who's talking! That's what I said to you about the backpacks, remember?"

"That was different."

"Why? Because you wanted something? If you must know," she responded, "I picked up some pouches of dried food my dad packed for me, a small plastic tarp, my mini flashlight, some stuff from my trashed medical kit, and … my pocket Bible."

Rico's eyes widened.

"Bible? What are you going to do with that?"

"Oh, bless your heart," Savi drawled. "I'm gonna read it!"

Savi went back into the cave and sat down next to Jade, who was still reeling from the traumatic events of the day. She curled up in the corner with her back to the entrance and cried softly. Savi sat down quietly next to her and gently laid her hand on Jade's shoulder. Then she bowed her head for a few moments and said a silent prayer for her friend. When she finished, Savi laid down on the chilly ground beside her new friend, and within minutes she, too, was fast asleep.

Chapter Twelve

A golden sunrise broke through the trees and ushered in a new morning. A noisy flock of Canadian geese flying in a distinctive V formation honked overhead. The squawking of the geese woke Jade from a fitful sleep. After a big yawn, she slowly sat up, rubbed her eyes, and looked around. Seeing the blood-soaked bandage on the side of Conner's face caused her to gasp. Instantly, the events and trauma of the day before flashed into her mind. She glanced around the cave and saw evidence of the bloody battle waged at the entrance only hours ago. Then she bowed her head in sadness and whispered to no one, "What am I doing here?"

Savi stirred when the geese flew by and after a few minutes opened her eyes. It took her a couple of moments to orient herself. Then she stood, and her eyes turned to Conner, still sleeping nearby. Seeing his bloody bandage, she reached into the medical kit and got some fresh gauze so she'd be ready to redress his wound when he woke. He was starting to move a bit, but she wanted to wait until he was fully awake before approaching him. All at once he let out a painful moan and opened his eyes.

"Hey, I'm here. How are you doing?"

"My head hurts like crazy. It feels like I lost half of my face."

Savi knelt down beside him. Then she took off the bandage to examine the injury.

"The gash has really swelled up." She reached into the kit, took out a cotton ball, and poured some peroxide on it. "This will help disinfect it, but it might sting a little."

Conner flinched a couple of times. "Ow! Go easy!"

"I know, but I've got to do it. We can't risk an infection. Now suck it up and hold on. I need to put a bit more on before I bandage you up."

He gritted his teeth, and in no time a clean dressing was applied on the wound.

Next, Savi walked to the entrance where Rico was on guard duty.

"Morning!" she greeted him.

"Hey, sunshine. How'd you sleep?"

"Awful."

"What, you didn't like the mattress?"

"Funny! That hard floor was lousy, and I was so cold. Worse, I kept hearing stuff all night."

"Well, we're all still alive. That's a good start."

"Let me check your arm. Oh, I need to change the bandage."

"How many do we have left?"

"We're good for now."

Savi looked out at the sun beginning to shine through the trees. In the glow of morning, the woods appeared harmless and innocent, but she now knew appearances meant nothing.

After everyone was awake and gathered at the front of the cave, their highest priority was finding food and water. No one had eaten anything except cookies since lunchtime the day before.

The night before, Savi had salvaged three small bags of dried food her dad had given her. When mixed with boiling water the ingredients expanded and became a hot meal. These were the same kind of dry rations he had used in the army. Fortunately, the pouches were sealed, so the bear had ignored them.

Rico and Savi went outside and returned to the area where the bear had mangled the backpacks. After searching a few minutes, to their relief they found another unopened food pack. Now assisted by daylight, they collected anything of value and retreated to the cave. In the process of searching, they found two water bottles and the lighter from Savi's tattered "Crisis Only" pack.

Rico feared that the smell of the food might attract more predators, so he led the group upriver a few hundred yards. After gathering some sticks, they used the lighter to start a small fire. They filled the tin canteen cup with river water and then heated it over the flame. Once it boiled, they poured it into the pouch and waited until the contents softened. Each of them took turns eating with the two forks and one spoon Rico had salvaged. All of them were grateful to get a little something to eat, but it wasn't enough to satisfy anyone's hunger.

Once finished, Rico put out the fire while Savi rinsed the canteen cup in the river. Then they headed back to the cave.

During the return journey, they stumbled upon a gruesome sight.

"Oh, my God!" Jade gasped as she looked down at a huge bloody glob of a mutilated carcass.

"That's so disgusting," Savi said, holding her mouth. "I'm going to puke," she warned . . . and then she did.

After vomiting up the small breakfast she'd just eaten, she did her best to clean herself up.

"Is that the bear from last night?" Conner asked as he surveyed the mess of remains.

Rico studied the one leg still on the carcass.

"Yeah, that's the same bear. See? There are the knife marks on his left leg."

"What in the world could have done this?" Conner asked, a look of bewilderment on his face.

Everyone knew the answer to the question, but no one wanted to be the first to say it. Finally, Conner answered his question with another question. "Could it be Vexel?"

Even saying the name, Vexel, sent chills down his spine and judging by the look on everyone's face, it did the same to them.

No one wanted to wait around to meet the culprit, so they hightailed it back to the cave. Now the goal was to figure out what to do next.

Just then, no more than a few hundred yards downriver, they heard the distinct thumping of a helicopter. In all likelihood, the aircraft was looking for them. Unfortunately, they were too far from the river for the crew to spot them. And little did they know that their abandoned raft had been located early that morning, nearly eighteen miles south of their current position. Because of the violent rapids and empty raft, the rescuers feared the worst and assumed the rafters had probably drowned.

Unwilling to give up the small sliver of hope that remained, the rescue team had sent three helicopters to the accident area to fan out in different directions. And despite their airborne viewpoint, the dense forest and rugged terrain made it difficult to see much of anything beyond the river.

Desperate, Rico sprung to his feet. "If I hurry, they might see me," he shouted and ran toward the river. "Over here! Over here!" he shouted and waved as he exited the dense forest near the edge of the river.

Regrettably, the helicopter banked left and headed off in the other direction after not seeing any clues or hint of survivors. Savi, Conner, and Jade, trailing well behind, got to the river a few minutes later. They arrived just as the helicopter vanished. The four of them stood crushed and speechless. Seconds later, the sound of the chopper was gone.

The group now knew they had a difficult decision to make. Should they stay in the area and hope that the rescuers returned? Waiting might mean facing more predators, maybe even Vexel. Or should they undertake the long and arduous journey through the wilderness back to Camp Arrowhead?

After a lengthy discussion, they came up with a compromise.

The group decided that Rico and Conner would return to the scene of the rafting accident. At the water's edge, they would tie Savi's shredded backpack to a tree and hope it might get spotted by rafters searching the river. Though the plan was smart, what they didn't know was that a rescue crew had just floated past the scene of the accident an hour earlier. Not seeing any trace of the missing teens, they continued downriver to search elsewhere.

After the boys returned, the group huddled together and continued to weigh their options. Following an extended discussion, they determined it was best to stay put for a couple of days so everyone could recover from their injuries. Then, if necessary, the team would begin the long journey back to Arrowhead.

"Do you think we're going to die out here?" Jade asked without hesitation.

"No! No way!" Savi shot back. "We're going to get through this together."

"She's right," Rico responded. "They'll probably find us. But if they don't, we'll figure this out on our own. Besides, we all came here for an adventure, right?"

"That's not even funny!" Jade said.

"Why did you come here, Rico?" Conner asked while holding the side of his face.

"I don't know. I guess the woods and camping bring back some good family memories. It makes me think back to when my mom was still alive."

"What happened to her?" Savi asked.

"She died of cancer, and after that everything changed. My dad quit coming home as often, and I ended up taking care of my two younger brothers and little sister a lot. Recently, my dad saw that I was burned out, and he knew I needed a break. Maybe he thought that time away in the mountains might cheer me up and take my mind off everything. He remembered how much I liked camping as a kid."

The deep sadness Rico carried about his mom's tragic death was now evident for everyone to see. They all realized Rico didn't often let people get this close to him or share emotions he hid on the inside. Jade reached over and placed her hand softly on his shoulder and squeezed him gently. Feeling exposed, he bowed his head and shook it back and forth as if already scolding himself for being so vulnerable.

Then he looked up and turned toward Jade.

"What about you? Why did you come to Arrowhead?"

"My reasons for being here seem so selfish after hearing that," she said with a sigh.

"Don't be so hard on yourself. Every one of us has a different story," Savi insisted.

"Well, I was raised in a Chinese family that valued boys and men over girls. Once I was old enough to understand that, I realized that I was a 'mistake.' My parents wanted another boy, but they ended up with me. Ever since I can remember, I've been a disappointment to both my parents but especially to my mother. She seems to enjoy pointing out my shortcomings. In her mind, I've always been and will always be a failure. Lately, I've started wondering if it's even worth living. Then a friend told my parents that I'd been cutting myself. They freaked out and decided to find somewhere to send me so I wouldn't shame the family. They got me certified as quickly as they could and shipped me off to Camp Arrowhead. I had hoped that maybe here I could accomplish something and prove I'm not always a failure," she concluded with tears streaming down her cheeks. Then she covered her face with her hands and lowered her head.

The others quickly scooted over, and with a keen sensitivity not to touch her injured shoulder, consoled her for the next few minutes.

"I already think you're special, even if you don't do anything spectacular. And don't listen to anyone that tells you otherwise," Savi encouraged her.

"You're one of the nicest girls I've met," Conner added.

"I don't think you're that nice, but you're super cute," Rico joked.

Everyone giggled, including Jade.

A few moments later, Jade looked over at Conner and urged him to share his reason for coming to the adventure camp.

"Do you mind if I pass?"

"No way, Hot Dog! You made me share why I came here. Now it's your turn," Rico insisted.

Conner hesitated and then let out a long sigh. "My story is simple. Every summer my parents travel somewhere in Europe. And every year they find new places to dump me off. This year I beat them to the punch and told them I wanted to come to Camp Arrowhead."

"Why Arrowhead?" Rico asked.

"Since I can remember, everything I've ever wanted was handed to me. I've never really had to work for anything . . ." Conner's voice trailed off.

"Go on," Savi urged him, "there's nothing to be embarrassed about."

Conner leaned away. "It's kind of hard to talk about."

Jade motioned with her hand. "Come on. I told you my story."

"The truth is I'm tired of having so much but feeling like it doesn't belong to me. I envy people like the ones who work for my father. They earn their money. Nobody gives them anything. I'm sick of being told by everybody that I 'hit the lottery' because I was born into the Swift family, even though it's true. I guess I just want to do something on my own, to prove I can."

"Yeah, I get that," Jade said sympathetically.

Rico reached over and gave Conner a light smack on the arm. "Hey, you proved you could do something last night. If you hadn't stabbed that bear after I got knocked down, anything could have happened."

"Yeah and now look at my face. I don't need a mirror. I can already tell my face will be scarred for life. Great way to get all the girls to turn their heads, huh?"

"You'll always be nice looking even with a scar," Jade said in a reassuring tone.

"This is so messed up," he shot back, exasperated.

"It is what it is. You can't change it now. Besides, once it heals, it probably won't be as bad as you think. Anyway, girls think scars are cool. Have you seen mine?"

Just then Rico lifted up the bandage on his left arm and winced in pain when he did. Then he showed them the wound the bear had inflicted on him the night before. Doing his best to mask his discomfort, he playfully taunted the girls. "Come on, look at my scar. It's kind of sexy, huh?"

Savi and Jade grimaced at first when they saw Rico's wound but laughed at his playful attitude. Conner smiled and conceded there was little benefit to stressing over his facial injury because it wouldn't change anything.

Suddenly, from outside they heard the distinct sound of a helicopter approaching their vicinity from somewhere downriver. This time, Rico didn't hesitate. He sprinted from the cave and ran to the river, as fast as his feet would carry him. Rico headed straight toward the sound of the helicopter.

Unfortunately, by the time he got to the river and broke through the tree line, again it was too late. He stood in stunned silence and listened to the sound of the rotors on the rescue chopper decrease to nothing. Dejected, Rico meandered his way back to the cave, realizing the hope of a rescue was rapidly fading.

Chapter Thirteen

Despite the sting of disappointment over missing the helicopter again, the group agreed to use the cave as a refuge to recover for the next couple of days. They reasoned that staying close to the accident site might increase their chances of being rescued.

In an effort to improve the quality of their sleep, the team gathered downed branches and pine straw to cover the cold, hard dirt floor of the enclosure. And in the event of another attack, they fortified the entrance of the enclosure. Fortifying the grotto involved sharpening the tips of several long and thick branches that had fallen from trees nearby. After trimming and carving them, they pointed the sharp end of the stakes outward to protect the entry. Next, Conner located a rather straight downed tree limb about five feet long. Then he followed Rico's example and used his pocketknife to shape it into a spear.

Even though Rico's shoulder still ached, he determined to suck it up and figure out how to do his part to help the group survive. Earlier, he had managed to salvage his collapsible fishing rod along with his reel and a small tackle box from his mauled backpack. Now it was time to put the gear to good use.

"I'm going to the river to see if I can catch us some fish," he said to the others.

Concerned, Savi objected. "Don't go alone. Let me come with you. I don't think any of us should be off too far away by ourselves. Besides, I can help."

Rico looked at Savi's cute but worried face and had to smile. "Okay, you can come with me on one condition. I'll catch 'em, and you clean 'em."

"What? That's the dirty job," she protested. "How 'bout I catch 'em, and you clean 'em?"

"You said you would help. Do you want to go or not?"

"Okay, flame down, Sparky. You've got a deal. But you better catch something."

The two of them slipped away and made their way to the water's edge, leaving Conner and Jade behind in the cave. They climbed over a number of rocks that jutted out over the river and ended up sitting on a big flat one about three feet above the swift current. While Rico prepared the rod and reel, Savi opened the small tackle box and looked over the lures. A green one with black spots and a silver stripe caught her eye, so she took it out.

"Here, use this one. It should land us a trout."

"How do you know about fishing?"

"Me and my dad fish all the time back in Mississippi."

"But how do you know there are trout in the Salmon River?"

"Because we looked online. We discovered the water is too cold for bass and most other fish but perfect for trout and salmon because they like cold water."

"Wow, aren't we smart!"

"It's a little early for salmon, so we need to fish for trout. And let me know if you need a fishing lesson," she said, grinning.

Rico enjoyed the playful ribbing from her and was genuinely impressed.

"Now you get why I gave you that lure? It's a trout lure."

"Really? Okay, let's test your theory."

Rico tied the lure on the end of his line and cast it out and reeled it back in slowly. The lure was weighted, so it sunk a few feet under the water. A few minutes later the small rod jerked forward.

"I've got one!" Rico yelled. "It feels pretty big. I told you we should use this lure," he joked. "You ready to clean, girl?"

"You reel it in, and I'll get it ready for the fire."

After a short fight, Rico landed a beautiful rainbow trout. He watched in amazement as Savi used her knife to cut off the fish's head and then slit its belly open and clean out its guts, which she promptly deposited in the river.

"You're the best fishing buddy I've ever had," he said, scratching his head in astonishment.

"Glad to hear it. But how about next time, I'll catch 'em, and you clean 'em?"

"Deal!"

Feeling encouraged by his success, Rico threw his line back in the river again. And just like before, another trout lunged at the lure and took the hook. He reeled the fish in close to Savi, who snagged the slippery creature, and in keeping with their agreement, cleaned it. After cleaning the second fish, she washed her hands vigorously in the cold river.

The two of them decided to cook up the fish there at the river's edge to keep the distinctive aroma as far away from the cave as possible. Gathering some sticks and pine needles, they stacked them, and using Savi's lighter, made a small fire. Rico carved a sharp tip on a small branch and skewered both fish onto it. Then he roasted the fish over the flames. Once they were finished cooking, they doused the fire with water to ensure it was out.

The duo headed back to the cave with the prized provisions, basking in the glow of success. Upon their return, Jade and Conner celebrated the catch, and they all quickly devoured everything until only bones remained. After the meal, Rico collected the fish bones and dumped them back in the river, just to be safe.

The traumatic events of the past twenty-four hours had left the foursome physically and emotionally drained. Rico, Conner, and Jade were very sore and still recovering from their injuries. Consequently, the teens elected to use the daylight hours to get some additional rest. They also decided that whoever guarded the cave's entrance would do a three-hour shift so everyone could get more sleep.

This time Savi insisted on being part of the rotation. Again, everyone agreed that Jade's injuries should keep her out of the rotation for one more night. Savi volunteered to take the first shift. So the others laid down on the dead leaves and pine straw they had piled on the cave floor. Within minutes, everyone was asleep but Savi.

After an hour of guarding the entrance, Savi reached into her vest pocket and pulled out her small Bible. She flipped through the pages until her eyes fell on the words, "Even though I walk through the valley of the shadow of death, I will fear no evil, for He is with me." She read the words of the Psalm over again and then her eyes filled with tears, and she began to cry. Suddenly, she was startled by something rustling in the cave behind her. She turned, only to see Jade walking toward her.

"Gosh, Jade! You scared the heck out of me," Savi whispered in an anxious voice, not wanting to wake Rico and Conner.

"Sorry, I didn't mean to frighten you."

Savi quickly wiped the tears from her eyes.

"Are you feeling better?"

"A little. I'm still pretty sore, but I feel way better than yesterday."

Then Jade leaned forward and studied Savi's face. "Have you been crying? What's going on?"

"I'm alright, it's nothing," she replied, turning away, embarrassed.

"Come on. What is it?" Jade asked. "And what's that little book in your hand?"

"It's my Bible."

"Is that what made you cry?"

"No . . . well, yes, I guess it did."

"What did it say that made you cry?" Jade asked with interest.

Savi showed her the words she'd been reading out of Psalm 23 and explained that she wasn't crying because she was sad but because the text brought comfort to her and calmed her fears.

Jade reached over and placed her hand gently on Savi's shoulder. "I'm scared, too."

All of a sudden, a rustling sound came from the far side of the clearing. Both of their hearts began to beat wildly. They bent down and peered in the direction of the noise. Then they saw movement about a hundred feet away inside the tree line. Savi felt nervous perspiration forming over her lip. Jade started to quiver from fear.

Squinting, they were able to make out a white-spotted brown creature lurking in the dense foliage. Then unexpectedly a large buck followed by a doe and a little fawn emerged from the woods.

Savi and Jade both let out sighs of relief at the welcome sight. They watched quietly as the family of deer fed on the green grass carpet in the large clearing. The deer grazed for a short time, and then, led by the buck, exited the glade and reentered the woods. The little fawn trailed behind and was the last one to disappear from view.

The red-orange sun was setting, and Savi's shift was coming to an end. Jade grabbed a water bottle, and the two girls took turns hydrating themselves. Then Jade put down her bottle and turned back to Savi. "How do you know that God is really watching over you?"

Savi thought. "My Bible tells me He is, and I believe it."

"Do you think he's watching over me, too?"

Savi nodded and smiled. "You can count on it."

"Does that mean nothing bad is going to happen to us?" Jade asked in a hopeful tone.

"No, Jade. It doesn't mean that at all. It just means that whatever we face, we don't have to face it alone."

Chapter Fourteen

Savi, Rico, and Conner had alternated guard duty throughout the night. A variety of birds burst into song signaling the start of a new day and the end of Conner's watch.

Rico yawned and wiped the sleep from his eyes on his way to join Conner at the entry.

"Man, do I feel better."

"I wish I did," Conner replied. "My face hurts like crazy."

"You've got to expect that those gashes are gonna take some time to heal."

"Yeah, I get it, but it still sucks. How's your arm doing?"

"It finally stopped bleeding. It's still raw, but starting to heal."

"Pretty quiet last night, huh?"

"We needed a quiet one."

"Hey, I'm gonna go wake up the girls."

Rico stepped into the grotto and stood over Jade.

"Hey, Sleeping Beauty. Time to get up," he announced.

Savi rolled over, opened her eyes, and sat up.

"You must be talking to me," she joked while glancing over at Jade, who was beginning to stir.

Rico smiled and looked down at Jade, who was now listening. "Yeah, I was talking to you. Who else would I be talking to, Conner?"

The morning's lightheartedness brought Jade to her feet smiling. Apparently, she felt much stronger than the day before.

Everyone had gotten a little rest, but they all woke up hungry. Unfortunately, the group had already gone through most of their food supply.

Savi grabbed Rico's fishing gear and started to climb out of the cave. "Come on, Rico. It's my turn to catch some fish and your turn to clean 'em."

"Okay, but first I've got to take care of some business in the woods."

"Really!" she shot back while holding her nose.

"What? You never have to go?" Rico questioned.

"Yeah, but I don't announce it to the world!"

Rico disappeared behind the rocks for a few minutes.

"Are you kidding how long you're taking?" she yelled. "We're all starving. Are you having problems with your diaper?"

"You'd better stop unless you want to clean fish again!" he yelled back.

"You know that's not happening."

Rico finally returned, and the two of them headed back to the fishing spot they had found the day before.

Savi reeled in three trout over the course of the next half hour. Two of them were about one pound each, but the last one was bigger, four pounds by Rico's estimate.

Rico cleaned the fish and skewered them onto a two-foot branch. Meanwhile, Savi lit a fire, and they cooked the fish. Upon returning to the cave, everyone ate the catch with a sense of gratitude. Afterward, just like the day before, Rico threw the bones in the river. But as he was returning to the cave, he was unaware that another rescue raft was floating past the shredded backpack that he had tied to the tree earlier. Unfortunately, the rescuers never saw it.

For the next hour, the group huddled in the enclosure to discuss an action plan. They concluded that the searchers probably wouldn't be able to find them anytime soon. So the group decided they had to begin the long journey back to Camp Arrowhead.

Convinced that bears would feed by the water, they chose to move inland and away from the river. The plan was to travel west for about a mile before turning north toward the camp.

Savi used the compass she had recovered from her tattered pack to lead the group in the right direction. Unfortunately, the only map they brought was in Doug's pocket, and when he fell from the raft, it went down the river with him.

"How'd you learn to use a compass?" Jade asked Savi.

"When I was a young girl and went fishing with my dad, we played a game together. After we got deep into the woods, he'd give me a map, a compass, and a set of coordinates. Then he'd go a few hundred yards away and wait. The game helped me learn how to use all three things to find him."

"Weren't you scared being out there alone?"

"At first I was, but I knew he was never that far away. The game taught me how to navigate my way through the woods alone. It took a while to get the hang of using a compass, but now it's pretty easy for me. Unfortunately, without a map, the compass will only help point us in the right direction."

"But how do—?"

Rico interrupted the girls' conversation. "Come on, let's gather up our stuff. We've got a long way to go to get back to Arrowhead, and we better get started while we still have plenty of daylight."

Within a few minutes, the group gathered up their belongings, including Rico's and Conner's spears, and they headed west away from the river. After about a mile, they stopped and took a water break.

"By my estimate, it's time to head north. It's that way," Savi said, pointing.

Rico led the way, determined to establish a good pace. Conner walked by Jade in case she needed help. Meanwhile, Savi was responsible for bringing up the rear, ensuring Jade and Conner stayed close behind Rico.

The woods were dense and loaded with thick underbrush, but the team worked hard and made steady progress over the next few hours. Finally, they agreed to stop for a well-deserved break.

"How long do you think it will take us to get back to Camp Arrowhead?" Conner asked.

Rico mulled over the question.

"I'm not too sure. The camp is probably twenty-five to thirty miles north of us. Maybe four or five days, depending on what we run into and how many miles we can cover each day. That's my guess anyway."

"How's your face doing?" Jade asked Conner.

"Probably about the same as your shoulder," he replied.

"Not so good then, huh?"

"No, not so good."

Conner got up, walked over to Rico, and sat down. "Before we take off again, I need to tell you something."

"What's up?"

"That was a crappy thing I said to you on the football field the other morning. I'm sorry, man. I really am."

"You're right, it was a cheap shot. But I already thanked you for that, didn't I?"

"Yeah, you did. That hit you gave me was worse than the stupid bear's paw!"

"You had it coming. But I appreciate the apology anyway. Why don't you lead the way and keep us on a good pace? I'll go back and check on the girls," Rico proposed. "Don't forget to check in with Savi to make sure we're going the right way."

The group headed out and hiked another couple hours.

Savi and Jade were tired and started to fall several yards behind Conner. The brisk pace was clearly taking a toll on both of them. Jade could see that Savi's limp was more pronounced than usual and that she was struggling.

When Jade saw Rico heading her way, she told him that she was tired and needed to stop. He and Conner were ready for a break as well, so they agreed to pause and take a twenty-minute rest.

During the rest stop, the girls decided to relieve themselves in the woods. They took turns keeping watch for each other. Jade went first. After she finished, she returned, and Savi took her turn.

Savi was gone an unusually long time. And Jade was starting to worry.

All at once, Savi yelled. "Jade, come look what I found!"

"What?"

"A huckleberry patch! There are berries all over the place. I saw some birds eating them, so I know they're safe."

Excitedly, the girls went to inform Rico and Conner. For the next several minutes they all stuffed themselves with wild huckleberries. Once they were full, they took Savi's plastic tarp that she had recovered from her pack and filled it with the delicious treat. Then they lifted the four corners and tied it together with a piece of rope that they cut from the coil. Everyone looked with satisfaction at their stash, knowing they had enough to feed on for at least a couple of days.

Now sporting purple hands and lips, the group felt revived and hopeful. The teens packed up and continued to make their way north toward Camp Arrowhead. After hiking what seemed like another few miles, they were exhausted from the long day's journey. It was time to find a place to sleep for the night. While looking for a new refuge, they came upon a small stream about ten feet wide. In need of a break, they stopped to quench their thirst and refill their water bottles.

"I never thought I'd be so happy to see water," Jade said after taking a sip from her canteen.

"Yeah, at home it's just always there when you turn on the tap," Rico added.

Savi glanced around at their surroundings. "I think there are a lot of things we take for granted. Things we always just expect to be there. Like food and water."

"If we get out of this, I don't think I'll ever look at a water faucet the same," Jade admitted.

Conner was just about to chime in when Savi interrupted him. "Shhh," she whispered. "Don't move."

The others fixed their eyes on Savi. For reasons unknown, something had startled her. She stood motionless, staring at something across the stream in the bushes about thirty feet away.

"What is it?" Jade whispered.

"Turn slowly, and you'll see!"

Chapter Fifteen

The others turned slowly to see what had caused the terrified look on Savi's face. Instantly, they understood.

Across the stream and next to a cluster of bushes a large, dirty gray wolf was standing. The wolf glared curiously at the horrified foursome. For a few moments, no one was quite sure what to do next. Then things quickly went from bad to worse.

Suddenly a second gray wolf emerged from the same cluster of shrubs. This one started to snarl and bear his teeth. This prompted the first wolf to do the same. Instinctively, everyone sensed that the wolves were ready to attack.

"Okay, slowly," Rico whispered. "Everybody take out your knives. Conner, you start moving upstream with Jade. Savi, stay close behind her. I'll watch our backs and bring up the rear. Conner, listen, no sudden moves but go as quickly as you can. Now go!"

Conner led the way as instructed, and the four of them moved methodically up the right side of the stream in a tight-knit formation. Both Conner and Rico had spears in hand and were prepared to fight off an attack if it happened. The girls likewise had their pocketknives out, knowing they might need them as a last resort.

But instead of charging across the stream, the wolves began to move up the left bank, mimicking the group's movement. Never imagining things could get worse, the group watched as two more wolves emerged out of the same cluster of bushes and joined the others. Now four feral creatures stalked them from across the stream. The wolves appeared content to bide their time and wait for the right moment to attack.

Keeping their eyes fixed on the wolves, the teens continued cautiously upstream for about a quarter of a mile. All of a sudden, they started to hear the distinct sound of water crashing. However, the noise seemed very different from that of the raging rapids. At first, they weren't sure what they were hearing. But they did notice that the further upstream they traveled, the louder the sound of the water became.

Meanwhile, everyone started to notice the stream was widening, which increased the distance between them and the predators on the opposite bank. After a while, the watercourse turned slightly to the left, and they saw a majestic waterfall with a huge circular pool in front of it. The water measured about a hundred feet in diameter and had a small sandy beach on the side occupied by the wolves. Behind the falls, a few feet above the waterline was a large rock ledge that led into a wide cavern behind the cascading water.

Across the way, the pack of wolves continued to train their eyes on the group and mirrored every step they took. Vicious growls reverberated with nearly every move the terrified teens made.

"Listen, if we can get onto that rock ledge behind the falls, it'll be almost impossible for the wolves to get to us," Rico yelled over the crashing waters. Then he turned to Conner.

"Take Jade and Savi and climb over those rocks," he said, pointing. "Make your way across the pool and get on the ledge behind the falls. I'll follow you once you're about halfway there. Now hurry!"

Conner led Jade and Savi over the rocks that jutted out above the pool in front of the ledge. On the way, Savi slipped and fell into the cold water just in front of the cascade. When she hit the water, she screamed as the chill shot through her body. Quickly, she hoisted herself up out from the pool and onto a nearby rock. Shaken but unhurt, Savi continued until she caught up with the others.

Eventually Conner, Savi, and Jade reached the flat ledge on the backside of the falls. The trio peered around the cascading water to see how Rico was progressing.

When Rico saw that the others were close to the ledge, he began moving up the right shoreline. But instead of going the same way as the others, he took a different route.

This move agitated the wolves and caused them to inch even closer to the water. As they did, they snarled viciously and exposed their terrifying teeth. Acting more aggressively than before, they watched Rico as he moved up the bank alone. Then the determined pack turned to glare at those standing on the ledge behind the falls.

One could almost see the wheels turning in the wolves' heads as they considered whom to attack first.

Suddenly a lone wolf moved away from the pack and attempted to climb around the backside of the waterfall. The determined creature was searching for some way to get to Rico. Soon the rest of the wolves followed his lead and quickly vanished out of sight.

Rico chose to take a narrow trail on the east side of the pool. Along the path were two large pine trees he had to pass before reaching the rock ledge where the others were waiting. As he walked by the first tree, his spear accidentally banged against it. All of a sudden, the sound of angry buzzing filled the air above him. When he looked up, there was a large mud hive with mad bees darting furiously in all directions. Rico ran for his life. But the bees pursued him and stung his neck, arms, and hands. The pain of multiple bites tore through his body.

Rico dove into the cold water, desperate to escape the onslaught. He swam under the falls and surfaced close to the ledge. Savi and Conner struggled to pull him from the chilly water. Savi leaned forward and plucked Rico's spear still floating in the pool. The spears were essential protection, particularly with the wolves lurking somewhere close by.

Rico was suffering from numerous bee bites, and the girls worked diligently to pull out stingers still embedded in the swollen wounds. While the girls attended to Rico, the wolves reappeared unexpectedly from behind the tree line. Boldly the pack inched closer and closer to the shore. The wolves crouched low by the water's edge and fixed their steely eyes on the shivering teens.

Conner spotted the wolves as, one by one, they emerged from a cluster of trees. Quickly, he seized his spear in the event they tried to swim to the ledge. Conner stood ready but felt fairly confident the pack of wolves wouldn't try to cross the water. Then unexpectedly, one of the wolves leaped from the shore over the water and onto a rock. And then he sprang again onto another one, this time a little closer to the ledge. The aggressive wolf, which appeared to be the leader of the pack, now was no more than ten feet away perched on a rock.

Conner squared up to the wolf and pointed the tip of his spear directly at the creature. The wolf stared at him with wild eyes and continued growling, but kept its place. The angry wolf figured out that the distance between them was too far to jump, so he plunged into the water and started swimming toward the ledge.

"Savi, grab Rico's spear and come now!" Conner yelled frantically. Without hesitation, Savi snatched the spear and positioned herself right next to her teammate. When the daring wolf reached the ledge, Conner and Savi drove their spears into its neck from opposite sides. The wolf recoiled and fell backward into the water, bleeding and howling loudly. Somehow, the wounded animal made its way across the pool to the water's edge. It hobbled out of the water and collapsed bleeding onto the sandy shore.

Conner turned to Savi. "Did you know wolves could swim?"

"I've never thought about it. But I guess if dogs can swim, why not wolves?" Savi replied.

"We've got to do something about that wolf! If Vexel smells its blood, we're over," Conner warned her.

She looked over at the wolf and knew it was dying, but it still twitched on the shore.

"There's nothing we can do at this point. Let's just hope it crawls away. I've seen at least two other wolves still lurking around in the woods over there. We've got to be careful."

Despite the danger, Conner was unwilling to let the wolf bleed on the bank and do nothing about it.

"If I don't deal with that wolf, we might as well put out a welcome sign for Vexel. I at least have to drag it into the pool so that the water will dilute the smell of the blood."

"No way are you going over there," Savi insisted.

"I thought that's what you'd say."

Then, without warning, Conner dove into the pool and headed toward the downed wolf.

"Conner!" Savi screamed.

Conner quickly swam to the shore, pulled out his knife and cautiously approached the dying wolf. Dodging snarling teeth, he used his knife to finish off the animal and put it out of its misery. Grabbing the hind feet of the dead animal, Conner dragged the carcass into the pool and hauled it through the water. He found a group of boulders near the center of the water and wedged the wolf's body between those rocks so it wouldn't drift back to shore. Exhausted, he took a minute to catch his breath before rejoining the others behind the falls.

"I can't believe you did that! What if the other wolves attacked you?" she questioned him angrily.

Dripping wet, Conner glared back at her. "Calm down, Savi. I had to do it. We already have enough problems without Vexel showing up. I did what I needed to do."

"I'm sorry. I just don't want to see anyone else get hurt or worse."

"I get it! We're all under a lot of stress out here. But with Rico down, I had to man-up and do that."

The sun slipped below the trees, and it was starting to get dark. Now that everyone realized the wolves could swim, there was more concern than ever about the rest of the pack still roaming around the area. Consequently, they posted two guards at a time all night long. They stationed a guard with a spear on each side of the ledge behind the waterfall. Rico was still hurting from over sixteen bee stings; but as the evening wore on he improved noticeably.

Savi had fallen into the pool earlier, and now that the sun was down, she started to shiver. She retrieved her life vest that she had hooked on Rico's backpack and draped it over her shoulders. Unfortunately, Rico and Jade were the only ones that still had backpacks. Savi and Conner took turns carrying Jade's gear because her shoulder remained sore from the accident and it couldn't support the weight of the pack.

Everyone kept an eye out for the wolves as they ate their fill of huckleberries and drank from the falls. Once they were all full and hydrated, Rico and Jade took the first three-hour watch. They took turns using Savi's small flashlight to ensure the wolves were not encroaching on their position. This time Jade felt well enough to participate in the rotation, which helped everyone to get some much-needed rest.

The long damp night behind the falls was interrupted several times by the eerie sounds of wolves howling into a moonless sky. Though no one saw the predators during the night, they knew the beasts were still in the area.

After a stressful night of guard duty, the morning sun shimmered through the falls and produced a beautiful rainbow in the mist. In the morning light, they could see that the wolf Conner had killed and wedged between the rocks was still there. No one had seen the wolves since late in the afternoon the day before. The hope was that they had moved on.

The chilled teens welcomed the warmth ushered in by the new day. The temperature rose rapidly once the sun climbed above the trees. Each person ate a few handfuls of berries for breakfast and drank water until they were satisfied. Then they refilled their canteens along with the water bottles and sat down together to discuss their next move.

"We've got to get out of here and head north," Rico urged.

"What about the wolves?" Jade asked concerned.

"We'll deal with the wolves when we need to," he replied. "But we can't stay here. There's too much blood around, and we're already running low on food. As much as I hate to say it, there's no alternative but to take our chances out there."

"I agree," Savi broke in. "We've got to keep moving. The compass says it's that way." She pointed past the waterfall.

"Before we go, I need to say something that I hope doesn't offend anyone. I know the water is cold, but we all smell pretty bad. We all need to clean up a bit. Especially you, Rico," Jade advised.

"Gee, thanks, Jade. What, I stink? Nice . . . I was in the water yesterday," he fired back.

"Well, it wasn't enough. Anybody got some soap?" Savi asked with a laugh.

"Oh great, now everybody thinks I stink. If you haven't noticed, I've been paddling down a river, cleaning fish, fighting bears, hiking for miles, and putting up with you guys for the past two days. I have a right to stink!"

"Wow, Mister Overreaction, we're just suggesting you take a little dip," Savi responded.

Once Rico and Conner surveyed the area to ensure no wolves were around, they appeased the girls and jumped into the brisk water.

"Hey! Do either of you have some bubble bath I can borrow?" Rico joked.

"No," Savi replied, "but I do have some deodorant."

Rico tried to splash her, but she was too far away.

After a couple of minutes, the guys got out, and Savi and Jade went in. The girls played around in the water as if they were two kids at a resort on vacation. Their laughter and giggles echoed through the trees. The sun was hot, so they decided to dry off by laying on a large rock jutting out in front of the falls. The two girls were chatting and as relaxed as they'd been in days.

Suddenly the wolves appeared out of nowhere just a short leap from the unsuspecting girls. They had secretly crossed back over from the other side of the pool and were waiting for an opportunity to attack. The sly pack inched forward, hoping to catch their prey by surprise.

Rico was the first to spot the predators. He picked up his spear and plunged back into the water. With urgency, he started making his way to the girls.

"Look out! Wolves!" he shouted. Just then, one of the creatures readied itself to lunge at the defenseless girls. Conner grabbed his spear and followed Rico into the water. Both of them were now racing to save Savi and Jade. Despite their best efforts, they couldn't get there fast enough. One of the wolves jumped onto a boulder. Seconds later, the beast sprang into the air landing on the far side of the rock where Savi and Jade were sitting. Both girls screamed simultaneously. Afraid to move, they weren't sure what to do next since they were unarmed. Meanwhile, another wolf leaped onto the rock that separated Rico and Conner from the girls. They were now surrounded and in a hopeless situation.

Suddenly the distinct crack of a rifle shot was heard, and the wolf near Savi and Jade immediately tumbled off the rock and floated motionless in the water.

Everyone was so overwhelmed that they froze in place. Then three more shots sounded in rapid succession. Instantly the wolf by Rico and Conner was hit as well. Startled by the gunfire, the last remaining wolf beat a hasty retreat into the woods and disappeared behind the dense foliage.

"What just happened?" Jade asked after she collapsed back onto the rock.

"Somebody saved our lives," Savi answered.

"Are you okay?" the guys asked once they reached the rock where Savi and Jade were sitting in shock.

"Yeah, we're all right," Savi replied with a heavy sigh. "But . . . who shot the wolves?"

Rico looked across the pool and noticed a lone dark figure wearing a camouflaged bush hat walking toward them. He carried an enormous backpack and toted a scoped rifle on his shoulder. Pointing toward the mystery man who was approaching, Rico finally answered Savi's question.

"I guess it was him!"

Chapter Sixteen

The astonished group moved out of the water as quickly as they could. Once on shore, they came upon the bloody remains of the second wolf that the stranger had killed. It had been shot in the head and appeared to have died instantly. The bullet had entered the wolf's head cleanly on one side, but it blew the other half of its face away.

Everyone was surprised and amazed as the young, tall, and rugged looking black man advanced toward the group. He walked up to them slowly but confidently and extended his right hand to Rico.

"I'm Luke."

Rico shook the stranger's hand with gratitude.

"I know I came out of nowhere, but don't worry, I'm a friend."

What Luke said seemed to put Rico at ease.

"Luke, I'm Rico."

"Pleased to meet you, Rico."

"Hey Luke, I'm Savi, and this is Jade," she said pointing at her friend.

"Glad to meet you girls," he said warmly.

"And who might you be?"

"Hi Luke, I'm Conner." They shook hands.

"What are you all doing out here in these parts?" he asked them.

"A couple days ago we were in a rafting accident and lost our guide," Rico answered for the group. "Now we're trying to make our way back to Camp Arrowhead."

"Well, you're heading in the right direction, but you've got well over twenty miles to go. And you'll be traveling over some pretty rough terrain."

"Do you have a cell phone?" Conner asked.

"Cell phone? What would I do with a cell phone out here? There's no service for miles, not until you get to Arrowhead anyway, and even then it's spotty."

"Is there anything around here?" Jade asked. "Someone that might help us get back or a place we can get some food?"

"There aren't any Burger Kings out here," Luke said jokingly.

"No, I was thinking more of a small town or some houses between here and Arrowhead. Or maybe even a ranger station."

He shook his head.

"I'm afraid you're out of luck, angel. There's really nothing and nobody out here. I mean, no one that you'd want to meet anyway. It looks like you've already met some of the locals," he said while staring at Conner's bandaged face.

"Where do you live?" Savi asked.

"About thirty miles southwest of here. The closest town to our cabin is twenty miles south," Luke replied.

Savi moved closer to Luke and extended her hand.

"Let me say thank you for saving our lives. You're quite a shot with that rifle," she said, glancing at the weapon on Luke's shoulder. "So why are you out here alone so far from your home? Are you hunting?"

Luke's face tightened, and he became noticeably agitated. Then collecting himself, he answered, "Yep, that's what I'm doing out here. I'm hunting."

The way he answered the question made everyone feel a bit uneasy. Something was disturbing, but no one could put their finger on why.

"Are you hunting for wolves?" Rico inquired.

Luke paused. "Nope, I'm hunting for Vexel."

It was as if all of them had seen a ghost at the same time. Savi looked at Rico, who turned to Jade, who then glanced at Conner. All four of them thought the same thing, but Jade broke the silence.

"Vexel? You mean he's real?"

"You bet. Vexel is real."

Rico felt the hairs at the base of his neck rise at Luke's answer.

"Why are you so sure?" Jade asked.

"Because he killed my dad three years ago," Luke replied in a sullen tone.

"Oh, no! I'm so sorry," Jade said. The others silently echoed her sentiments with sympathetic nods.

"What happened?" Savi asked.

For the next hour, Luke told them all about Vexel, including how the mysterious beast had tracked down and killed his father during a hunting trip.

"That evil beast devoured my dad until all that was left were his bones."

Luke also told them the promise he made standing over his father's grave three years earlier. He vowed that day he'd hunt down and kill Vexel, or he'd die trying, not only to avenge his dad's death but to rid the world of the hideous creature. He made the pledge when he was seventeen years old. Now he was twenty and still had not fulfilled his vow.

"Two weeks ago, I started looking for him again. I finally picked up his trail about four days ago. And I've been tracking him ever since. That is until I came upon you all last evening."

"How did you find us?" Rico asked.

"Between the four of you, you were making enough noise to raise the dead," he said half-joking.

"You mean you've been here all night?" Conner asked.

"Yep."

"Why didn't you let us know you were around last night?"

"No need to do that. You all seemed to be doing just fine on your own. But today I could tell you needed a little help."

"If it weren't for you, we'd probably all be dead right now."

Luke accepted the compliment, but then became deadly serious. "Listen up, you guys. I'm going to give you a few things to take with you and some words of advice. Then I'll send you on your way. I've got to get back to tracking Vexel. Have any of you ever used a pistol?" Luke asked.

Both Savi and Rico nodded and raised their hands.

"No offense, missy, but I think I'll give this to Rico." Luke handed him a small caliber pistol. "Use it wisely and remember it's only a six shooter. After you fire all six bullets, it's only good for a hammer," he said with a grin.

"Savi, here's a map. It's pretty beat up, but it will help. I see you've already got yourself a compass. You know how to use it?"

"She sure does," Jade bragged.

Luke then reached in his backpack and gave them a bag of dried fruit and another one filled with deer jerky.

It was enough to last them at least a couple of days. Luke also traced out on the map his thoughts about the best way to get back to Camp Arrowhead. Everyone saw the journey would be difficult, just as Luke had told them. The teens now learned they had to cross a challenging mountain range to get back to the camp. Luke also highlighted a few camping spots along the way. And he showed them the area with a hidden cave in the mountains. He said it would serve them well as a final night's camping stop should they need it. Finally, he cautioned them about snakes.

"There are lots of harmless snakes around these parts. No need to worry about those. But it's the venomous ones that are the problem. Just be sure you steer clear of any rattlesnakes. There are two kinds of rattlers you may encounter. A single bite from either one can kill you. One species is called the Great

Basin Rattlesnake, and the other is known as the Northern Pacific Rattlesnake. These snakes aren't naturally aggressive unless they're cornered, stepped on, or taken by surprise. But you've got to keep your eyes open," he warned.

Before Luke departed, he pointed out the last natural obstacle they would have to cross to get back to the camp. It was a river about a quarter mile wide called the Susquehanna.

He informed them that every year on September 1, just five days away, the Clayton Dam was opened for fourteen days. After the dam had released its water, the river was virtually impassable. Then he told them that if they didn't make it across the Susquehanna River by August 31, they would be stuck on the wrong side of the river for at least another two weeks.

Luke glanced at each of teens one last time and shook hands with Rico and Conner, who both thanked him for everything. The girls each gave him a warm farewell hug and echoed their thanks as well. They all watched and waved as Luke disappeared into the trees to fulfill his vow. Obsessed by his pledge to kill Vexel, he left the struggling teens to make it back to Camp Arrowhead by themselves. The group stood in stunned silence and secretly wondered if their paths would cross again.

Luke had deliberately withheld one vital piece of information during his visit. He decided it was best not to tell them this one thing since it would only increase their already high level of anxiety. Vexel was in the area, and he, too, was moving north.

Chapter Seventeen

The team anticipated a long day of hiking, so they drank freely from the waterfall and filled their canteens and water bottles again before heading north. Rico took the lead followed by Jade and Savi. Conner's job was to bring up the rear and ensure no one fell behind. From the outset, the terrain was treacherous, and the going was slow.

After a grueling morning of trekking through the woods, the foursome stopped for a midday break. Lunch consisted of the deer jerky that Luke had given them and the last few handfuls of the huckleberries. By the time they finished eating and recovering, it was early afternoon. Everyone knew they still needed to travel another four miles through dense forest and heavy underbrush to get to the destination Luke had suggested.

During their time together, Luke was kind enough to sketch out the most direct route to Camp Arrowhead. He also provided them with a tentative schedule that would get them to the Susquehanna River by the afternoon of August 30. Following his timetable ensured that they would arrive a full day before the Clayton Dam opened. But if they were late, the river would become impassable for at least two weeks.

The plan required that they travel at a reasonable pace and cover about five miles a day. He also advised them that the last days would be the slowest and hardest because they would have to cross over a formidable mountain range. The mountains were the last major obstacles before they reached the Susquehanna River.

Traveling through the dense forest was difficult enough, but the heavy underbrush made it even more challenging. The journey was so demanding that every half mile or so, the hikers would become so exhausted that they had to stop and rest. Savi informed the others that they had already fallen behind Luke's suggested timetable. But there wasn't much they could do since everybody had been giving their all.

The day dragged on as the group navigated its way through the dense wilderness. By late afternoon, they were about a half mile from reaching their destination.

Exhausted, Jade looked at Savi and asked, "Can't we just camp here for the night? I don't think I can go much further."

"We're getting close. You just have to push yourself. We'll be there soon," Savi replied.

"I can't. I need a break," Jade insisted.

Everyone's arms and legs were scratched and bleeding because of the dense underbrush. Savi realized Jade wasn't able to go on, so she yelled ahead.

"Rico, we need to stop. Just for a few minutes."

"No way, not now. It'll be dark soon. We've got to keep moving. It's just a little farther. Then we can stop."

"I'm not going another step without a break," she shot back angrily.

Then Savi stopped and sat down against a tree. Following her example, Jade collapsed to the ground and let out an enormous sigh of relief.

Savi reached over and handed Jade her canteen and a piece of dried fruit. Tired, but grateful, Jade drank her fill of water and then ate the small bit of fruit.

"Are you kidding me?" Rico shouted when he turned around and saw the girls sitting on the ground.

"Thanks, Savi. I'm trying to keep up, but it's hard. I don't know how you're doing it with your ankle and all."

"Believe me, I'm hurting, too, but we're almost there, and then we can rest for the night."

Anxious to get moving again, Rico walked back a few yards to where Savi and Jade had stopped and compelled them to get up. "Come on, girls, it's time! We've got to go before it's too dark to travel. Let's go!"

Savi got up like a woman five times her age. Then she reached out her hand to Jade.

"Come on, Cinderella. Get up before your carriage turns into a pumpkin."

Jade grabbed Savi's outstretched hand and used it to pull herself up to her feet.

"What I need are ruby slippers like Dorothy had in *The Wizard of Oz*. I'd click my heels together and say, 'There's no place like home. There's no place like home.'" She started to walk again.

After hiking a few minutes, Jade looked over at Savi.

"As bad as this place is, the truth is it's better than being at home. It's weird, I've only known you a few days, but I already feel like you're one of the best friends I've ever had."

"What about me? Do you love me, too?" Conner asked her from behind in a mocking voice.

"Shut up, Conner!" she snarled. "And what are you doing eavesdropping on our conversation anyway?"

"I'm just trying to learn a little more about my next girlfriend!" he replied in a playful tone.

"Dream on, lover boy," she fired back.

Following the exchange, everyone lapsed into an extended period of silence. The weary hikers trekked methodically through the darkening forest one tiresome step at a time. Although the hike seemed like it would never end, they finally arrived at the destination Luke had marked on the map.

After they had caught their breath, Savi walked over to Jade, who was propped up against a large rock. She put her hand on Jade's good shoulder and gave it a soft squeeze.

"I'm really proud of you, Jade, for pushing through today. And so you know, I heard what you said about me back there. And I'm really glad that you feel that way. I feel the same way about you. I'll bet we'll be friends for the rest of our lives," Savi added.

"I hope so, too," Jade replied.

Luke had chosen a great place for them to spend the night. It was on a relatively secure hilltop about forty feet high and had steep rock walls on all sides. The natural outcropping, thousands of years in the making, was practically vertical all around. That made it almost impossible for predators to climb. The narrow goat trail that zigzagged up the east side was the only way to get into the camp. The single entrance made guarding the fortress a lot easier.

After reaching the elevated vantage point, their view was unobstructed for about a quarter mile in all directions. The clear line of sight afforded them a sense of safety and security they hadn't experienced since the accident on the river.

The night air was cooler than usual because of a brisk breeze blowing in from the north. The unusual conditions seemed to indicate a possible change in the weather. Or worse yet, an approaching storm.

Once the group settled in and had a chance to recover, they rehydrated themselves and ate some more of the food that Luke had given them earlier in the day.

Conner and Rico went back down the goat trail to gather small branches and wood to build a fire. Once they returned and lit the fire, everyone happily surrounded it and gradually began to thaw. At first, they sat quietly and relished the warmth and a few moments of relative safety.

Eventually, Jade broke the silence. "Do you think we'll make it to the river by the last day of August?"

"I hope so," Conner replied. "But we're going to have to press hard. Tomorrow will be another tough day, so we'd better rest up."

"I think we only need one guard per shift tonight. Let's make the rotation three hours long. Everybody good with that?" Rico asked. "How about I take the first watch?" he added.

The others nodded, laid down by the fire, and quickly fell asleep.

Rico began his vigil and walked slowly around the approximately fifty-foot oblong hilltop. As the moon slipped behind a gathering of ominous looking clouds, the visibility decreased noticeably. In the distance, Rico saw flashes of lightning illuminate the night sky, followed by loud thunderclaps several seconds later. It was now apparent that rough weather was approaching their exposed position.

Rico found an open spot to stand near the fire. Though the flames were gone and only glowing embers remained, the warmth they radiated felt good to him. Not far away, Conner was snoring softly. Rico glanced over at the girls who were on the other side of the fire and sound asleep. The rocky hilltop didn't provide much when it came to creature comforts, but at least it felt relatively safe.

All of sudden in the distance, the sound of an airplane caught his attention. It appeared to be flying moderately low and moving quickly toward the hilltop. Rico quickly realized that what he was hearing could be a nighttime search plane looking for them. In just a few moments, the aircraft was within sight and flying no higher than a thousand feet, he guessed.

Instantly, he dropped his spear and attempted to pull the lighter out of his vest pocket so he could signal the plane. Then he remembered that after lighting the fire he had given the lighter back to Savi. The plane was now directly overhead, and Rico waved frantically hoping to get the pilot's attention.

Unfortunately, since the fire had gone out, the hilltop was dark, and Rico and the encampment went unnoticed.

In a matter of moments, the plane flew out of sight. Rico kicked himself for giving the lighter back to Savi instead of holding on to it. After the aircraft had already passed by, he also remembered she had a small flashlight. Rico stood alone on the hilltop discouraged beyond despair. He now faced the reality that a rescue was improbable. They were stranded and alone. Now their mission was to get across the Susquehanna River by August 31, or else. He was reasonably confident they could do that if they stayed on pace. Unfortunately, nothing could prepare them for what the next day would bring.

Chapter Eighteen

Following the airplane incident, all was quiet for the rest of Rico's shift. Jade was next in line for guard duty, but to give her extra time to sleep, Rico extended his shift by an hour. After being on watch a little over four hours, he was weary and resolved that it was time to wake her.

Rico gave Jade several gentle nudges before she finally opened her eyes. She rose to her feet and let out a big yawn. A few minutes later, she was fully alert and ready to assume her guard shift.

"It was hard to get up," she said, following another yawn. "I would have slept till morning if you didn't wake me."

"It's good you got some solid rest. You'll need it for tomorrow," Rico said.

"I'm sure you're ready for a few hours sleep, huh?"

"Yeah, I am."

Rico looked at Jade and noticed her beautiful face glowed, even on the moonless night. She glanced up at him with a girlish smile and studied his handsome features.

"Why are you staring at me that way?" he asked somewhat defensively.

"Oh, so I can't look at you without you questioning me?"

"No. I'm not saying that."

"Then what are you saying? Either you like me looking at you, or you don't. Which is it?" she pressed him.

Rico knew he was on the spot but didn't answer her question. Jade folded her arms and stood directly in front of him waiting. When he still didn't answer, she raised an eyebrow and asked him again. "Well? Which is it?"

Before she knew what had happened, he pulled her close, wrapped his arms around her, and then kissed her firmly on the lips. Her first instinct was to pull away. But instead, she melted into his strong arms and kissed him back. At first, he squeezed her so tightly that she nearly lost her breath. Following the unexpected but welcome kiss, she placed her head gently on his shoulder, and they enjoyed an extended embrace. Suddenly, Rico pushed her to arm's length and studied her beaming face. She stood hypnotized and gazed back into his dark brown eyes. Without hesitation, he kissed her again, this time softly.

"Do I stink now?" he asked with a wry smile.

"Yeah, just a little."

"I can't believe you just said that."

She laughed and batted her eyes playfully. All at once, a look of concern swept over her face.

"What's wrong?"

"Right now, there's probably some big brown bear or even Vexel climbing the side of this hill. And I'm standing here making out with you. May I remind you, I'm supposed to be on guard duty."

"You're right. We shouldn't have done that," Rico replied, pretending to be serious.

"I didn't mean—" she started to say.

"What did you mean?" he said with folded arms. "Good night, soldier. We're counting on you to protect us and guard the camp. See you in the morning."

Jade watched Rico walk away. Her eyes followed him until he found a spot to lie down near the others. Soon he was asleep.

Stunned, Jade stood alone and reflected on what had just happened to her. As she gazed into the dark expanse of the forest, she felt a warm rush of emotions flood her entire being. For the first time, she wondered if this was what it felt like to fall in love. Though it had been about two years since a boy had first kissed her, from this night forward, she would always consider Rico's kiss to be her first because she'd never been kissed with such passion.

For the rest of Jade's shift, all she could think about were the precious minutes spent with Rico. She wondered how she'd been swept off of her feet so quickly and easily by just one kiss.

Before Jade knew it, her shift was over. Conner was next in line for guard duty, so she shook him gently and whispered that it was time for him to get up. Once he was fully awake, he asked her to stay up and talk with him for a while. To his dismay, she declined. Though she claimed to be tired, in actuality she wanted to continue to savor the tender moments she and Rico had shared together. Her heart and mind still raced so fast that she worried she wouldn't be able to sleep at all. But shortly after she lay down, her eyelids grew heavy, and she fell fast asleep.

A profound feeling of loneliness overwhelmed Conner as he stood alone on the hilltop. It had been years since he had allowed himself to feel this depth of emotion. He had become a master at hiding his deep-seated feelings of abandonment. One of his ways to distract himself was surrounding himself with lots of friends and participating in lots of social activities. He also used his false bravado to cover up his insecurities. Now, the pain of his facial wound, the stress associated with being stranded in the wilderness, and a crushing sense of isolation all combined to bring him to tears.

Alone in the cold and the dark, he sobbed quietly for nearly an hour.

Conner's night shift seemed to drag on forever. Finally, it came to an end, and he woke Savi to take his place. Right away, she could tell something was wrong. Conner's customary cocky attitude and stride were missing. He appeared sullen and troubled like she'd never seen him before.

"What's up?" she asked.

"Not much. I think I'm just tired. And . . . I'm not sure what else," Conner mumbled.

"It's been a rough few days out here."

"I don't think it's about being out here. . . ." He hesitated a moment. "Oh, just what you need, to listen to my stuff, huh?"

"Why not? It's not like I've got a lot to do," Savi replied. "And sometimes, talking helps."

"I guess, but I'm not good at talking about serious stuff or trusting people," he confessed. "Seems as if every time I trust someone, I end up getting hurt."

"Maybe you're trusting the wrong people," Savi said.

"What do you mean by that?" He sounded annoyed.

"Just what I said. Maybe you're not trusting the right people."

"So how do you know who to trust and who not to trust?"

"I consider what people do, not just what they say."

"What do you mean?"

Savi thought for a moment, "How about I answer your question with another question. Suppose somebody told you they were honest, but you consistently caught them lying, what would you think?"

"I'd assume they were a liar. Even though they said they were honest."

Savi nodded.

"I totally agree. So the bottom line is that I've learned to trust people based on what they do more than on what they say."

"That makes sense," Conner admitted.

Savi stepped forward, wrapped her arms around him, and gave him a big hug. Rising on her tiptoes, she whispered in his ear, "I'm glad you feel that way." Then she looked down at his watch. "It's late. You'd better get some sleep. We'll be leaving in a couple hours, and you need some rest."

"I think you figured out that I don't usually talk to people about this kind of stuff. So don't go telling those guys what we've talked about, okay?"

"Shucks, Conner, I was just going to wake them both up and tell 'em everything," Savi said with a big smile and her best southern accent. "Now go get some sleep."

"Good night, Savi. You're pretty smart for a little squirt," he joked, leaving them both smiling as he walked away.

There would be no majestic sunrise on this day because ominous clouds covered the ordinarily blue morning sky. At first, only a few raindrops fell. But soon the rain came down so hard that it hit the faces of those sleeping and woke them up. Before long everyone was up and about, getting ready for the next segment of the journey.

When Jade saw Rico, she greeted him with a girlish smile and went on about her business as if nothing had happened the night before. Rico acknowledged her with a raised eyebrow and returned the friendly greeting. He, too, carried on as if nothing between them had changed. Both of them were doing a good job of pretending, except when they would catch each other sneaking a peek.

After breakfast, the group decided to sit down with the map and go over the route Luke traced out for them the day before. Since it was tucked away in Rico's backpack, a short distance away from where they were sitting, Savi got up and went over to retrieve it. On her way to get the map, she glanced back when she heard Jade laughing at something that Rico said. For a moment, she lost track of where she was going and stumbled into Rico's pack that was leaning up against a rock.

Instantly, they all heard a loud rattling sound.

Rico shouted, "Savi, stop! Stay still!"

Confused about what was happening, Jade looked to see what was the matter. Her eyes focused on something moving next to Rico's pack. Instantly, she realized what she was looking at and let out a blood-curdling shriek. The scream made Savi flinch, which alarmed the rattlesnake coiled up next to her. Before Savi had time to react, the snake sprang forward and clamped its venomous fangs through her wetsuit and into Savi's right calf. Instantly, she crumpled to the ground writhing in pain with the snake still clinging to her leg.

Immediately, Rico leaped forward and used his spear to knock the snake off of her. Then he pulled the pistol out that Luke had given him and deposited three bullets into the rattler's head. He killed it, though it continued to squirm around for the next several seconds.

Conner ran to Savi. She was rolling on the ground in severe pain, holding her calf, and wailing loudly. He bent down and pulled up her wetsuit above the wound. Then, not knowing what else to do, he put his mouth over the snakebite and sucked as much of the poison out as he could. All through this painful process, Savi writhed in agony and continued to scream hysterically. Every couple of seconds, Conner would spit the venom out and then repeat the same procedure.

Savi became quiet and started to shake. Jade sat down next to her and cradled Savi's head in the crook of her arm. She tried her best to comfort her friend but feared she might be dying.

"Savi," Jade pleaded, "come on, stay with us."

Rico quickly whipped off his belt and used it to tie a tourniquet on her upper right leg. Pulling out his knife, he cut a straight incision between the two fang marks, which caused blood to flow freely. Savi screamed and tried to pull away, but she didn't possess the strength to do so. Rico, following Conner's lead, then sucked more of the venom and blood out of the wound and spat it to the ground. Finally, Conner disinfected the spot where Rico made his incision and then carefully bandaged the snakebite.

Feeling distraught, Jade turned to the guys with tears streaming down her face and asked in an anxious whisper, "Do you think she's going die?"

Conner and Rico looked at one another and then back at Jade.

Rico leaned forward and answered for the two of them. "Only God knows."

Chapter Nineteen

Jade had not left Savi's side since she was bitten. She watched her friend carefully and monitored her every move and breath. For several hours Savi slipped in and out of consciousness. She had been lying still for about thirty minutes when suddenly she began to twitch and shake uncontrollably. Frightened and unsure of what to do, Jade yelled for Rico and Conner. They dashed over to the girls to see what was going on.

Savi's breathing was shallow and her pulse hard to detect, but she was alive, and that's all that mattered for now.

Once they felt Savi had stabilized again, Rico motioned Conner to follow him. They moved to the far side of the hilltop so that they could talk without being overheard.

"She's too sick to move anywhere," Rico confided after he made sure they were out of earshot. "We're going to have to stay here at least another day, maybe two."

"I agree," Conner replied. "I'm not sure what else we can do for her."

"We've got to keep loosening the pressure on the tourniquet about every ten minutes for the next couple hours. It may lessen the amount of toxin that passes through her body. Besides that, I can't think of anything else we can do, except to try and keep her warm."

Jade began to sob as she looked down at her friend's motionless body. At this stage, even the slightest motion or sound from Savi was reassuring. Any movement helped Jade retain a sense of hope that Savi might still recover.

Jade sat helplessly gazing down at one of the first friends she'd ever really trusted. More than anything she wished there was something she could do to save Savi's life. But the only thing she knew to do was wait.

As Jade studied Savi's face, she noticed there was something about her that was pure and wholesome. But she was also fun and feisty at the same time. Savi exuded confidence but had a humility that made her endearing. Everyone knew that she read her Bible but she never sounded preachy or judgmental. She lived her faith, instead of only talking about it.

All at once, Savi started to shake again and let out a horrific scream.

"Savi! Can you hear me? It's Jade! You're going to be okay, just hang on!"

Gradually, the shaking slowed and eventually stopped. Within minutes, Savi slipped back into unconsciousness, and her body lay motionless.

Jade noticed the top of Savi's little book sticking out of her front vest pocket. Curious, she reached for the book. Jade still remembered the words Savi had read to her and thumbed through the little Bible searching for something called Psalm 23. Somewhere close to the middle she found it.

Rico and Conner were talking privately on the other side of the hilltop. After they had finished chatting, they returned to where Jade was sitting with Savi and sat down.

"How are you doing?" Rico asked, placing his hand softly on top of hers.

"Not good. I'm so afraid she's going to die. I just feel so helpless."

Rico looked at her sympathetically, "Listen, there's a lot of things in life we can't control, Jade, and this is one of them."

"Maybe that's why she was reading this book," Jade said.

"What are you talking about?" Conner asked.

"Savi was reading from her Bible the other day. And when I asked her what she was reading, she showed it to me. It's funny, but something about the words I read touched me in a way I can't explain."

"What did it say?" Conner asked.

"I don't remember exactly. That's why I want to look at it again."

"I want to hear what it says, too. Will you read it out loud?" Conner asked.

"Okay."

Jade glanced at Rico. "Do you mind?"

"No, I don't care, go ahead and read it."

Jade lifted the small brown book and began reading the words Savi had shared with her.

"Even though I walk through the valley of the shadow of death, I will fear no evil, for He is with me."

Then Jade lowered the book along with her head and immediately started to sob. Rico and Conner sat quietly, not sure what to say. In an attempt to comfort her, they each placed a hand gently on her back. After she had stopped crying, the three of them sat silent for the longest time and stared down at Savi. She lay so quiet and still before them, but nonetheless, they all knew she was fighting the biggest battle of her young life.

It was now late afternoon, and Jade still hadn't moved from Savi's side since early morning. Again, Rico and Conner walked a few feet away and spoke for a few minutes in hushed tones. When they returned, the boys advised Jade she needed to take a break. They offered her some water, a little of the remaining dried fruit, and a piece of jerky that Luke had left. Though she didn't like the idea of leaving Savi even for a minute, she knew a short break and having a bit to eat and drink might revive her.

Conner volunteered to sit with Savi during Jade's absence. Rico and Jade found a large rock to sit on about ten feet away from where Conner was attending to Savi.

"I just can't bear the thought of losing her. I've only known her a few days, but she's like the best friend I've ever had."

"She may be small, but she's a fighter. If Savi was going to die, I guess it would have happened by now. She's still not out of the woods, though." Rico paused a moment. "Did I just say that?"

A half-smile crept across Jade's face as she punched Rico hard on his good arm.

"Quit joking around," she said in a scolding tone.

"Okay, calm down. It was just a slip. You know how much I want Savi to pull through," he added sincerely.

"I know. But I'm afraid she might die."

Conner sat next to Savi holding her hand. Suddenly, she squeezed his hand tight and yelled out, "Killed my brother! And just five years old!" Then her grip lessened on Conner's hand, and a moment later, she slipped back into unconsciousness.

Jade and Rico heard Savi yelling and ran over to her.

"What's going on?" Jade asked anxiously looking at Conner.

"She's just delirious. She yelled something about her brother. That somebody killed him!"

Jade pressed him. "Do you think that really happened?"

"Who knows, but I wouldn't take too seriously anything she says in her condition. Savi's system is trying to fight off the venom. A lot is going on in that little body of hers right now."

The clouds had looked threatening all day, but the rain never materialized until now. All at once, a heavy downpour started.

In a matter of minutes, everything and everyone was soaking wet. Though they tried their best to protect Savi, before they knew it, she was lying in a large puddle of water. This new difficulty added to an already challenging situation.

"We've got to move her quickly," Rico advised. "Let's get her onto that flat rock. If we don't, she's going to get pneumonia on top of everything else she's fighting."

"Are you sure we should risk moving her?" Jade asked.

"We don't have a choice," Conner replied.

Carefully, the three of them lifted Savi and carried her about ten feet to the top of a flat rock. The trio did their best to dry her off and covered her with the small piece of tarp that once held the berries.

The rain continued for the next few hours and well into the night before it eventually stopped. Soon after that, the dark clouds vanished, revealing a half-moon and star filled sky. Thankfully, not only had the rain moved on but also the chilly air left with it. Everyone was grateful that the temperature was now more moderate rather than achingly cold as it had been earlier.

Rico and Conner cautiously worked their way down the goat trail to gather twigs and wood so they could make a fire. The plan was to build a fire as close to Savi as possible without endangering her. They hoped the warmth of the fire would keep her comfortable and hasten the time to dry her clothes.

While Rico and Conner were gathering wood down below, Jade returned to Savi's side. She had just sat down when, suddenly, Savi started convulsing uncontrollably. This time she shook violently for several seconds. Then as quickly as the shaking began, it stopped, and her body went limp.

At this point, Jade feared the worst and immediately bent down and placed her ear over Savi's mouth to see if she was still breathing. To her relief, she was, but just barely. Saddened by Savi's dire condition, Jade leaned back, sighed deeply, and started to sob.

Then, without any warning, Savi opened her eyes and whispered, "Jade, can I have some water?"

Shocked, Jade gently squeezed Savi's hand.

"Oh Savi, it's so good to hear you talk again. I'll be right back with some water."

Jade hurried to find a water bottle and quickly returned. Carefully, she propped up Savi's head and held the bottle while she drank slowly. Over the next couple of minutes, Savi downed about a quarter of the bottle's contents.

"Oh my God, we thought you were going to die. You've been in and out of consciousness for almost a day. How are you feeling?"

"Like I got . . . bit . . . by a rattlesnake. My leg . . . killing . . . me," Savi whispered brokenly as she closed her eyes and nodded off.

Rico and Conner finally made it back up the slippery goat trail to the hilltop. Both of them were carrying big bundles of wood. When Jade saw them, she shouted, "Savi woke up and talked to me!"

Rico and Conner dropped the wood they were carrying and ran over to see how Savi was doing.

"What happened?" Rico asked.

"Savi woke up and asked me to get her some water. I couldn't believe it. She knows a rattlesnake bit her and everything. I thought we'd lost her for a while, but now I think she's getting better."

"Maybe somebody is watching over her," Rico said, "because, honestly, I thought she was history. Listen, it's been a crazy day. You guys stay close to the fire and get some sleep. I'll stand guard a few hours and keep an eye on her. Conner, help me bring some of the wood closer to the fire. I want to keep a flame going for Savi as long as we can."

"How do you think she'll feel by tomorrow? Do you think she'll be well enough to travel?" Jade asked.

Rico paused. "I sure hope so. Because we only have four days left to get across the Susquehanna before the dam opens."

Chapter Twenty

Conner placed a butterfly bandage over Savi's wound to pinch it closed to lessen the bleeding. Finally, she had stopped shaking and was no longer delirious.

Savi struggled through the first part of the night and seemed more aware of the painful wound on her calf. Sometimes while half asleep, she would reach for her calf and groan in agony if she touched it. Once Jade saw this, she'd grab Savi's hand whenever it started to move toward her leg to keep her from hurting herself.

Late in the night, Savi woke up and requested food for the first time since the rattlesnake had bitten her. She also drank a full bottle of water. Pain and discomfort from the wound were still written all over her face, but at least the injury had stopped bleeding.

It took quite a while for her to finish the food and drink she'd requested. But soon after, she closed her eyes and immediately fell back to sleep. The fact that her thirst and appetite were increasing served as a great encouragement to everyone. For the first time since the incident, Savi was showing indications that she was well on the road to a miraculous recovery.

By morning, Savi was sitting up, still woozy but talking more like her old self. During breakfast, the others informed her about the craziness she had missed while still unconscious. Regrettably, Savi's injury had forced them to extend their stay on the hilltop. Now the provisions Luke had given them were almost gone. Though she was feeling much better, Savi was still too weak to hike through the woods. Everyone knew the time they had to cross the Susquehanna River was rapidly ticking down. Obviously they wouldn't be leaving the hilltop anytime soon. They all determined that a new plan was needed if there was any hope of crossing the river by the deadline.

The teens all huddled together. Rico shared his idea to help the group move north again toward Camp Arrowhead. Rico had modified his backpack to serve as a carrier for Savi. He suggested that he and Conner would use the modified pack to alternate carrying her through the woods until she could walk on her own.

At first, Savi vehemently objected. She popped right up and attempted to show everyone that she could walk unassisted, only to fall after just a few steps and lay on the ground writhing in pain.

Conner sprang to his feet, helped her up, and protested sharply. "For such a smart girl, that was a stupid thing to do!"

"We don't have time for this!" Rico interrupted him. "Now listen, we've got to move now. We're low on food, out of water, and running out of time. If we want to cross the river before the dam opens, we've got to get moving!"

"You might be able to walk better tomorrow, but today you can't," Conner added emphatically to Savi.

"I think it's a good idea" Jade interjected. "At least we'll be moving again, and let's face it, Savi, you're in no condition to walk right now."

Savi bowed her head and thought for a few moments about what they were all saying. Convinced they were right, a sign of resignation settled over her. "Alright, I'll let you carry me if you guys promise me that as soon as I can walk,

I'm out of the baby seat. Deal?"

"Deal," everyone agreed.

Savi was tied in place and rode on the crude carrier made out of Rico's altered backpack. Obviously, the mode of transport was extremely uncomfortable for her, but despite the pain in her calf she refused to complain. In fact, she was deeply touched by the concern and care the others were showing for her.

The group surveyed the camp one last time and felt grateful for the hilltop retreat that had been their home for the past couple of days.

Carefully, they eased their way down the slick goat trail until everyone had reached the bottom and the edge of the tree line.

Once they entered the woods again, Rico focused on making sure that Savi's injured calf stayed clear of the dense underbrush. It was now late morning, and the blazing sun made carrying her that much more challenging. After about a half an hour, they came upon a small stream where they drank freely and rested. Before leaving, they refilled their water bottles and canteens. Conner could see that Rico was tired and volunteered to take a turn at carrying Savi. Rico strapped his pack to Conner's back and then helped secure Savi to it. Minutes later, they were on the move again.

"Hey Savi, how's the ride back there?" he quizzed her.

"The truth is, it sucks," she shot back wearily. "Nice horse, but lousy saddle."

"You must be getting better. You're feisty again," Conner joked between breaths. "I hope you tip well."

"Here's your tip," she said sincerely. "I really appreciate what you're doing for me."

"Was that a compliment? Next you'll say you like me or something."

"Whoa," she shot back. "Don't get carried away. I'd never say anything that crazy."

"You're killing me," he laughed. "But seriously, I need a break, or I'm gonna drop you."

Realizing he had carried her for about a half an hour, Rico and Jade gently helped her down and instantly Conner collapsed to the ground. After they had tended to Savi, everyone rested and drank. During the break, Rico agreed to carry Savi for the next leg of the journey. This rotation continued throughout the remainder of the day.

Rico and Conner were thrilled to see Jade feeling much better. Since the rafting accident she had recovered slowly, but now she carried Conner's spear and did a good job keeping up with the pace. Though she was understandably tired, like everyone else, she looked healthier than she had been in days.

The boys continued to take turns carrying Savi until they could hardly walk. By early evening, they were still a mile away from the stop Luke had marked on the map to spend the night. Completely spent, Rico and Conner could go no further and conceded they'd have to settle down for the night in the open woods, exposed.

After an extended time of rest, the group decided to set up the camp. To fortify their position, they stacked branches four feet high in a circular area about eight feet wide. They completed the structure by forming a narrow opening that served as a passageway in and out of the camp. They eventually finished the makeshift fortress just as the sun was setting.

Darkness had fallen. And though there was plenty of water to drink, the group had depleted the supply of dried fruit and was down to the last three pieces of deer jerky. Jade knew that Savi hadn't eaten much of anything since the snake had bitten her. Rico and Conner, famished from carrying their friend all day, also needed food to replenish their strength. Appreciative of their hard work and touched by the compassion they showed Savi, Jade responded in kind. Taking out the last three pieces of jerky, she handed one to each of them. When they protested, Jade joked she wasn't hungry and said she needed to watch her figure.

"I thought that was my job," Conner crowed.

"You sound like you sucked in too much rattlesnake venom," she replied with a wry smile. "Now, eat your jerky and—"

"Don't say it! I know. I know. Shut up!" he said before she did.

"Thank you. You're smarter than you look!" Jade smiled.

Everyone was too hungry and tired to argue about the jerky. So they simply thanked her and happily wolfed down the last few strips of dried deer meat.

Suddenly, in the distance, they heard wolves howling. Fortunately, the creatures sounded like they were at least a mile away, if not farther. Nonetheless, the thought of wolves instantly sent cold chills up the girls' spines, bringing back horrible memories of the waterfall incident.

Rico and Conner had mustered the energy to gather wood, and after doing so, they started a fire. Everyone leaned in close to the warmth of the rising flames which contrasted the chill of the night air. They spent time recuperating from the day's exhausting hike and talked about the schedule for guard duty.

Moments later, a branch snapped a short distance away from their position, and then another.

"Quiet!" Rico whispered. "Something is close and getting closer."

Conner grabbed his spear, and the girls pulled out their knives. Rico reached for his pistol and was just about to stand up when the group heard a voice.

"Hey now, don't go shooting at me," Luke yelled out, half-kidding.

Then he suddenly appeared in front of the branch barricade surrounding the teens.

"You scared us to death, Luke. What are you doing here?" Jade asked.

"How 'bout I sit with you guys for a couple of minutes?"

"Come on in," they replied in unison, motioning Luke to the entrance.

Luke squeezed his way into the camp through the narrow passageway. And after exchanging pleasantries with everyone, he sat down in front of the fire.

"Honestly, I expected you guys to be a lot farther along than this." Concern tinted his voice.

"Savi was bitten by a rattlesnake yesterday morning and almost died," Rico told him. "We couldn't move her until just before noon today. Conner and I took turns carrying her. She's still having a difficult time walking."

"You probably shouldn't have moved her this soon." Luke looked Savi over. "Sounds like you've had a rough go of it. Where'd it bite you?"

"On my leg," she pointed to her bandage.

"How are you feeling?"

"I'm getting better. Maybe I'll be able to walk by tomorrow," Savi hoped.

"Well, don't overdo it. It'll take a couple of days for that venom to leave your system."

Luke paused a moment and studied Savi's smudged face glowing in the firelight.

"You're lucky you made it, missy. People die from bites like that out here, especially when there's no doctor to treat them."

Then he looked at the injuries each of them was sporting and shook his head.

"I wish there was a good doctor around here because you all sure look like you could use one."

"No kidding," Jade agreed.

"Now be careful to keep those wounds disinfected and as clean as you can," he cautioned.

Then Luke asked them about how their provisions were holding up. At first they hesitated to admit the truth. But finally, Conner confessed that they were all out of food. Hearing this, Luke reached into his pack and gave them what appeared to be half of his provisions.

"No, we can't," Jade protested. "It wouldn't be right."

"It wouldn't be right to leave you here to die of starvation." He flashed a smile at her. "I'll be alright. There's plenty of stuff to eat out here."

"Are you sure?" Rico asked.

"I insist. And before I leave, I'll show you some berries, mushrooms, and nuts out here that you can eat."

"Thanks so much, Luke," Jade said with heartfelt appreciation.

"I don't believe that any of us would still be alive if it weren't for you."

"I'm not sure that's true. But I'd like to see you get back to Arrowhead safely," he said.

"It's great to see you again," Savi admitted.

"Glad you feel that way, and believe me, the feeling is mutual. Unfortunately I didn't only come for a social visit," he said. "I'm here to warn you."

"Warn us? About what?" everybody asked at the same time.

"Vexel. I've been tracking him. And I'm convinced he's close by."

Chapter Twenty-One

The flames in the campfire receded until all that remained were glowing embers. One by one, the weary hikers began to nod off. Luke was also tired, but he understood the importance of staying vigilant because Vexel often hunted at night. Earlier in the day, he had picked up the beast's trail. He felt sure he was closing in on the creature and decided to continue tracking him instead of packing it in for the night.

Luke had already said his farewells and hoped to depart quietly so as not to disturb the weary teens. Suddenly the others were startled awake by the hideous sound of animals fighting in the distance. The yelping and crying noises made by a wounded animal in desperation were horrible to hear. The violent nature of the encounter suggested that they were listening to the brutal work of Vexel.

Luke said a quick goodbye and then hurried out of the camp to track his prey. After he had departed, the terrified foursome turned and looked at one another. A stunned expression crept across each of their faces. There was grave concern over the horrific noises they had just heard, especially in light of Luke's warning about Vexel prowling the area.

Rico knew it would be a tense night and decided to put more wood on the fire. He also volunteered to take the first shift, but this time, Savi overruled him. She knew Rico and Conner had labored extra hard lugging her through the woods, and they needed a good night's sleep. Rico was too tired to resist her offer. He laid down with his trusted spear by his side and fell asleep in a matter of minutes.

Rico gave Savi the pistol before he bedded down. She tucked it away safely in her front vest pocket. Besides the gun, she also had Conner's spear nearby. It was leaning up against the wall of branches near the passageway, only an arm's length away. In the event of trouble, she'd have both weapons instantly at her disposal.

The first two hours of Savi's shift were uneventful except for the occasional howling of wolves in the distance. By her estimate, the creatures were probably a mile or so away from the makeshift camp. As she stood alone by the dwindling fire, Savi prayed the wolves would remain occupied elsewhere.

Earlier, Jade offered to take the second watch, and it was nearing the time to rouse her. Savi tossed a few branches on the fire and then woke her friend.

Once Jade was fully awake, Savi carefully lifted the pistol out of her vest pocket and gave her a lesson on how to use it. Both girls hoped the gun wouldn't be needed, but they also thought it wise to be ready just in case.

After chatting softly for a few minutes, Savi slid over a few feet from the glowing fire and promptly went to sleep.

Jade felt a sense of relief that during her shift everything was calm and peaceful. Except for the hooting of an owl, all had been quiet. It was three hours into Jade's watch when Rico woke up on his own. After taking a drink from his water bottle, he moved over and stood by her.

"Sleep well?"

"Like a rock. After carrying Savi yesterday, I was so wiped out," he admitted. "What about you? How long have you been up?"

"Just a few hours. I slept okay. Those animals fighting freaked me out," Jade replied as she took a slow look around. "Rico, can I ask you a question? And please don't mock me."

"Sure, anything."

"Do you think we're going to make it?"

"Are you talking about making it to the river on time or making it out of here alive?"

"Both!"

"Why wouldn't we make it? Luke's hunting Vexel, and we're only about eighteen miles from Arrowhead. All we need to do is keep moving north. But getting to the river on time will be tough," he acknowledged. "It all depends on how fast Savi's leg heals and how quickly she'll be able to walk on her own. Today will be an important day. We've got to get started early and go at least five miles if there's any hope of crossing the river before the dam opens."

Jade grabbed his hand tenderly and then turned to look at his rugged but handsome face.

"I probably should have asked you earlier, but do you have a girlfriend?"

"I'm not going to lie to you, Jade, I do," he admitted.

Instantly, Jade dropped his hand and turned away. "Then why did you kiss me the other night?" she asked angrily.

"Because you're the one I'm talking about," he replied with a sly grin.

Quickly, she turned back and grabbed his hand again. "I can't believe you did that to me." Then her face lit up, and she batted her eyes, "Really, you think of me as your girlfriend?"

"As long as we're out here I do."

"Rico! Come on! Do you really think of me as your girlfriend?"

"Yeah. Is that okay? Or maybe you still have a thing for Conner," he joked.

"You know better than that."

Just like he had done the other night, Rico pulled Jade close and kissed her softly. Afterward, she rested her head on his shoulder, and the two sat down in front of the fire for the next several minutes looking like a couple in love.

Jade lifted her head and looked at Rico blissfully and thought to herself, *This is the happiest I've ever been in my whole life.*

Nearby, a variety of birds began to stir as the morning light increased minute by minute. The forest started to come alive and welcome in a new day. The chirping of crickets decreased gradually and was replaced by the merry whistling of songbirds.

Rico woke Savi and Conner at daybreak and encouraged them to begin collecting their gear. Because of the extended length of the day's hike, the group needed an especially early start. Following a quick breakfast of dried fruit and water, the foursome finished packing up and left the enclosure. Their next destination was the campsite Luke had marked on the map for them, about five miles north.

In the morning light, everyone could see that Savi was walking much better than anyone could have expected, particularly since a rattlesnake had bitten her just two days earlier. Obviously, her improved mobility was a welcome re-lief to Jade but even more so to Rico and Conner, who no longer had to carry her.

"How's it feeling, Savi?" Rico inquired.

"It's still sore, but it feels a lot better. I should be able to walk on my own, at least for a while."

"Give it a try and see. But you have to tell us if you need help, promise?" Conner pressed her.

Savi agreed. "C'mon. We've got a long way to go, and I'm sure my leg will eventually slow us down."

Soon the enclosure they had built was out of sight behind clusters of trees, shrubs, and bushes. The morning air was crisp but they all knew that before long they would be hiking in the heat of the day.

Conner and Rico chose to set a moderate pace in order not to overwhelm Savi. The slower pace enabled her to keep up and helped the group to make steady progress. Unexpectedly, the terrain abruptly changed. Leaving the thick underbrush and dense forest, they found themselves in an open meadow at least a half mile wide and a mile or so long. Upon entering the open grassland, they came across a small stream where they drank freely and refilled their canteens and water bottles.

Following a short break, they proceeded across the meadow. The unobstructed walk was a welcome change from the thick underbrush and dense forest of the last few days.

Unhindered by obstacles, they were all now able to double their pace, including Savi. However, by mid-morning her limp worsened, and the pace slowed once more.

The group now had to take rest stops about every fifteen minutes to avoid having to carry Savi again. While they relaxed near the end of the large meadow, they noticed behind them a herd of elk crossing the open plain. Then, without warning, the elk burst into a run and started to head straight toward them.

At first, they were uncertain as to what was happening. But when a pack of wolves emerged from behind the stampeding elk, everything became clear.

The elk zigzagged back and forth in an attempt to shake the pursuing wolves. But the wolf pack was relentless. They mirrored the herd's every move with lightning-fast reactions. Turn for turn, cut for cut, they were right on the elks' heels.

"We've got to make a run for the tree line!" Conner shouted.

"Savi can't run," Jade yelled back. "It's too far. She won't make it!"

"You're right!" Rico agreed. "Let's get in a tight circle and face out. Savi, take my spear. I only have three bullets left. So I'll stand behind you guys in the middle with the pistol and try to shoot at least three of them. The rest, we'll have to hold off with the spears and knives."

The elk ran wild as they bore down on the encircled group. They all understood that they would be trampled to death if the stampeding herd didn't turn aside quickly.

"Alright, here they come!" Rico yelled. "We've got to guard each other's backs."

Suddenly, Jade panicked and started screaming. "We can't stay here. We're going to die!"

"Jade!" Savi yelled. "Pull it together!"

"We're going to die!" she screamed hysterically.

Then, Savi, positioned next to Jade, slapped her hard across the face. The sound of flesh striking flesh was so loud that the others heard it, even over the noise of the charging elk.

Jade, shocked by what Savi had done, immediately stopped screaming.

"Unless you pull it together, we are going to die!" Savi shouted at her in anger. "Now stop it!" Jade quickly resumed her position, as did Savi. Now the charging herd was just fifty feet away and closing fast.

Chapter Twenty-Two

The charging elk perceived the group to be an obstacle or a threat, and, at the last moment, veered off to the right. The herd of about forty blew past the teens leaving them shocked and in a thick dust cloud. After the herd had passed by, the terrified onlookers expected to see the wolves appear, but they never did. Instead, to their amazement, they saw the wolf pack hundreds of yards away. They had downed a straggler from the herd and were in the process of devouring the helpless animal.

Although relieved for the moment, they understood the wolves would eventually finish eating the carcass and turn their attention elsewhere. So without hesitation they made a beeline for a cluster of trees that were about a quarter mile away. Once hidden inside the tree line, they paused to catch their breath and take a drink. Just before they resumed their trek, they looked back in the direction of the wolves. Despite successfully taking down their prey, the wolves were fighting with one another over different parts of the fallen elk. This welcome development convinced the group that they were no longer in imminent danger. Unwilling to take any chances, they hurried away from the wolves as fast as their legs could carry them.

About a half hour later, exhausted from the forced march, the group needed to pause for a break. Once they stopped, Savi made her way over to Jade, who was less than excited to see her.

"I'm sorry for slapping you the way I did. I hope you can forgive me?"

"No! I won't forgive you. You hit me really hard," Jade said in an angry tone. "Just like my mother slaps me."

"I'm so sorry, but it looked like you were losing it out there, and I didn't know what else to do," she confessed.

"I've been slapped in the face since I was old enough to remember, and I hate it more than anything," she fumed. "I never thought you'd do something like that to me."

"I get that you're angry, Jade. You have a right to be. And again, I'm sorry. I've never slapped anyone like that before. And I don't plan on ever doing it again. I just want you to know how awful I feel."

"I don't care how awful you feel! I'm the one that got hit," she railed.

Just then, Rico interrupted. "Let's go, you guys. We've got to keep moving. We lost a lot of time back there. Those wolves could be finished with that elk and headed in our direction. Savi, you come up here and walk with me. Conner, you keep Jade in front of you and guard the rear."

"Sounds like my kind of job," Conner said with a grin.

"Shut up, Conner," Jade said with a snarl.

As they commenced moving north again, Rico could tell that Savi was struggling. Not only was she hurting physically, but she was also devastated by Jade's apparent unwillingness to forgive her. Savi's limp was now more pronounced than ever, and she was walking with her head down, obviously distressed about her situation with Jade.

A few minutes into the hike, Rico placed his hand on Savi's back in an attempt to encourage her.

"For the record, you did the right thing back there, Savi. Don't get me wrong, I'm not suggesting that you make a habit of slapping people around, but in that situation, it was necessary."

"Thanks for saying that. But it doesn't change the fact that Jade's still really mad at me," Savi conceded. "I feel bad that I slapped her at all, but the fact that I hit her so hard makes me feel even worse. I think I was just scared, and I knew we needed her head in the game."

"Give her some time. She'll get over it," Rico assured her.

They had traveled about three miles since leaving their overnight camp and now were only two miles away from reaching the day's final stop.

"Hey, Jade, how are you doing up there?" Conner inquired.

"Leave me alone," she replied harshly.

"Hey, don't bite my head off," he replied in an exasperated tone. "I was just checking on you."

"I'm just mad at Savi. And besides, I don't want to talk right now."

"Why are you so angry at her, because she smacked you?"

"Duh!"

"Well, guess what? We had to do something. We were in trouble back there, and we needed your help. You panicked. Someone had to get your attention."

"Oh really!" she shouted back. "This coming from a guy that hid in the back of the raft after Doug fell out. Nobody is going to hit me in the face ever again without getting whacked back. Got it?"

"Sounds like you get slapped a lot, huh?" Conner questioned.

"Shut up!" she blurted in a huff. "I'm done talking to you."

"Fine. Whatever."

It was now late afternoon, and they had been hiking since early morning. Savi was hurting and totally spent, and there was still about a quarter mile to go before they reached the spot that Luke had marked on the map. Rico realized that the group could not make the last quarter mile without an extended break, so they elected to take one.

During the rest stop, everyone drank most of their water and ate the remaining stock of food Luke had so kindly provided. Jade and Savi sat apart from each other, separated by about ten feet. The guys ate and drank together and then Rico walked over to Jade and sat down. Conner went to sit with Savi.

"I heard you yelling at Conner back there. What were you arguing about?" Rico inquired.

"Nothing. Everything's fine," Jade said, bitterly turning away.

"Okay, if that's how you want to play it," Rico shook his head and started to leave.

"No, don't go! I'm just really mad at Savi," she grumbled. "And then, Conner had to go and open his big mouth."

"What did he say that made you so crazy?"

"He said he thought that Savi was right to slap me."

"Well, she was," he insisted.

"What! You think so, too?"

"Yeah, I do. We needed you to be strong out there, and you were freaking out. What do you think she should have done?"

She turned away in anger. "I'm done with this conversation. I can't believe you're taking Savi's side over mine."

"I'm not taking anyone's side. I'm just telling you the truth," Rico said with a sigh. When Jade wouldn't look at him or respond, he got up and walked away.

The tears welled up in Jade's eyes until she couldn't hold them back anymore. Then she began to cry. Savi started to get up to console her, but Rico grabbed her arm and held her firmly.

"No, she's got to work this one out on her own," he told her. "I think it's better if we leave her alone for now."

The break lasted about an hour. Jade sat alone for the rest of the time. Once they were all revived, Rico instructed them to gather up their stuff and prepare to hike the last quarter mile to the camp. Still weary, hurting, and feeling somewhat stiff from the extended break, everyone struggled to get to their feet.

This time Conner led the way, with Jade close behind. Savi was next, and Rico brought up the rear.

Rico and Conner were becoming increasingly concerned that they might have to carry Savi again. Her limp had worsened, and it seemed inevitable if they wanted to keep up a steady pace. But when they saw the determination on her face, they knew she was committed to gut out the hike on her own.

The last quarter mile was brutal, but eventually they reached their destination. And to everyone's astonishment, Savi was able to make the final leg of the journey without assistance.

By this time, it was early evening. There was just enough light to see that the place Luke had picked out for them was perfect.

They quickly discovered a small stream surrounded by several large clusters of huckleberry bushes and a good supply of edible mushrooms. Across the current, there was a rock formation with a narrow but deep cave that could serve as their refuge for the night. All of them were relieved to see that the only access to the enclosure was through a small opening that was three feet wide and four feet high. The narrow opening meant the cave would be that much easier to guard against potential predators. The opening was so small that even Savi had to duck in order not to bump her head on the top of the entrance.

Although everyone was tired, they all had tasks they needed to perform, in particular setting up and securing their new camp. As they had done the last couple of days, Rico and Conner gathered wood for a fire. They also carved sharp tips on several branches and used them to fortify the cave entrance against unwelcome visitors. Down by the stream, Savi gathered enough huckleberries and mushrooms to last the group for the next few days. Jade's task was to fill everyone's canteen and the extra water bottles.

Rico lit the fire, and the exhausted teens gathered around the welcome flames. Once settled, they ate berries and mushrooms and drank till they were filled. Though their physical needs were satisfied, an air of tension still hung over the group. The strain was apparent because no one talked.

After about twenty minutes of awkward silence, suddenly Jade spoke up.

"I've thought a lot about what happened today. And I need to apologize for how I acted out on the field." She dropped her head. "And for my bad attitude afterward. When I saw the elk charging at us, and the pack of wolves behind them, as you know, I freaked out. Obviously, I didn't handle myself well. I started to panic and wanted to run. Savi, I get it that when you hit me, it wasn't done to hurt me, but it did. I forgive you for what you had to do, and I'm sorry for letting all of you down out there."

Jade then reached over and took Savi's hand. "I know you felt bad about slapping me. But I just wasn't ready to hear it at the time. You guys need to know that my mother has slapped me in the face for as long as I can remember. And honestly, I hate her for it. When Savi slapped me, it brought all that stuff up for me. I'm just so sick of being hit," Jade said, sobbing.

Rico and Savi immediately put their arms around Jade.

"I'm so so sorry," Savi whispered. "I had no idea what you've been through before you came out here."

"You did what you had to out there, Savi. I guess I needed it for once. God knows it worked."

"I'm super proud of you," Rico said to encourage her. "I know what you just said wasn't easy, especially with what you told us about your mom."

"Have you ever told anybody about this before?" Savi asked, choking back tears.

"I told my aunt, but she said if people found out, it would bring shame on our family. So I've just kept it to myself."

"Jade, abuse is illegal. I've been swatted, too, on occasion, especially when I was young. Most of the time it was for being disrespectful, but there's a big difference between a swat and being hit in the face continually."

"She's right. What your mom's doing to you is not okay. You have every right to report her. You know, to the police."

Jade paused and thought for a minute. Suddenly she straightened up. There was a look of determination on her face.

"Here's my promise. If I ever get out of this mess alive, I will tell my mom that if she hits me again, I'm calling the police."

Everyone sat quietly and reflected on Jade's promise and the implications of her commitment. Then Jade looked across the dancing flames of the fire, "I'm sorry to you, too, Conner. I know you were just telling me what I needed to hear earlier, and I snapped at you. I hope you can forgive me."

A broad grin burst upon Conner's face. "Only if you let me have your share of the berries tomorrow. I'm not getting enough to eat around here."

Until then, Jade hadn't smiled all day. In fact, everyone was now laughing. Even Rico thought Conner's quip was funny. It seemed like it had been a long time since they'd all had a good laugh. Unfortunately, they wouldn't be laughing for long.

Chapter Twenty-Three

The campfire died down until there were only hot embers illuminating the darkness. Conner used water from the stream to extinguish what remained of the fire.

Earlier, Savi went through the medical kit and used some of its contents to redress Rico and Conner's injuries. Rico's arm showed no signs of infection and was healing well. But Conner's facial gash was still raw and inflamed. Savi cleaned it by pouring on the remaining bit of peroxide to prevent it from getting worse. After gently sterilizing the claw marks, she bandaged the cuts to keep them covered and clean.

Once inside the cave, the group discussed a plan for guard duty. Everyone acknowledged that they were physically and emotionally exhausted from the day's grueling journey. Each of them also admitted concern about staying awake for a two-hour shift after such a hard day. Consequently, they decided to reduce their watch times to just one hour. Though still very fatigued, Rico reluctantly volunteered to take the first shift.

Immediately following the discussion, the weary girls disappeared into the cave. As soon as they sat down on their makeshift pine needle mattresses, both of them started to doze. In a few minutes, they were fast asleep.

The guys had fortified the entrance to the cave in the usual way. They strategically placed several sharpened stakes at the cave's opening to make it difficult for any mischievous predators to get into the enclosure.

After they had set up the protective barrier, Conner elected to stay up a few minutes to chat. He took out a water bottle he had filled earlier, leaned forward, and offered Rico a drink. He gladly accepted the bottle and sucked down several healthy gulps.

"I think you've done a great job out here, man," Conner said sincerely. "You and Savi have proven yourselves to be strong leaders during some tense moments."

"Thanks, that's a nice thing to say. And since we're tossing around compliments, you're not half the jerk I thought you were when we first met."

Conner stared at him with a puzzled look on his face. "Was that supposed to be a compliment?"

Rico flashed him a quick smile. "That's how I meant it."

After shaking his head and smiling back, Conner glanced into the cave at the sleeping girls. "Wow, can you believe that Savi? She's really something."

Rico glimpsed at her. "Yeah, I'd say so."

"I've never met anyone like her before. She's such a good person, but at the same time, super tough," Conner said with admiration.

"I wonder if that's how they raise 'em in Mississippi, a Bible in one hand and a pistol in the other," Rico laughed.

"And how about Jade? You're lucky she's all into you. I thought I had a chance with her at first, but now it's clear you're the man," Conner conceded.

"I'm glad you figured that out. Saves me from having to tie you to a tree and leave you behind for Vexel."

Conner looked over at Rico and again shook his head in disbelief. "That's a pleasant thought before I go to sleep. Thanks for that. I'd better get out of here before you find some rope to tie me up. See you in the morning."

"Goodnight, Hot Dog."

Conner looked back at Rico one last time, smiled and shook his head again. He quietly slipped into the cave. Then he stepped around the girls and disappeared into the darkness of the enclosure.

Rico stood alone at the cave's entrance intoxicated by the scent of pine mixed with the lingering smell of the extinguished fire. In a short time, Conner was snoring softly, and everyone but Rico was asleep. Rico had worked hard all day and late into the evening, and it all finally caught up with him. Only forty minutes into his watch, he started to nod off. Instead of standing up and walking around, Rico foolishly chose to sit down behind the stakes by the entrance. In no time, he drifted off to sleep.

Unbeknownst to everyone, a cunning group of predators lurked nearby not far from the cave. This new pack of wolves detected a tempting scent and had followed it to just outside the enclosure. Crouching low, they inched their way toward the opening with quiet and deliberate steps.

Inside, Rico slept like a baby, oblivious to the deadly threat slinking toward him. The lead wolf gently placed his front paw on a rock by the entrance. He used the strength of his hind legs and silently lifted himself up. Now his head was high enough to see what he had only smelled up to this point. The wolf's steely eyes darted back and forth and then fixed on Rico sleeping behind the wooden stakes just a few feet away. The others crowded forward behind the lead wolf sensing a killing moment.

Suddenly one of the predators lurched forward and tussled with another wolf hoping to get a better look at their unsuspecting prey. The aggravated wolf spun around and instantly bit the overly aggressive member of the pack. All at once, the wounded creature yelped in protest.

Startled awake, Rico reached for the pistol just as the lead wolf leaped in the air toward him.

"Conner!" Rico shouted.

Alarmed by Rico's cry, Conner sprang to his feet and grabbed his spear.

Both Savi and Jade were frightened awake and screamed simultaneously. The scene was terrifying and chaotic.

The lead wolf let out a horrible shriek when it failed to hurdle the stakes guarding the cave's entrance and impaled itself on a couple of them. The predator's pitiful wails filled the air as it struggled to free itself just a few feet away from the terrified group.

Rico knew what he had to do. He quickly lifted the pistol and shot the wolf once in the head. Instantly, the beast died on the stake barrier. After hearing the gunshot, the other wolves made a hasty retreat.

Blood gushed from the dead wolf's multiple wounds onto the cave floor. Traumatized by the incident, everyone took a moment to catch their breath. Then they all turned angrily on Rico.

Savi stared at him in anger and disbelief. "How did the wolves get so close to the cave without you waking us up?"

Rico hesitated before answering. In fact, he took so long that Savi decided she needed to repeat the question.

Rico was tempted to lie. Instead, he reluctantly told her the truth. "I fell asleep."

"You what?" Savi raged.

"I told you already. I nodded off," Rico repeated shamefully.

"Oh, that's just great. You fell asleep!" Everyone protested at the same time.

"That's what I said. How many times do I have to tell you? I fell asleep!"

"Really! That's something I'd expect from Conner, not from you," Savi scolded.

Immediately, Conner shot a look of disappointment in Savi's direction. "Gee thanks. I'm glad to see that you have so much confidence in me."

"Sorry," Savi replied continuing to stare a hole through Rico. "I just can't believe you didn't wake one of us up. Instead, you put all of our lives at risk."

All at once, they heard growls outside the cave very near the entrance. This time everyone was prepared and had their weapons in hand. The teens quickly moved toward the opening and glanced around.

Instantly, the collective tension level rose when they noticed the relentless pack of wolves had regrouped and were advancing slowly but steadily toward the enclosure.

Rico whispered, "I've only got two shots left in the pistol, and I see four of them."

"Savi, you said you could shoot a gun, right?" Rico asked.

"Yeah, I can shoot," she replied.

"Okay, take this, and I'll use the spear. There are only two bullets left. You've got to nail two of them. Take good aim and don't miss," Rico added firmly.

Then Conner and Rico stationed themselves behind the dead wolf impaled on the stakes. Side by side, they pointed their spears at the approaching wolves. Savi stood between them one step back with her pistol raised. Her heartbeat steadily increased as she waited patiently for a good shot. Jade hid behind everyone. She had a knife in hand, and her body was shaking from fear.

Savi leaned forward and whispered, "I've got a clear shot at the one on the right."

"When you're ready, take it," Rico whispered back.

Moments later a shot rang out, and the targeted wolf crumpled to the ground. Immediately, the remaining wolves made a quick retreat into the woods.

"Great shot, Savi, you got 'im!" Conner yelled excitedly.

"One down," Rico added.

"Here they come again," Conner warned.

Again the unrelenting wolves began advancing toward the enclosure. The three remaining predators moved aggressively, growling with every step. With the element of surprise now gone, they pressed boldly forward without hesitation.

Just as she had done before, Savi trained her pistol on the lead wolf. He snarled viciously as he steadily crept ever closer. She took aim and again waited patiently for the right moment. Suddenly she fired the last bullet. The wolf fell to the ground. It quivered momentarily and then became still. The remaining two wolves appeared to have had enough and disappeared across the creek and into the woods.

"Savi, that was unbelievable," Jade said from behind her.

Rico grabbed her shoulder, spun her around, and hugged her.

"You weren't kidding when you said you could shoot."

"All that target practice on the farm has finally paid off," Savi said with a sigh of relief.

After taking a minute to calm down, they used Savi's small flashlight to survey their surroundings. It was a bloody mess. One wolf was dead on the stakes just inside the cave's entrance, while two other animals lay still and bleeding a few feet apart just outside the enclosure.

Suddenly in the distance they heard two rifle shots. Savi perked up and turned to the others.

"Listen, we have to get out of here. Now! I'll bet that was Luke firing at Vexel. Do you remember when he told us that Vexel is attracted to the smell of blood? Look around. There's blood everywhere."

They quickly agreed and in a matter of minutes grabbed their gear and fled the cave. Savi and Conner accidentally got blood on themselves while climbing over the dead wolf at the entrance. So they cleaned off the blood in the stream before leaving the area. Savi knelt and quickly used her map and compass to figure out the best route to the next camp. As soon as she plotted what appeared to be the most direct route to the new location, they all headed out.

Secretly Savi feared that Vexel was stalking them and gaining ground. She hoped the rifle shots meant Vexel was finally dead. But she had a nagging feeling inside that he was still very much alive. Then her thoughts shifted to Luke. She prayed the shots they heard weren't his final defense before the beast overtook him.

Moving through the dark wilderness, Savi wondered for the first time if her dad would ever walk her down the aisle the way she'd always dreamed, or if instead he'd be attending her funeral. Her mind swirled with thoughts of home and how much she missed everyone she'd left back in Mississippi. Then a low hanging branch that Jade brushed against snapped back and hit Savi in the face, bringing her back into the moment.

"Ow!" she blurted out.

"What's wrong?" Jade asked, turning around.

"A branch hit me in the face," she grumbled.

Concerned, Jade stopped. "Are you okay? Do you need a minute?"

"No, we've got to keep going," Savi, insisted. "I'm okay."

Just as they were about to continue, they heard the gruesome sound of vicious animals fighting, no more than a half mile away. The violent encounter ended with ferocious roars that sent chills down everyone's spine. No one said a word. They just kept slogging through the woods as swiftly as the conditions allowed. But they each had the same nagging question running through their mind:

Has Vexel found us?

Chapter Twenty-Four

Walking through the dense forest at night was difficult enough. But trying to do it quietly was nearly impossible, especially with the moonlight hardly showing through the thick canopy of trees. Just as before, Savi used her small flashlight, map, and compass to determine the shortest possible route to their next camp spot.

Now it was one o'clock in the morning, and the group had traveled only a couple of miles from the blood-soaked cave.

The teens felt exhausted from fighting off the wolves, a lack of sleep, and the challenging hike. But they had no choice and were forced to stop and take an extended break. Initially they discussed the idea of setting up camp where they had stopped to rest. However, after thinking about the awful sounds they heard earlier, everyone concluded it was best to keep moving.

While studying the map, Savi saw an alternative campsite that Luke had circled. She remembered he told her it could be a backup if the group didn't need to stop and felt well enough to hike further. She calculated that it was now only about a half mile from their current location. With a renewed sense of purpose, the weary adventurers agreed to make the alternative refuge their new destination.

Fortunately, soon after resuming the journey, the forest thinned out. The unexpected development dramatically improved the visibility and revealed a bright three-quarter lit moon. This welcome change made moving through the woods faster and significantly easier.

Before long, they arrived at the area where Luke had assured them there was a safe and sheltered campsite. Initially they couldn't find the enclosure, so they spread out and began to search for it. After scouring the area for several minutes, Conner was the first to locate the hidden encampment. It was situated halfway up a hill behind some large rocks and tucked behind a group of pine trees. The cavern was so hard to see that they realized without the map and Luke's help they would have never found it.

Savi and Jade decided to use the remainder of their strength to gather up pine straw. Like before, they used it to cover the floor of the cave and lessen the chill from the cold ground. At the same time, Rico and Conner gathered thick tree limbs and sharpened them into stakes to fortify the entrance to the enclosure just as they had done before. After a brief discussion, the group agreed not to build a fire for fear they might give away their hiding place.

The cave's entrance was situated so that the moon shone directly into the first several feet of it. The weary foursome sat down together in the moonlight. For the next few minutes, they ate yesterday's berries and drank their fill of water. After she finished eating, Savi took the time to check Conner's facial wound. To her surprise, she saw a marked improvement over the day before. The open edges of the wound seemed to be fusing.

Everyone was so tired they could hardly speak. They sat quietly for the next several minutes just recuperating. Finally, Jade broke the silence.

"I hope Luke's alright," she said, in between sips of water. "When we heard those shots earlier, I'll bet he was shooting at Vexel."

"Well, judging by the horrible sounds after that, he must have missed him," Conner lamented.

"Hopefully, the three dead wolves we left behind gave him plenty to eat for the time being," Savi added.

Rico had been unusually quiet since the wolf incident and looked troubled. Savi asked the question on everyone's mind. "Rico, what's going on?"

He didn't answer, instead sat silently with his eyes down. Slowly he lowered his chin, letting quiet tears fall onto his folded hands. Though Savi, Jade, and Conner were dog-tired, they each quickly slid over by Rico.

"What's going on?" Jade whispered softly.

After a few moments, he lifted his dust-covered brow. The moonlight showed the fresh tear tracks on his sad face. Again, Rico ignored Jade's question as he had done to Savi's earlier. After several torturous moments, he finally answered.

"I—I almost got us killed," he confessed. "I really messed up when I fell asleep on my shift."

After admitting his blunder, he dropped his head again in shame. Savi let him sit quietly for a minute before she gently lifted his chin and turned his face toward hers. She looked him in the eyes and spoke in a gentle tone.

"Yeah, Rico, you did fall asleep, and that wasn't good. But it's been like hell out here. Since the rafting accident you've been a great leader and super responsible up until you fell asleep on your watch. We're all wiped out, and it could have happened to any one of us."

Then she paused a moment as if a new thought had popped into her head.

"And one other thing, I was too hard on you back at the cave, and I want to apologize for that."

"Savi's right, Rico. You've been an awesome leader and have done your best to protect us ever since we lost Doug," Jade added.

"It's true, man. It could have been any one of us. Glad it was you and not me, but it could have been any one of us," Conner said clumsily.

"Nice, Conner, that was helpful," Savi fired back.

Rico shook his head and fought back a smile. Then he took a few seconds and studied the faces of his new friends.

"I feel stupid. I don't think I've cried in front of anyone since my mom died."

"Ever so often we all need a good cry," Savi said. "I've heard someone say 'it cleanses the soul.'"

Rico reflected on Savi's words.

"You're probably right. It's been rough since my mom died. My dad still hasn't recovered, and he's gone a lot. I've been trying my best to take care of my brothers and sister. I guess there's a lot on my shoulders right now."

After a long pause, Rico continued, "I feel like you guys are already more than just friends—and we've known each other less than a week. I've already told you more than most people know about me. Thanks for forgiving my screw-up. And I'm really sorry I put your lives in jeopardy. It won't happen again. I promise."

"We know it won't," Savi said to reassure him.

Again, he looked slowly at the others one by one and said, "I wouldn't want to be out here with anybody else but you guys. That is except for you, Conner," he joked.

"Gee, thanks for the love," Conner countered, shaking his head in amusement.

Rico laid down on his back near the entrance. Clasping his hands behind his neck, he gazed up at the brilliant three-quarter moon and drifted into his thoughts. After a few minutes, Jade came over and sat down next to him. She lowered her head gently to his chest. No words were exchanged between them nor did there need to be. Rico was comforted with Jade's open display of affection and immediately put his arm around her and caressed her tenderly. Before long the two of them were sound asleep.

Conner volunteered to take the first shift and encouraged Savi to retire into the cave so she could get some rest. Dog-tired, she entered the enclosure, pressed together some pine needles, and made a small bed. Before going to sleep, Conner watched Savi kneel down on the cold hard ground and spend a few minutes praying. When she finished, she rolled on to her pine mattress and fell asleep.

Conner elected to extend his watch by an hour so the others could get some much-needed extra rest. But after a time, he started to fade and knew he had better wake Savi.

Conner stayed up with Savi a few minutes before going to sleep to give her time to collect herself. Once he was certain she was ready to assume the night shift, he retreated into the enclosure and fell asleep on the pine straw bed Savi had made.

It was now three-thirty in the morning, and all was calm and quiet. Besides crickets chirping and the occasional croaking of frogs, the night passed peacefully.

As Conner did before her, Savi also decided to lengthen her shift by half an hour before waking Jade. When she tried to rouse her, Jade moaned and rolled over, but Rico woke up instantly.

"Go back to sleep," she whispered to him. "It's Jade's turn."

"No, let her sleep. I'm awake now," he insisted.

There was no argument out of Jade, and instantly she settled back into sleep.

Just before Rico took over guard duty from Savi, he glanced over at her. There she stood by the entrance holding Conner's spear with a determination that he'd rarely seen in other girls. The sight of her brought a smile to his face. Moved by her tenacity, he rose to his feet, walked over, and put his arm around her shoulder.

"You were right to come down hard on me after I fell asleep on my watch," he said sincerely. "There's no excuse for that. I put everyone in danger."

"Yeah, that's true. But we've already talked about that, and nobody's perfect. We all make mistakes."

"True, but if somebody else did that . . . I would have had a hard time forgiving them," he admitted. "You seem to be able to get over stuff quickly. I wish I were more like that."

Then Savi moved out from under his arm and turned away. "I've had a lot of practice at forgiving, Rico. Way more than you can imagine."

He gazed at her with a puzzled look on his face. "What do you mean?"

"I don't mean anything," as she started to walk away. "I'm going to get some sleep now. I'm super tired."

"Savi, wait. Tell me what you're talking about."

"Not now. It's too complicated, and I'm too tired to talk about it," she said with tears welling up in her eyes. "Let's talk about it another time."

"Promise?"

"I promise. Now I need to get some sleep. Good night, Rico."

"'Night, Savi."

After she had disappeared into the enclosure, Rico wondered what kind of secret could be troubling Savi so deeply. For now, all he could do was guess. But before long, he knew she'd keep her promise, and then he would know the answer to the mystery.

By the end of his shift, the dawn shimmered golden sunbeams through the woods and into the enclosure. The warmth of the sun brought welcome relief from what had been a chilly night.

Rico decided it was time to wake Savi. After she had rubbed the sleep out of her eyes, he asked her to grab the map and sit with him. The map indicated they were about eleven miles from the Susquehanna River. Unfortunately, they still had to cross over a mountain range to get to the river and ultimately, Camp Arrowhead. Luke had predicted that the last part of the journey would be difficult and slow going. Savi glanced over at Rico with a worried look on her face and told him what he already knew.

"Today is the twenty-ninth of August. We only have three days left to get across the river."

Chapter Twenty-Five

Savi and Rico both felt a renewed determination and a keen sense of urgency. Jade and Conner woke up and were encouraged to pack quickly and prepare for a long day's journey. Savi calculated that they were about nine miles from the base of the mountain range they had to cross before reaching the Susquehanna River. On the map, Luke had pointed out a sheltered encampment at the base of the range. This was where they intended to spend the night before traversing the mountains to reach the river.

The nine-mile hike ahead of them would be the longest they had attempted until now. Fortunately, everyone felt well rested and ready for the day's trek. When they made it to the camp, they would be only a day's journey from the river, and that much closer to safety.

The group headed out early knowing it would require all day and possibly a good part of the evening to get to the remote campsite.

Just as they were leaving, everyone heard the thumping sound of a helicopter nearby. Instantly, their adrenaline surged, and for a few fleeting seconds, they envisioned the possibility of a rescue. But soon their hope was crushed just like it had been before. Within a minute, the copter turned away and flew toward the river, which by now was over a mile to the east of them.

Though failing to get the attention of the rescue helicopter did discourage them momentarily, it also seemed to bolster their resolve to survive.

They decided to press on. Fortunately, the weather conditions were ideal for hiking, and within the first hour, the terrain changed noticeably in their favor as well. This welcome development allowed them to make swifter progress. The thick underbrush was gone, and the dense forest had thinned out significantly. By mid-morning, they had already traveled over three miles, leaving them six miles to go to reach the base of the mountains and the targeted campsite.

"Keep your eyes open for anything to eat," Rico told Savi after his stomach rumbled. "We finished the last of the berries and mushrooms this morning, and I'm starving."

"I've been looking for food since we left early this morning but haven't seen a thing," she replied. "There's a lake on the map where we might be able to catch some fish, but it looks too far out of the way. I'm sick of berries and mushrooms, but I'd eat anything right now."

"Oh look, is that a Taco Bell?" Conner shouted from the back.

"Shut up, Conner," Jade scolded. "That's not even funny right now."

"Okay, Jade, now for sure you're not getting any of my Burrito Supreme."

"Whatever!"

Suddenly a clap of thunder was heard in the distance, interrupting their banter.

"Great, just what we need, a thunderstorm," Jade whined.

"The guys are starting to smell again. A little rain might not be all that bad," Savi joked.

"That's true," Jade said, holding back a laugh.

"I heard that," Rico hollered from behind.

"Me, too," Conner added.

"Good, so take the hint," Savi said playfully.

Fearing another severe weather system was heading their way, the teens pressed even harder toward the camp. It was now mid-afternoon, and according to the map, they were just two miles from their destination. But the forced march had taken its toll and gradually wore them down. Equally concerning, the weather was changing from bad to worse with each passing minute. Before long, a thick mist that reminded Jade of a foggy summer morning in San Francisco engulfed the weary foursome.

Besides the fog, there were also sporadic downpours. When the driving rains pelted them, the fog briefly decreased. But after the rain let up, the dense mist returned thicker than before.

"Savi, try to keep the map dry," Rico yelled. "You better lead the way because I can't see ten feet in front of me and have no idea where we're going."

"Okay, but we've got to stop a minute so I can double-check where we are on the map," she replied.

"Seriously, no one has anything to eat?" Conner said in a desperate tone. "I'm dying here."

"Want some of my Burrito Supreme?" Jade quipped.

"Don't be annoying, Jade. I'm really starving," he fired back.

"Hey, blankie boy, not so funny now, is it?"

"Really! Can you two stop for a minute?" Savi barked. "I'm trying to figure out where we are."

"Okay," Conner reacted. "You don't have to bite our heads off."

"Alright, I think we're here . . . and we need to go that way," she pointed northwest.

"Are you sure?" Rico asked.

"As sure as I can be," Savi replied.

"Okay, you lead the way," Rico advised. "Conner, you follow Savi. Jade, you go behind Conner. I'll watch your backs."

By this time, the rain had stopped. In its absence, the mist had grown so thick that everyone feared if they weren't careful, they would lose sight of each other. Plodding their way through the endless fog was beginning to take a toll on all of them. After walking another half an hour in the soupy conditions, everyone's confidence in Savi's ability to navigate began to waver.

"Savi, it feels like we're going in circles," Conner said with concern. "Are you sure you know what you're doing?"

"I'm doing the best I can. I've never operated in these kinds of conditions. Here's the compass. Do you want to try?" Savi questioned him angrily.

"Come on, Savi. We're all wiped out, and we just don't want to hike any farther than we have to or go in a wrong direction," Rico said.

"I get it!" Savi replied hotly. "I need you guys to chill out. If you can't trust me, at least trust the compass. I'll have you know that I didn't sign up for this. Now quit whining and keep up!" She stormed off ahead of them.

"You guys, stop it!" Jade snapped. "Leave her alone. She's trying her best. Can't you see she's already got enough pressure on her without you two questioning her every move?"

After a few minutes, Savi stopped dead in her tracks, looked back, and waited for the others. Once they caught up, without saying a word, she turned and kept pushing forward through the dense mist despite increasing protests from Rico and Conner. Unconcerned by their lack of confidence in her, Savi remained focused, while periodically checking her map and compass. After trudging through some very muddy ground for nearly an hour, everyone was exhausted, soaked, hungry, and extremely annoyed at Savi, including Jade. Their tempers had all passed the boiling point. Jade, who had earlier defended Savi, was also starting to question her friend's navigational skills.

"Savi, are you sure we're not just going in circles?" she asked.

"Yeah, this is ridiculous. You don't have any idea where we are or where we're going, do you?" Conner blurted out from behind Jade.

"We can't keep marching around like this any longer," Rico objected angrily.

Savi was limping noticeably and had a strained look on her face. She turned toward the others and shouted, "All I know is that the compass says we're moving northwest, and I believe it. That means we're about a half an hour from the camp. If we stop now, we're in the middle of nowhere. We've got to keep moving. Now all of you need to suck it up and quit moaning," she chided them. "My ankle and leg are killing me. If we don't find the camp in forty-five minutes, I'll give up myself."

Somehow, the group mustered the courage to continue slogging through the fog filled woods in spite of their uncertainty. In front of her, Jade heard Savi plead out loud, "Lord, please show me the way. We've got to find this camp."

"Oh, that's great! Now Savi is praying that we find the campsite. That's just perfect," Connor objected vehemently.

By this time, another half hour had passed, and the verbal protests were multiplying by the minute.

"Enough!" Rico yelled from the rear. "We need to stop, right now!"

"No, we've got to be close. Five more minutes is all I ask," Savi pleaded.

"No way, Savi, it's over!" Conner yelled.

"They're right, I can't go on anymore," Jade added. "We have to stop now. I'm over." Then she collapsed in a heap onto the muddy ground.

Savi let out a big sigh. "So it's come to this? Are we just going to lie down here and die? Well, not me! The map says we're right on top of the camp, and I'm going to find it."

"You can't just go off by yourself," Jade warned. "You'll get lost out there. We won't be able to see you in this mist after you go ten feet."

"I'm not giving up, not yet anyway," she shot back.

"You're staying with us. That's it!" Rico yelled angrily.

"You're not my mother!" Savi screamed. "I know we're close. And I'm going to look around. Like it or not!"

Resolute, she hobbled off and spent the next fifteen minutes searching in the dense mist for the elusive campsite without success. Weary and discouraged Savi came back limping to the spot where she'd left them. When she got close to where she thought they were, she yelled out for them. Fortunately, they heard her shouts; and she followed the sound of their voices until she found them again.

Though the mist was still thick and the rain had stopped, no one had the energy to talk, least of all Savi. Visibly puzzled, once again she pulled out the map and tried to figure out where the camp could be. As soon as Rico, Jade, and Conner saw her with the map in hand, they started taunting her again.

"What now, Savi? Are you going to tell us we have another half an hour to go? Lots of good your prayers did, huh!" Conner said mockingly.

"It's over, Savi, put the map away," Rico grumbled.

"You tried, but we're lost. Just let it go," Jade said.

"I'm going to look for some food," Conner moaned. "I'll eat anything at this point."

"I'll go with you," Rico responded.

Savi sat hungry and exhausted, wondering what she had done wrong. She used the compass to guide her path and the map to check her bearings. She couldn't understand why she had missed the camp. Frustrated beyond measure, she bowed her head and began to sob. Jade was so tired from the walk that she didn't have the strength to move over to console her. So Savi sat alone crying in the thick mist wondering why her compass, map, and God had failed her.

Rico and Conner had been searching for something to eat for about ten minutes. Suddenly, Rico yelled, "Where are you guys?"

"Here we are!" Jade shouted.

A minute later, Rico and Conner appeared out of the mist with strange looks on their faces. They rejoined the girls and told them to follow them.

"Did you find some food?" Jade asked anxiously.

Neither Rico nor Conner answered. Rico just lifted Jade to her feet, and Conner reached down and tried to pull Savi up as well, but she protested.

"What are you doing?"

"Just get up and come with us. You've got to see this," Conner insisted.

Savi stood up, and the two of them led the girls through the forest for several minutes, when all of a sudden some big rocks became visible. Then Conner grabbed Savi's hand, pulled her forward, and pointed.

"Look, it's the cave we've been trying to find. You did it, Savi! You led us here."

Instantly, Savi started to cry. She dropped to her knees, bowed her head, and whispered softly, "Thank you, Lord."

Rico, Jade, and Conner watched as the faithful little warrior knelt before them on the muddy ground and wept in gratitude. The three of them felt ashamed as they thought about how badly they had treated her. In a matter of minutes the mist lifted miraculously, and to everyone's amazement revealed a beautiful blue and cloudless sky. Now was the first time since midmorning that everyone could see their surroundings.

As they surveyed the area, they saw they were in what appeared to be a magical and enchanting place in the middle of the woods. A few hundred feet away a pond the size and shape of an ice rink was now visible. The pine forest sparkled in the late afternoon sunlight, and the birds began singing again for the first time since early morning. The setting sun ignited the moisture on an infinite number of pine needles, and they glistened beautifully. The view around them was nothing short of majestic.

The cave that was so difficult to locate was now visible and just a few feet in front of them near a large rock formation. The enclosure itself was about fifteen feet deep, and the best part was that it was dry inside. The only thing they lacked now was food.

Savi and Rico tried to fish the pond for a while, but they didn't even get a nibble. They were just about to give up, but Savi decided to look inside Rico's small tackle box one more time. She found a little green cricket made out of soft plastic with a tiny hook on it. It took just a few seconds to tie the lure onto the end of the line and then cast it out a few feet. Savi let the plastic cricket float on the surface of the pond and waited. Soon there were small swirls around the lure. Suddenly a fish took the lure under the water. Savi set the hook by jerking back on the line and quickly caught the first fish of the day. It was only about six inches long, but at least it was something.

Rico immediately took the fish and cleaned it. Then he gathered some dry twigs and found a place to prepare a small fire. Savi continued walking and casting around the pond until she had caught seven fish in all. The largest measured about eight inches.

Once Rico cleaned the rest of Savi's catch, he lit the fire and cooked the fish. As usual, they ate every bit of their meal and left only the bones. After dinner, Conner took the bones and buried them a long distance away from the camp to ensure the lingering scent of the fish was nowhere near the cave. Once he returned, everyone gathered at the entrance to rehydrate themselves and rest a few minutes before fortifying the refuge for the evening.

After the group had finished reinforcing the entry to the grotto, they went inside for the night. Rico, Jade, and Conner sat close to each other. But Savi moved a few feet away from them and sat alone in silence. No one spoke for the next few minutes. They were all very tired and lost in thought. It seemed like no one wanted to be the first one to talk or say the wrong thing. It had been a challenging day, and as awkward as it was, the silence felt right. But Savi wouldn't be quiet for long. Tonight was the night she'd tell her story. It was a story sure to deepen their insight into her heart and character.

Chapter Twenty-Six

The group sat quietly for a long time. Though the silence was increasingly uncomfortable, no one was sure how to begin the conversation. Finally, Rico broke the ice and spoke on behalf of the others.

"Savi, we all need to apologize to you for how we acted on the way here. We were wrong, and you were right. You knew what you were doing and none of us trusted you. Worse than that, we made fun of you which didn't help anything, either. I'm really sorry for doubting you and adding to your stress back there."

"Me, too, Savi," Conner echoed. "I feel like I made things worse for you, too, and I'm sorry. Especially for taunting you when you were praying. God knows I should pray more myself."

"I'm sorry, too. I doubted you and added to the pressure you were already feeling," Jade said, her eyes cast downward. "That was a lousy thing to do to a friend."

Savi listened with head bowed and digested the words of her repentant friends.

Still unsure if Savi was willing to forgive them, they tried to apologize again.

"Savi, can you forgive us?" Jade pleaded.

"Come on. Talk with us," Conner begged.

"Why won't you say something?" Rico questioned.

Finally, Savi looked up with a compassionate expression on her face. "You don't have to keep apologizing. It's over. I'm not holding anything against any of you because you doubted me. The truth is, I doubted myself. I've never been in a situation like that before. I couldn't rely on anything but Luke's directions, the map, and my compass. It was the compass I never doubted," she confessed. "Can I show you something I learned?"

"Sure, why not?" they all agreed.

"What do want to show us?" Jade asked curiously.

"You'll see. For now, just do me a favor. I know you're tired but stand up a minute. Come on, do this for me," Savi insisted and then waited till they all stood to their feet.

"Now, I'd like each of you to close your eyes and point in the direction that you think is north." Savi waited as Rico, Jade, and Conner tried to figure out which way was north. After a few moments, each of them pointed in the direction they thought was north. "Now continue to point the way you are, open your eyes, and look at each other."

Just as Savi had instructed, the three of them opened their eyes and looked at one another.

"Do you see that you're all pointing in different directions?" she noted. "According to the compass, none of you knows where north is. Actually, the compass shows that north is that way." She lifted her finger and showed them the direction the compass needle pointed.

Savi now had her teammates' full attention.

"I'll never forget something my dad told me when I was a young girl.

He taught me, 'In this life, two things will never lie to you, your Bible and your compass.' I've never forgotten those words. Especially today, when you doubted me, and I doubted myself. One thing I knew for certain, my compass wouldn't lie to me."

Rico, Jade, and Conner sat down and quietly stared at their friend who seemed much wiser than her years. Her maturity dumbfounded them, especially since she was the youngest in the group.

Then Jade spoke and asked Savi the question that had been on her mind for days.

"We've all shared about why we came on this trip, except you, Savi. You haven't told us your story yet. Tell us why you came to Arrowhead."

Savi hesitated a moment before she answered. She appeared to search deep within herself for an extra measure of courage. Then she began to speak softly and slowly.

"Four months ago, my uncle accidently killed my five-year-old brother, Josh," she told them in a somber tone.

Shocked, Rico interrupted her and blurted out, "Wait! What are you saying? What do you mean, he killed your brother?"

Savi stayed calm and focused.

"On April twenty-sixth my Uncle Ray came to our house drunk and asked my dad for some money. When my father refused, he stormed out of the house, got into his car, and backed over my brother Josh who had pulled into the driveway behind him on his bike."

She paused as tears rolled down her face.

"Josh died in the ambulance on the way to the hospital. And my uncle Ray was arrested and charged with involuntary manslaughter. He's now serving a six-year sentence in a Mississippi prison."

"Oh my God, Savi. That's awful," Jade sobbed. "You must hate your uncle's guts."

Savi looked at her and paused. "Actually, I recently forgave him," she said to everyone's surprise. "And so has the rest of my family."

Rico, Jade, and Conner sat in stunned silence. Jade's tears wet her face while Rico and Conner looked mesmerized by the story.

"Forgiving my uncle was the biggest test of my life. At first, I hated him like I'd never hated anyone else. Everybody in my family went through a really dark time. Then my dad told us what we already knew about forgiveness. He reminded us that we should forgive the way we've been forgiven.

"Gradually, my heart started to change toward my uncle. It was just three weeks ago that I went with my dad to the prison and saw him for the first time since the accident. He cried like a baby and accepted full responsibility for his actions. He begged me to forgive him. He said he'd understand if I couldn't but hoped that someday I would. I believed he was sincere and genuinely sorry, so I put the palm of my hand up against the glass window that separated us. I told him over the phone that I forgave him. That made him cry even harder, and then he lifted his hand and placed his palm on the glass over mine.

"At that moment, something happened inside of me, and my heart softened toward him. I looked into his eyes and saw a broken man who would live a lifetime of regret for the foolish mistake he made that cost Josh his life." Savi paused and fought back her tears.

"So that's why I came to Arrowhead. My mom and dad thought a change of scenery and some fun might do me good after such a rough patch. And wow, am I having fun out here," she scoffed with her first smile of the evening. "Let's get everything set up for the night. I've got to believe that there are some berries or mushrooms around here somewhere. That fish didn't even put a dent in my appetite."

Everyone sat silently for the next couple minutes. Finally, Jade spoke up. "Savi, I'll never forget the story you just told us, not for the rest of my life."

"Neither will I," Rico agreed.

"Me, neither," Conner added. "Thanks for trusting us with your story and forgiving us."

They all got up and began to work on preparations for the evening. But nobody could get the story Savi had told them out of their heads. Jade filled the water bottles and canteens at the pond. Then she helped Savi gather pine straw to cover a portion of the cave floor. They also scoured the area for berries or anything else to eat. The boys gathered wood for the fire. Afterward, they positioned sharpened stakes at the entrance of the enclosure in the usual way.

Fortunately, the girls found some blackberry bushes near the backside of the pond. They quickly picked several handfuls and wrapped them inside of the plastic tarp. When they brought them back to the cave, everyone gobbled them down within a matter of seconds.

The night unveiled a clear starlit sky and a brilliant orange moon rising over the trees from the southeast. Everyone knew the mountains they had to cross were nearby, but they had not seen them because of the thick mist blanketing the woods all day. The challenging range ahead was the last major obstacle they would encounter before finally reaching the Susquehanna River.

It was evident to all that having extended guard shifts was risky because they were all so tired. Consequently, they decided to break the shifts down into one-hour blocks to minimize the possibility of anyone falling asleep on guard duty.

Savi graciously volunteered to do the first watch. So the others retired into the grotto and went right to sleep.

It was a quiet evening except for the chirping crickets and frogs croaking near the pond. Savi felt unusually tired and knew that she had to stay on her feet throughout her watch or risk nodding off to sleep. She feared if she sat down even for a minute, she'd be sleeping in no time. Fortunately, her hour passed quickly, and before she knew it, it was time to wake up Conner.

When Conner relieved Savi and started his guard duty, he hugged her goodnight and watched her slip quietly into the cave. Before she closed her eyes for the night, Savi took one last glance at the magnificent starlit sky.

All at once, a shooting star appeared. The light trail that followed the falling star glowed brightly for several seconds before swiftly disappearing. Savi looked over at Conner standing tall in the pale moonlight and wondered if he had seen the falling star as well. He pointed up and confirmed that he had seen it also. For the next few moments, the two of them marveled at the extraordinary event they had just witnessed. Then Savi nestled into her pine needle mattress, closed her eyes, and drifted off to sleep.

The stars gradually disappeared in the morning light and the once brilliant moon was barely visible. The birds started to chirp and sing in celebration of a new day. Jade stood guard on the last guard shift and watched eagerly as the forest around her came alive with sounds and light.

Luke had warned them days earlier that the journey over the mountains would be slow and strenuous, so Jade decided it was time to wake the others so they could get an early start. Once everyone was up, she and Savi combed the pond area for more blackberries. Fortunately, they found enough berries so each of them could have a generous amount for breakfast. Following the morning meal, everyone drank extra water because they knew the long day's journey ahead would be especially challenging.

The teens packed up quickly and took one last look around the encampment that had served them so well. Then they headed out with Savi leading the way and Rico, Jade, and Conner following close behind.

Savi had plotted out the course the night before and again used the map and compass to navigate. The route led them in the direction of the mountains toward two possible campsites. The first camp was at the base of the range and the second much farther away and near the top of the mountain. If they made it to the summit camp, the map indicated they would be only two and a half miles from the Susquehanna River, which was just a half mile from Camp Arrowhead.

A feeling of optimism filled the group as they set off on the day's trek. The realization that Camp Arrowhead was within striking distance gave each of them a renewed sense of determination to get there. They had traveled less than a half mile when unexpectedly the forest ended, and they entered into a vast open and rocky area. Then for the first time everyone saw the mountain range they had to cross to get to the river.

One by one they stopped in their tracks and gazed at the daunting test before them. Instantly the confidence they had felt just minutes earlier vanished.

"Luke warned us about this," Savi reminded everyone.

Jade sat down and scanned the mountain range looming before her. All at once she began sobbing.

"There's no way we can make it over those mountains and cross the river in three days," she groaned.

Savi bent down and put her hand on Jade's shoulder.

"You're right, Jade. Because today is August thirtieth and we only have two days, not three, to get across the river."

Chapter Twenty-Seven

Savi's warning intensified the stress they felt. Except for the sound of Jade's sobbing, it was eerily quiet. Savi, Rico, and Conner stood in shocked silence and absorbed the severity of their new obstacle.

After Jade had stopped crying, she stood and joined the others without saying a word. As Savi studied the map, she estimated the mountains were about a mile and a half in front of them. Even a skilled mountain climber would certainly describe the range as steep and treacherous.

As daunting as the mountains appeared to be, everyone knew the clock was ticking. There was no time to waste.

"We're not going to get across the river standing around here," Savi advised the group. "I know we're tired, and this looks bad, but if we get moving, we might make the camp near the summit by nightfall."

Luke had marked two different campsites on the map that they could use depending on how vigorous they felt. The first was near the base of the mountain they were approaching. Everyone agreed they had to press on, so they set their sights on a second campsite near the top of the mountain. Though reaching this site was an ambitious goal, they had to push themselves hard if they would have any chance of crossing the river by September first.

The crisp, clean air and open terrain made the journey much easier than it had been the day before. The fatigued yet determined hikers made steady progress in spite of the number of large rock formations they had to traverse to get to the base of the mountain.

The group took a short break and afterward seemed to be rejuvenated, displaying a new dose of courage and confidence. It seemed that they left behind the discouragement that had overwhelmed them earlier. Methodically, and with an undeniable commitment to succeed, they moved ever closer to the base of the towering peaks.

"Savi, how long do you guess it will take us to get over these mountains?" Rico asked.

"It's hard to say. The map shows that the mountains are high, but it looks like a short distance down the other side. When we get to the summit, there's a good chance we'll be able to see the river," she added. "Once we pass the first camp spot, we've got to go a bit west. Luke said there's a snake trail up the side of the mountain which is a hard climb, but it will save us tons of time."

"We've got no choice," Rico said, resignation lining his voice. "If we don't make it to the river on time, we're in real trouble. You make the call, Savi. No one will question whatever you think is best." He assured her. "Go ahead and lead the way, and I'll make sure the others keep up." He studied the ground around them. "Just be sure you keep an eye out for rattlers, though. Luke told me there were plenty of snakes in these parts. He said they love these rocky areas."

"You bet I will. One bite is enough for me."

The resilient teens reached the first camp at the base of the range a little after nine in the morning, which meant they had most of the day to climb the mountain and reach the camp at the summit. The plan was to spend their last night at the refuge before crossing the Susquehanna River the next morning.

Before beginning the challenging ascent, everyone filled their canteens and water bottles in a gushing stream, no doubt one of many that flowed down from the jagged peaks above. They also found an abundance of berries to eat and enough to pack away for later.

After leaving the lower camp, they headed west about a quarter mile, walking parallel to the mountains. Eventually, they came upon the snake trail Luke had highlighted on the map. The trail was narrower than they expected, and worse yet, it hugged the edge of the mountain for as far as they could see.

"Now I understand why Luke said this part would be slow going," Conner grumbled.

"It's gonna take us forever to climb that trail," Jade complained.

"Yeah. That's why we've got to get going now," Rico said emphatically. "Let's do this, you guys. Conner, you bring up the rear. I'll stay up front between Savi and Jade. We've got to move at a steady pace. Jade, you've got to keep up. Conner, make sure she does."

"That's why I carry a spear."

"Oh, I'm the problem child," she shot back. "We'll see who can't keep up."

"You go, girl!" Conner encouraged. "I like it when you play like you're tough."

"Shut up, Conner. Have I mentioned that you annoy me?"

The short break had given them time to refresh before initiating the grueling ascent. At first, the trail was unusually steep and a bit slippery. But after awhile, the path flattened and began to zigzag back and forth across the face of the mountain. Since the climbing was arduous and took every bit of strength each hiker possessed, few words were spoken to conserve energy.

Savi and Rico watched carefully for snakes as they hiked on what could barely be called a trail. Adding to their tension, they noticed several discarded snakeskins on the path, but much to their relief, neither of them saw a live rattler all morning.

By noon, they had ascended nearly halfway up the mountain. The worn climbers decided to celebrate their impressive achievement with a much-needed break.

The view from the side of the mountain was majestic. For the first time, everyone could see the course of the Salmon River, and the miles of wilderness they had passed through to get to their current location. Jade looked over at Conner and became concerned because he looked pale and sickly.

"Are you okay?"

"Uh, no. Not so good," Conner grunted. Immediately, he began throwing up the little that was in his stomach.

"What's going on?" Rico inquired, putting his hand on Conner's back.

Rico waited for him to recover a bit and then repeated his question. "What's up, Hot Dog? You okay?"

"Yeah, I'm alright," he replied unconvincingly.

"Come on, man," Rico insisted. "Tell me what's going on."

"Well . . . it's just that . . . heights freak me out . . . " he confessed in a hushed voice hoping the girls wouldn't hear him. "I looked down a few minutes ago, and all of a sudden my head started spinning and I got sick."

"You're afraid of heights? That's nothing to be ashamed of—if you're a girl," Jade teased.

"That's mean," Savi nudged Jade.

"I'm just messing with him the way he always does with me."

"She's right. I do tease her. So since I just puked my guts out, I guess there's no goodnight kiss tonight, huh, Jade?"

"Now I'm gonna puke!" she replied, holding her hand up to her mouth.

"You must be feeling better. Come on, let's keep going," Rico directed.

Again, they began moving back and forth across the face of the mountain. About ten minutes from where they had taken a break, they heard a horrible noise near the base of the range. They looked down toward the sound and saw two animals engaged in a gruesome battle. Though it was hard to see clearly from their distant vantage point, they could tell that the one animal was four-legged and light brown like a mountain lion or cougar. Unmistakably, the animal was severely wounded because it could not flee from the monstrous looking beast that was mauling it.

The aggressive creature looked to be an enormous brown bear. Even from half a mile above, the teens could see that the creature was gigantic. Its roar was ferocious as it overwhelmed and taunted its prey. Then the beast pounced on the wounded animal with a fierceness that chilled them all. In moments, the fight was over. The aggressor killed his prey, tore it apart, and devoured it piece by piece. At the sight of this, Jade was woozy and grabbed on to Rico so she wouldn't fall to the ground.

"What's going on now, Jade?" Rico asked frustrated, while holding her up.

"Are you kidding? That could have been any one of us."

Jade started to shake. Rico grabbed her firmly and pulled her close. "You need to calm down, right now! It's time to toughen up! Why don't you act more like Savi?"

"We're not gonna make it!" she cried. "We're all going to die out here."

"Shut up, Jade, and get a grip," Rico said tersely.

"You shut up!" Jade replied sharply. "And don't tell me how to act."

"Come on, you guys. Stop! Nobody is dying out here. The river and camp are on the other side of these mountains. And we're going to get there," Savi said.

After Savi had spoken, no one else knew what to say. They just stood silently and stared down at the bloody disturbance below.

Just then the brown creature lifted his head and roared. He made the worst sound anyone ever heard or even imagined. All at once, the creature stopped and glanced up in the direction of the onlookers.

"I think he spotted us!" Rico whispered.

"I know he did!" Conner replied. "Let's go, now!"

Without a moment's hesitation, the group scurried up the snake trail as fast as possible. No one needed to say anything. It was clear they had just witnessed

Vexel killing another animal. Now the hideous monster was most likely stalking them, and there was no time to spare.

Savi calculated at the last break that they had another two miles to reach the summit camp. According to the time they were making, it meant another three to four hours, and it was already half-past two.

"We've got to get to the camp and fortify the entrance as soon as we can. If Vexel is following us, that's our only chance. God, I wish I had some bullets right now," Savi lamented.

"Even if we had bullets, no pistol could stop that thing," Rico replied. Then he turned and in a hushed voice spoke to Conner. "Man, we've got to pick up the pace. If that thing catches us, we're sitting ducks on this open trail. Unless we get to the summit camp in a hurry, it's over."

"I know. I'll do my best," Conner replied.

"No, we need to do better than that!" Rico chided.

For the next two hours, the group pushed themselves to their absolute limit. Concerned that Vexel was pursuing them up the mountain, they stopped only occasionally for a quick drink. Savi now figured that they were only about one more hour away from the camp at the summit.

Beyond wasted, the tired travelers finally had to stop for more than a short rest. The air was thinner at this altitude, and the teens could hardly breathe. After two hours of an unrelenting pace, the group was forced to take another extended break. The hikers were so exhausted they weren't sure if they could continue.

During the lengthy break, Rico decided to take another look down at the spot where they had seen Vexel devouring the animal. From their present position, he could hardly make out the images below. But one thing was for certain, Vexel was gone, and where he might be was now anyone's guess.

"Okay, time to go," Rico commanded. "We've got to get to the summit camp."

"I'm dead tired," Jade complained.

"Well, if you want to be tired and dead, just sit there," Conner warned.

Rico was frustrated with Jade and chose to ignore her comment. Instead, he turned to Savi. "How's your ankle? I noticed you were really struggling a few minutes ago."

"It always hurts when I climb," she responded. "But when it's a choice between walking in pain or dying, I'm all for walking."

"Do you think Vexel will catch us?" Jade asked anxiously.

"Not if we get moving," Savi replied. "Besides, Conner said he'd eat him for lunch. Remember, at the campfire?"

"Or was it the other way around?" Jade replied in a snarky tone.

"Come on, Jade. Let's save our breath for the hike," Savi urged.

The next section of the journey was the hardest of the day. Even after their long rest, the teens' energy was waning, and the snake trail was the steepest since they began their ascent. Each step became increasingly difficult. Dismayed by their slow progress, they had to abandon their hope of reaching the camp in an hour. After another hour of hiking, they were still over thirty minutes away from the summit and the encampment.

Eventually, they all crumpled to the ground and reached for their water bottles. The climb had not only taken its toll on each of them, but it had nearly depleted their water supply. Though they still had a little left, they needed to find more water soon.

"We've only got about a half a mile to go," Savi said between winded breaths. "We've got to keep moving. Let's go. One more push," she struggled to her feet.

"I need a few more minutes," Jade protested.

"We don't have a few more minutes!" Rico shot back. "We've got to go now. We need to get to the shelter. We're too exposed out here."

"Okay, okay, will you help me up?" Jade asked Rico.

Though aggravated with Jade's constant whining, Rico helped her up.

"You're acting more like a drill sergeant than a boyfriend," she complained.

"Right now, I am your drill sergeant," he said emphatically. Then Rico grabbed her hand and looked at her squarely. "Listen, Jade, right now my priority is keeping us all alive. So suck it up and let's get moving!"

The final half hour hike to the summit camp turned out to be about forty minutes. When they finally arrived at the refuge, they discovered Luke had directed them to a place that was more than they could have hoped for.

Just like the last cave, a narrow entrance to the enclosure made protecting it less difficult. The covered area was spacious and provided them plenty of room to sleep. A small creek flowed on the eastern side of the cavern about fifty feet away, and just as important, several clusters of ripe and luscious berries hung delicately on the branches of some nearby bushes. It was easy to see why Luke had suggested such a hospitable haven.

Rico and Conner immediately worked to secure the cave's entrance while Savi and Jade refilled the canteen and water bottles, picked berries, and gathered pine needles to insulate themselves from the cold ground in the cave. Once all the preparations were complete, they all sat down behind the sharpened wood stakes that protected the entrance. Rico and Conner placed more than the usual number of stakes at the entrance, knowing they might need additional security if their greatest fear came to pass.

The sun had barely set when to their horror, they heard crackling sounds in the trees nearby. Rico hushed everyone and they all peered outside in the direction of the noise. Again branches snapped, but they couldn't see anything yet.

Terrified, Conner whispered the obvious question on all of their minds. "Is it Vexel?"

Chapter Twenty-Eight

The teens were afraid and heard more movement in the woods across the small clearing. Raising their spears and knives, they prepared for what was sure to be the ultimate showdown. All of a sudden, a slender, tall and familiar silhouette emerged from the dark woods.

"Oh my God, Luke!" Savi practically shouted.

"Is that you, missy?"

Everyone let out a huge sigh of relief and quickly dismantled the barrier they had constructed at the entrance. Once finished, everyone rushed to greet Luke. The girls hugged him tightly, and Rico and Conner shook his hand enthusiastically and exchanged fist bumps.

"I can't believe you're here. We thought you might be dead," Jade admitted. "We heard two gunshots and then after that, nothing."

"Well, rumors about my death are clearly false," he boasted. "And about those shots—a man has to eat, doesn't he? I had a clean shot at a deer, and I took it. The second shot was to put it out of its misery."

"How did you find us again?" Savi asked.

"I came across your tracks on the snake trail," he replied. "Earlier in the morning, Vexel doubled back on me. Somehow he got behind me, so I knew I needed to climb the mountain and get some distance between us. I followed you guys up the trail to ensure he wouldn't overtake you by surprise. The added height gave me a bird's-eye view of everything. That's when I saw Vexel at the base of the mountain killing that big mountain lion. I had him in my sights for a second, but then he dragged the lion behind some rocks, and that's when I lost sight of him. I also knew if I fired and missed him, it would give away my position."

"We saw him, too," Conner insisted. "He was tearing that animal apart. You say it was a big cat?"

"Yeah, a good size mountain lion. There are plenty of them in these parts. That creature must have gotten in a scuffle earlier with another cat and was wounded. Usually, those fights are over a female. Just like in town," Luke said with a laugh. "Vexel must have smelled blood from the wound, tracked the lion down, and finished him off."

"Luke, are you sure that was him?" Savi asked.

"Oh, that was Vexel alright," he affirmed. "And believe me, he's not only vicious, but he's also smart. Like I said, he doubled back on me this morning. Thank God he found that injured mountain lion because it distracted him. That bought all of us some extra time to get a good distance away from him."

"How can you be sure it was him?" Savi questioned a second time.

"Because I got a good look at him," Luke replied. "And now I know the rumors are true."

"What rumors?" Rico wondered aloud.

"Rumors about the fire and the bear."

"Go on," he insisted.

"About ten years ago, there was a devastating fire south of here. Acres of forest burned and hundreds of animals got trapped in the blaze and were killed. There was a rumor that a huge grizzly bear got trapped under a burning tree that fell on it. Somehow the bear managed to survive but was disfigured due to the burns that covered much of its body. I saw him from a distance today, but I was close enough to see that Vexel is most likely that bear. He is the most fearsome looking beast I've ever seen, and man, is he big. If my guess is right, he's about twelve feet tall on his hind legs and has at least a five-foot shoulder span. And on top of that, I'll bet he weighs close to a thousand pounds. Much bigger than any Idaho grizzly I've ever seen, so he's got to be a coastal transplant."

"What do you mean a coastal transplant?" Savi asked.

"My dad told me that twelve years ago, the forest service relocated some huge bears from the West Coast, specifically, from Washington State up near the Canadian border. They moved them to Idaho to thin out the grizzly population on the coast. He has to be one of those bears," Luke assumed.

"So did he start killing people after the fire?" Conner asked.

"Oh no, he killed the first person before that. Most people thought Vexel died in the fire, but to everyone's surprise, six months after the blaze the killings started up again. At first, he just went after animals, and then he started killing people as he had done before. Once a grizzly has tasted human blood they never forget it. They're like a Kodiak bear that way. We have to hunt and destroy bears that attack humans, or they will keep on slaughtering people indiscriminately, just like Vexel killed my father," he said sadly.

"Do you think Vexel followed us up the snake trail?" Savi asked Luke.

"No, not right away. I stopped about halfway up the trail and waited for several minutes to see if the beast was pursuing us. He never showed up. But that doesn't mean much. That trail is not the only way for a bear to get up the mountain."

"What do you mean?" Jade asked nervously.

"I mean that a bear doesn't need a snake trail to get up the mountain," Luke declared. "He just climbs right up."

She let out a nervous breath. "Do you think we should stay here tonight? I'm not feeling very safe in this place anymore."

"I suggest you all get a good night's sleep," Luke answered. "I feel rested, and I'll keep watch for as long as I can tonight. You all must be exhausted, and you need to get some shut-eye. By sundown tomorrow, you've got to try to get across the river. The dam releases water into the Susquehanna the day after to-morrow. There's no telling what time they'll open the gate. If you get caught on the river when it opens, you haven't got a prayer," he warned them solemnly.

Luke paused a moment and continued, "There's one final thing that might help you sleep a little better. When I killed that deer, I cut out its liver and some of the other organs. I packed them in plastic bags and then sealed them in two more plastic bags to mask the smell."

"That's so gross," Jade complained. "And you said that would help us sleep better?"

"Well, yes. Because on my way up here, I left some of that stuff around to keep him distracted and away from us. I've got a few more parts here in these plastic bags if you'd like to see them." Luke reached for his pack.

"Um, yeah, no thanks," Jade said as politely as possible. "I think I'll pass if you don't mind."

"No problem," he said with a smirk. "I'll just keep these gizzards for Vexel and me. They're nice to have around if you get real hungry."

Jade's usually fair complexion turned a slight shade of green. She scooted away as quickly as possible, fearing that Luke might pull something else out of his backpack that she'd rather not see.

After Jade had excused herself, Savi asked if he'd give her one of the plastic bags filled with the deer's internal organs. She told him that she wanted it just in case they ever got into a jam. Luke graciously agreed and gave her a plastic bag that she tucked away in her backpack.

The security of knowing Luke was standing guard gave everyone a much-appreciated sense of safety. This secure feeling, coupled with their ex-haustion from the day's hard mountain climb, made falling asleep that much easier.

Luke stayed up and kept watch most of the night. Finally, at four, he woke Rico. Then Luke slept for about an hour while Rico stood guard till the sun rose.

At morning light, Rico woke everyone and encouraged them to pack up so they could get an early start. Before leaving, Luke gave each of them a strip of jerky. The famished teens also ate several handfuls of berries they found the day before. Then Luke traded his machete for the empty pistol he gave Rico a few days earlier.

"Okay, listen up," he told them. "There are some things you need to know before you leave here today. It's a steep descent down the mountain. And the snake trail ends about halfway down. I showed Savi one last encampment on the map, in case you need it. But I sure hope you don't have to stop before the getting to the river. Try to get there as quickly as you can. When you reach the river, it's about a quarter mile swim across it. Once you're on the other side, it's only about a half mile to Camp Arrowhead."

Then Luke turned to Conner and Jade. "You guys go ahead and fill all the containers with water from the stream and collect at least a day's supply of berries. Savi and Rico bring the map and come with me. I'll give you a glimpse where you're going."

Conner and Jade started filling the canteens and water bottles, while Luke grabbed all his gear. Savi and Rico followed him on a narrow path that rose quickly up the hill past the cave. Luke led the way, and the trio hiked up the steep incline for about ten minutes. Finally, Luke reached the summit and stopped. Savi was first to join him, and Rico arrived soon after that. The three of them stood on the mountaintop and gazed in amazement at the panoramic view of the valley below. From this grand vantage point, they saw the steep decline of the mountain Luke had spoken about earlier. They also noticed the emerald green forest in the distance, and best of all, their first glimpse of the turquoise Susquehanna River. Then Luke pointed in the direction of Camp Arrowhead though it wasn't visible from their location.

"That's where you're going." He took a step forward and leaned over the edge.

"It will take you the better part of the day to get down this mountain. Once you do, you'll be about a mile and a half from the river. Savi, let me have the map a minute."

Luke highlighted the spot where they were and then moved his finger northward. "See here. There's a safe cave if you should need it, less than an eighth of a mile from the river."

Then he stood up and motioned Savi and Rico to come closer. Again, Luke pointed toward the Susquehanna, "Do you see the small sandy beach on the other side of the river?"

"Yeah," they replied in unison.

"Well, directly across from that in the river, there's a small sandbar. When you're swimming across the river, that's a great place to take a break if you need one. Once you get to the beach on the other side, Camp Arrowhead is straight ahead through the forest about half a mile. Before I go, there's one last thing. Watch out for mountain lions. There are a lot of them up here. It's mating season, and they're edgy. If you surprise one or catch them hungry, they'll attack you without hesitation," he warned.

Savi and Rico looked at one another with concern but didn't say anything.

"I've got to go now," Luke said in a determined voice. "I've never been so close to getting Vexel, and I'm not letting him get away this time."

"You're leaving?" Savi said with disappointment.

"Yep, it's time for me to go. You've got a rough road ahead of you," Luke cautioned them. "It's obvious to me that you two are the leaders in the group. So get Jade and Conner back to Arrowhead safely. I probably won't see you again. So be careful, and may God bless you all and keep you safe."

Luke extended his hand for Rico to shake then gave Savi a parting hug. The two thanked him once again for everything he had done for all of them.

Savi began to cry as she wrapped her arms around Luke a second time to say goodbye. "I'll never forget you, Luke. Not as long as I live. I'll always be grateful to you. All of us owe you our lives," she said appreciatively through her tears. "Promise me you'll be extra careful. Remember, you told us Vexel is smart. So you better be smarter."

Then Savi reached into her vest pocket and took out her small Bible. She quickly thumbed through the pages until she got to Psalm 23, then she tore the page from the book and handed it to Luke.

"I have nothing to give you but this simple Psalm. I hope you find as much comfort in it, as I have. I pray that God blesses and protects you," she said through tears.

Instantly, tears welled up in Luke's eyes.

"Missy, no one's done anything that kind for me in a long time. I promise I won't forget you, either, not any of you. Now go, before I start bawling like a baby. You all have a big day ahead of you."

Savi and Rico watched as Luke descended the mountain, entered a grove of pine trees, and then disappeared. Once he was out of sight, they quickly made their way back to camp and reconnected with Jade and Conner, who were ready and waiting. As instructed, they had filled the canteens and water bottles and picked enough berries to sustain them for at least a day.

After they had picked up their belongings, everyone followed Savi up the steep path that led to the summit.

Upon reaching the top of the mountain, they began heading down the backside of the range. Within minutes, Luke's warning about the steep and treacherous descent proved accurate. The snake trail was narrow and challenging, so as a precaution, the team used a rope to connect themselves together, just in case anyone fell.

Savi led the way, followed by Jade, Conner, and Rico. Conner's fear of heights came into play at every turn. He hugged the mountain wall and refused to look down. Instead he kept both eyes on Jade's back and put one foot in front of the other. Several times, Rico had to pull Conner along with the rope connected between the two of them to keep him moving.

"Conner, I won't let you fall," he assured him. Then he turned and glanced at his terrified face, adding with a laugh, "Chico's got you covered, Hot Dog, just follow me."

Conner glanced over at Rico and tried to muster a smile, but he was so terrified that his face wouldn't cooperate.

Up front, Savi and Jade moved along the trail at a steady pace. From time to time they felt the rope tighten behind them, signaling Conner's resistance. Suddenly Savi stopped dead in her tracks. Immediately Jade sensed something was wrong.

"What's going on?" Jade asked anxiously.

Savi was white as a sheet and could do nothing but motion with her finger. Jade glanced in the direction that Savi was pointing and then let out a blood-curdling scream.

Chapter Twenty-Nine

Rico was startled by Jade's scream and rushed forward to see what was happening. When he reached the girls, he saw the reason for Jade's outcry. There, perched on a rock about ten feet in front of Savi, was a large rattlesnake. Its tail was making that familiar sound Savi had heard once before, only too late. Quickly, Rico moved in front of the girls and unclipped himself from the rope. Using his spear, he carefully inched toward the deadly creature. The snake's head rose instinctively indicating it was ready to bite.

Rico used his spear to poke at the rattler and entice it to strike at him. Whip fast, it did.

Both girls screamed as the snake sprang toward Rico. He quickly jumped backward and used the tip of his spear with precision to swat the rattlesnake off the rock and onto the trail. The agitated serpent raised its head again as Rico continued to prod it with the spear. Then, for a second time, the rattler lunged at him violently. This time it landed a couple of feet short of him. Hurriedly, he swung his spear tip across the path, scraped up the serpent, and flung it several yards down the mountainside.

Now that the rattlesnake was no longer a threat, Rico promptly ushered the others around the spot where the serpent had been and down the trail about fifty feet. They regrouped and all breathed big sighs of relief.

"What else can happen to us?" an exasperated Jade shouted.

"A lot can happen to us," Conner answered without thinking.

"Thanks, Conner. Did you know you have a gift for always saying the wrong thing?"

"How kind of you to say," he said jokingly.

"Will you guys knock it off?" Rico pleaded. Then he turned to Savi. "Hey, are you okay?"

"I think so. I've never attracted a lot of attention, but the snakes sure seem to love me."

"You do appear to be quite the snake charmer," Conner quipped.

"You see what I mean?" Jade said rolling her eyes. "You're unbelievable!"

After a careful inspection of the area, Savi sat down on a rock. It was evident that she needed a bit more time to catch her breath and recover from the incident. Once she was calm, she looked over appreciatively at Rico. "Thanks so much for helping me. I don't think I could have handled that without you."

"Don't underestimate yourself. You could have done it, but didn't need to with me here."

"No really, I'm not sure I could have dealt with that—especially after just being bitten."

"Well, that's what friends are for." Then he looked over at Conner. "How about you, Hot Dog? You alright?"

"I'm surviving, but I've got to get off this mountain soon. If I had any food in my stomach, I'd be puking my guts out every few steps."

Rico chuckled and reattached himself to the rope. He motioned to the others, and soon they all started moving down the trail again. When they had gotten about halfway down the mountain, it was finally safe enough to untie themselves and walk freely on their own.

About fifteen minutes later, without warning, the snake trail ended abruptly. This unwelcomed development meant that once again for safety reasons, they had to stop and reattach themselves by rope to one another.

Following a short break, they reattached the line and continued down the rocky hillside. From the time the trail ended the descent down the mountain was much more demanding and challenging.

As the morning progressed, Savi led the others down the steepest part of the range by moving from one tree to another. Occasionally, all of them would fall, which caused minor injuries and slowed their progress. These delays made their trip wearisome and more than a bit frustrating.

By noon, they were about two-thirds of the way down the mountain. To their relief, the altitude was less of a problem the lower they descended. But the thin air still made moving down the decline hard, and they were all desperate to stop for another break.

Unfortunately, what they couldn't stop was time. The relentless ticking of the clock hung over the group like a dark cloud. So instead of stopping they decided to press on.

"At this pace, do you think we'll make it to the river by the end of the day?" Jade asked Savi.

"I don't know. But if we keep going like this, we just might. Come on, let's save our breath and get off this mountain."

Finally, the group noticed the range began to flatten out, and the severity of decline decreased significantly. The roped team was finally able to untie themselves again and hike freely. This newfound ease allowed them to move much faster down the remaining base of the mountain.

Ultimately the team realized they had reached the bottom of the range. It was three o'clock in the afternoon, and the weary foursome took a few minutes to hydrate and celebrate their accomplishment. Now that they had surmounted the final obstacle before the river, a new surge of hope filled each of them.

They sat silently for a moment and cherished the realization that they were getting closer and closer to safety with every step.

The map indicated they were now just one and a half miles from the Susquehanna River and a little over two miles from Camp Arrowhead.

"We're on the homestretch," Savi crowed. "I can almost see the finish line."

"I need a longer break," Jade moaned. "I'm wiped out."

"Hey, you guys. We both need a few more minutes," Savi said in a winded voice and a big sigh. "Let's sit for a while. I need something to eat."

"We're good with that," Rico and Conner acknowledged.

The tired foursome continued to sit together and surveyed the mountain they had just descended. After rehydrating themselves and finishing the remaining berries, they lay down on the ground and enjoyed an extended rest.

"Conner, you must be feeling better, huh?" Savi asked.

"I'd say. I puked so many times up on that mountain I lost count," he lamented. "No one said anything in the camp brochure about mountain climbing."

"You know I've been thinking about the people back at Camp Arrowhead. I'll bet they assume we're all dead," Jade pondered aloud. "Boy, is everyone gonna be surprised when we come walking into camp."

"I'm sad about what our parents and family must be going through," Savi said with regret. "They've probably cried their eyes out by now."

"My parents are probably happy they don't have to pay for my college," Jade grumbled.

Savi shook her head. "Jade, that's not true. They're probably sick with worry."

"It looks like I may get to find out. You know, I didn't believe we'd make it until now," Jade admitted.

Rico stood to his feet. "Okay, let's get moving. I've got this creepy feeling that Vexel is following us. We've got to get to the river before dark."

The group journeyed over the flat terrain toward the river. Savi made several course corrections as they continued to move forward. By four o'clock, they were less than a quarter mile from the Susquehanna. Spent, they decided to stop one last time for a brief break before tackling the final leg of the journey that would get them to the river.

Everyone sat near a cluster of large rocks and within speaking distance of one another. After they all had caught their breath, they drank the last of the water.

"I'd guess we're twenty minutes from the river," Savi exclaimed excitedly.

"Can you believe it?" Conner said. "We've come such a long way since the rafting accident."

"What's the first thing you're going to do when you get back to Arrowhead?" Savi asked Jade. Before she could answer, they both saw something move in a wooded area behind Conner.

Terrified, the girls hushed and studied the trees behind him where the movement had originated. Suddenly a mountain lion appeared out of the woods, and both of them screamed. The dangerous intruder had snuck up on them and was now perched on a rock formation several feet away, directly above where Conner was sitting.

"Nobody move," Rico commanded as he slowly reached for his spear. Conner had his back to the danger and had no idea what was happening. Startled by the look on the others' faces, he quickly reached for his spear. Instantly the large cat leaped from the rock onto him.

Rico immediately jumped to his feet and charged the mountain lion that was now mauling Conner's arm. Conner was writhing in pain and doing his best to fight back the beast but to no avail. Rico advanced and plunged his spear into the hindquarters of the cat and wounded it.

All of a sudden, the injured animal turned on Rico. Savi ran toward Conner and grabbed his spear while Jade screamed in horror and cowered behind a small pine tree.

The mountain lion quickly overtook Rico and tossed him to the ground, clamping his jaw on Rico's lower leg. In a desperate move, Savi lunged forward and drove Conner's spear into the lion's side. Instantly, the animal started to shake violently and released its bite on Rico's leg. In seconds, the creature fell to the ground in a pool of blood. It squirmed wildly in the wet red dirt, giving Savi time to grab Rico's spear. With all the strength she could muster, she jammed the sharpened tip into the downed creature's neck and finished it off.

After she was sure the lion was dead, she rushed first to Conner. His agonizing screams were awful to hear, and his arm was a bloody mess. But despite his loud and terrible cries, it was apparent that Rico's injuries were far worse than Conner's. His lower leg was bleeding badly and riddled with nasty bites. He was on the ground moaning in pain and clutching at his wounded leg.

"Jade, hurry!" Savi shouted. "Get the medical kit out of my pack. Rico, just hold on," she pleaded. "The lion's dead. Just listen to my voice and stay awake."

Jade quickly handed the medical kit to Savi, and she took out the last two rolls of gauze, some large bandages, and an Ace wrap for binding the wound. "Here, go help Conner!" She gave Jade the gauze and bandages.

"Rico! Stay with me and keep your eyes open." His eyes opened a little. "That's it. Now listen to me. Your calf is really chewed up. I need you to put this in your mouth and bite down on it." She handed him a short, thick stick. "I've got to close your wound, and it's going to hurt. Do you understand?"

Rico could only grunt and nod.

Savi put the stick in his mouth and started to work on the wound. Before attempting to close it, she removed his belt and used it as a tourniquet to slow the flow of blood. He bit down on the stick and agonized as Savi pinched the wounds closed and bandaged them tightly in a desperate attempt to stop the bleeding. Meanwhile, Jade tried to calm Conner down so that she could treat his bites and scratches. He was hysterical and crying for help.

"Savi, what do I do?" she yelled.

"Come over here and finish putting this bandage on Rico's leg," she commanded.

Then Savi left Rico and rushed to Conner's side. Unsure of what else to do, she grabbed him by the vest and shook him.

"Conner! Conner! We can't help you unless you stop," she exhorted. "I know you're hurting, but you've got to let us work on you."

"My arm! It's on fire. I can't stand it," he moaned.

"I know. Now let me help you."

"Savi!" Jade screamed. "Rico's losing consciousness."

"Don't let him," Savi shouted back. "You've got to keep him awake. Hang on. I'll be right there."

Savi quickly wrapped Conner's arm and slowed the bleeding. Then she hurried back to Rico.

"Go over there and stay with Conner while I work on Rico," Savi ordered.

"Is he going to die?" Jade cried out in a panic.

"Not if I can help it, he's not. Now get over there and tend to Conner. Now, Jade!"

The chaotic scene gradually calmed down. Savi, with Jade's help, had bandaged both Rico and Conner's injuries, and after nearly an hour, their wounds had all but stopped bleeding. Savi used every resource at her disposal to steady them both. Conner had finally quieted down though he was suffering terribly. Across the way, Rico's leg wound was deep and his injury severe. The mountain lion had clamped down multiple times on his right calf and buried his fangs deep into his lower leg. Rico also had several scratches on his chest from the cat's claws. Though still in a lot of pain, he appeared to be somewhat stabilized.

"What do we do now?" Jade blurted in a panicked voice.

"We slow down and come up with a plan," Savi replied calmly.

"What kind of plan?"

"Listen to me right now, Jade. You've got to pull it together in a hurry. I need your help, and so do they. You've got to toughen up and quit freaking out on me. We've got big problems here, and I don't need to add you to the list. Got it?"

Savi turned away and brushed the tears from her eyes.

"Sorry," Jade shot back in frustration. "I live in San Francisco. I don't see this kind of stuff every day."

Savi wiped her eyes.

"Do you think we fight animals in the streets of Mississippi? This stuff is overwhelming for me, too, Jade. But we've got to keep it together, or we're all going to die out here."

"Okay. But please don't yell at me. I'm just really scared." Jade confessed while doing her best to compose herself.

"Oh really? I hadn't noticed! Now listen, I don't mean to yell at you. But I'm frightened too, Jade. And I just need you to help me."

"What can I do?"

"Go and check on Conner," she replied. "And please quit asking me questions for a while, okay? I need to think."

Jade went to check on Conner while Savi worked on Rico's injuries. Though the bleeding had slowed significantly, Savi was still concerned. But she was encouraged that Rico was sitting up and leaning against a rock.

"I'll bet that hurt worse than my snake bite," she said to him with a smile.

"My leg feels like someone hit it with an ax," Rico moaned. After a moment of groaning, he spoke again. "I can't believe you killed that lion, Savi."

"Well, I didn't have a lot of choices. You guys were lying around crying like middle school girls after a breakup. Somebody had to do something."

Rico forced a smile for the first time since the attack. "Hey, I need you to do me a favor," she asked him. "Tell your girlfriend to get it together. She's driving me crazy."

"You know she's just afraid," he grunted as he looked down at his blood-soaked leg and jerked in pain. Then he looked up at her. "I can't walk on this leg, Savi. With me slowing things down, you guys won't make it to the river in time. It's already almost six o'clock."

Then he looked into her eyes and said the words she didn't want to hear. "You need to leave me here and try to save yourself and the others. I can't go any further. You have to leave me here, Savi!"

Chapter Thirty

Rico's request to be left behind infuriated Savi. She glared at him angrily and then shook her head in refusal.

"You've got to be kidding me! No one is getting left out here alone, especially you."

Realizing what she had just said, Savi blushed and quickly tried to cover her tracks. "I mean, you've gotten us all this way, and I would never leave you out here by yourself. No chance," she said emphatically.

"I didn't . . . get us here alone," he said between groans. "It was as much you . . . as it was me."

"Whatever you say. But I'm not leaving you behind," Savi said resolutely. "My dad was in the army, and he taught me that you never leave a wounded soldier on the battlefield. Either you come with us, or we all stay here."

"Can Conner walk?"

"I'm sure he can. The lion bit his arm, not his leg."

"Okay, I'll try. But you've got to help me up," Rico implored her. "I don't think I can put any weight on my leg."

Savi struggled to help Rico to his feet while he wailed from the pain of moving. They quickly discovered the damage was so severe that he couldn't stand or put any pressure on the mauled limb.

Realizing that he couldn't walk without support, Savi bowed her head curiously. After a couple of moments, she helped Rico to a nearby tree and carefully propped him up against it. Then she withdrew the bloody spear from the side of the dead lion and brought it over to Rico.

"Here, try using this to lean on and see if it helps," Savi encouraged him.

Rico took her advice and a few short steps. He discovered he could hop and hobble forward by using the spear to support himself.

"Okay, let me help you sit back down, and then I'll go and get Conner ready," she told him.

When Savi headed over to Conner, Jade immediately went back to sit with Rico.

"Are you alright? I thought that the mountain lion was going to kill you," she said through tears. "I'm so sorry. I didn't know what to do to help you."

"Stop crying. There's nothing you could have done about what happened. But you can do something now."

"What?" Jade asked.

"You've got to stay calm and help Savi," he said. "Do whatever she tells you. She's the one who's going to lead us out of here. Promise me you'll try to stay calm and help her."

"I promise. And I've already told Savi that. Do you think you can walk on that?"

"I'll try my hardest. But I'm not sure how far I'll get."

Across the way, a sobering thought crossed Savi's mind. She looked around and saw blood was everywhere. Suddenly she remembered that Vexel was attracted to the smell of it and declared they had to leave the place immediately.

Conner stood with Savi's assistance for the first time and realized he could walk, despite the burning pain in his arm.

Then Savi returned to Rico and informed him and Jade that they had to leave as quickly as possible. She directed them to bring Conner's spear, their knives, the rope, and anything else vital that they could carry in their vest pockets. Everything else they were instructed to leave behind. Just before leaving, Savi reached into her backpack and pulled out the plastic bag Luke had given her and stuffed it in her back vest pocket.

"Why do you need that?" Jade asked her.

"Who knows? We might need it later to distract Vexel," she replied.

When everyone was ready, Savi checked her map and compass and pointed the way they should go.

"Jade, you're way taller than me. So you help Rico. He'll have to lean on you and the spear. Make sure you tell me if he starts bleeding again," she cautioned her. "Conner, you come up here with me and walk close behind me."

"Okay, we'll try to keep up. But, you've got to go slow. Rico won't be able to go very fast."

"Yeah, I know. I'll keep an eye on you guys," Savi assured her.

The girls guided their wounded comrades slowly through the wilderness toward the river. Unfortunately, they had to stop every few hundred feet so Rico could catch his breath. Jade was struggling to keep him moving and upright. The last quarter mile to the river was grueling and seemed to take forever.

Savi realized it was now nine-thirty at night on August 31st. The dam was scheduled to open the next morning, and no one knew at what time. The weary foursome also understood there was no way they could cross the river in the dark. And complicating the situation, it was plain that without some assistance or a float of some kind, neither Rico nor Conner could make it across the quarter mile wide river they needed to traverse.

After hours of relentless struggle through the dark woods, Savi finally heard the distinct sound of flowing water.

Rico and Conner had been moaning and agonizing since they departed the scene of the attack. They were both bleeding freely again. Savi and Jade were thoroughly exhausted both from the grueling trek and helping their injured companions.

After a few more minutes, Savi and Conner stumbled their way over a short incline and finally broke through the trees into a vast clearing. Both of them fell to their knees onto the sandy beach that lined the edge of the waterway. Gazing out onto the slow-moving current, they watched moonbeams dance upon the river. Savi bowed her head quietly, no doubt thanking God for helping them to reach the Susquehanna River.

Utterly spent, Jade and Rico collapsed onto the beach several minutes after Savi and Conner. A while later, with considerable effort, Savi lifted herself up. She collected the water bottles and canteens they had packed in their vests. Then she limped several steps to the river and, one by one refilled them. When she finished, she staggered back to the others and handed each of them a container.

"Here, drink as much as you can. There's a river full out there."

Savi walked over to Jade and tossed her a water bottle. Then she downed most of her canteen. When she had finished, she glanced back at Jade.

"You did so well. I'm really proud of you. There's no way I could have gotten the guys here by myself."

"Thanks for saying that," Jade replied. "I know you said not to ask you any more questions, but Rico's bleeding pretty badly again. Can you help me figure out how to stop it?"

"Conner is bloody, too. How much is Rico bleeding?"

"There's a lot of blood on his ankle and foot."

"I'll check on him," Savi replied. "And Jade, the question thing? It was a bit stressful back there. I just meant no more questions at the scene of the attack. You can ask me whatever you want now, okay?"

"Well, I wasn't sure if you meant ever or what."

"Jade, you know better than that," Savi sighed. "Now go and refill the water bottles and make sure these guys get plenty to drink. I'll go check on Rico, and then I'll see how Conner is doing."

Savi removed the bloody gauze from Rico's calf. Since they were out of clean bandages, she washed the blood-soaked dressing in the river and did her best to clean it. She also used the last drops of the peroxide to treat his wounds. After squeezing the bandage to dry it off, she rewrapped Rico's injuries.

Savi shifted her focus to Conner and inspected the damage the lion had done to his arm.

"How are you doing, big guy? That was quite a bite," she said while examining his arm.

"You mean when I bit the lion? I still have hair in my mouth."

"That's disgusting but funny. Are you feeling any better?"

"Not really. My arm is still killing me." Then Conner looked over his shoulder. "How's Rico's leg doing?"

"It's pretty bad, and you can bet he won't be playing football anytime soon. Or even walking on his own."

Savi pulled the map from her vest and studied it. She noticed Luke had circled a cave that looked to be only a few hundred yards away from their current position. She reminded everyone that it was too dangerous for them to stay out in the open all night, and against their protests, advised them she was going off to try to find the cave. No one had the strength to restrain her nor could they have stopped her anyway. So off Savi went in search of the much-needed refuge.

Fifteen minutes later Savi located the cave right where Luke had indicated it would be. After spending a short time inspecting the enclosure, she headed back to tell the others. Upon returning, she roused them to their feet, and they made the slow and painful journey through the dark and dense woods to the new hideaway. Unfortunately it took three times as long for them to get to the cave as it had for Savi to find it. After finally reaching the grotto, Savi and Jade began preparing the enclosure the way they had seen Rico and Conner do it.

"Jade, help me pick up some pine straw so the guys can lay on it. Then we'll take a break and finish fortifying the entrance."

"Okay. But I can't wait to lie down. I feel like I carried Rico half the way here."

"You did. And I know he's grateful."

After they had finished gathering the pine straw, the girls dragged some downed branches over to the cave's entrance to use as stakes against predators. When all the preparations were complete, Savi and Jade collapsed in a heap next to Rico and Conner, who were by now fast asleep on the floor of the cave.

"You said I could ask you questions again," Jade declared. "So here's one. What are we going to do?"

"Honestly, I don't know," Savi replied. "I need a few minutes of quiet time to pray and think."

"Well, when you figure out a plan, let me know, and I'll help."

"I know you will. For now just get some rest."

Jade laid her head down next to the guys and in the next few minutes was sound asleep.

Savi stood alone at the entrance to the enclosure and looked up at a nearly full moon and myriad glimmering stars. Then she looked down at her friends and bowed her head for the longest time. Every few minutes either Rico or Conner would wince in pain and let out a painful groan before falling back to sleep. The constant moans were unsettling and awful to hear.

Savi stood by herself and continued to pray for guidance.

Like the others, she was exhausted. But she realized she needed to stay awake or risk a possible attack from a predator. After standing watch for a while, she pulled out her pocket Bible and her flashlight, hoping to spot some words of inspiration. She thumbed through the pages until her eyes fell on a verse she did not recall reading before.

"Greater love has no one than this, that he lay down his life for his friends."

She closed the book and for the next hour or so pondered the words she had read. When she was too tired to stand any longer, she woke Jade to take the next guard shift.

Once Jade was ready to take over, she put her hand on Savi's shoulder and looked into her eyes. "Did you think of a plan?"

"Yes, I believe I've got one," she told her, "but you're going to have to be brave and strong to help me pull it off."

Jade looked concerned. "What do you mean I'm going to have to be brave and strong?"

"Just what I said. Here's what I'm thinking. We're going to use the rope we brought with us and the machete Luke gave us to construct a small raft for Rico. Tomorrow morning at first light, we'll build it, and then we can use it to float Rico across the river. You and Conner are going to have to kick as hard as you can to propel the raft across the river before the dam opens. Once you get to the other side, you'll only be a half mile from Camp Arrowhead. Can you do that for me, Jade?"

"Wait, where will you be?"

"Don't worry about me for now. I'll be okay. Now can you do what I asked you?"

"Yeah, I'll try my best. It sounds like that's our only option. I can't believe you thought of that on your own."

Savi smiled. "I didn't. I had some help."

For a moment, Jade wasn't sure what Savi meant. But then she pointed up and nodded with a grin.

"Now I've got to get some sleep. At dawn we'll build the raft. Let's not wake the guys until we're through making the float. They need to rest, and they can't really help us anyway."

Besides occasional moans from Rico and Conner, the night passed without incident. Jade stood guard on the last watch as the sun appeared over the horizon. As soon as there was enough light to work, Jade woke Savi. The two of them used the machete to cut pine branches and fir boughs about five feet long and four inches in diameter. Then they cut three lengths of fir to tie across the bottom of the raft to stabilize the timber and keep it flat. Savi remembered that fir branches were unusually buoyant. They would be useful to help the raft float, especially with Rico's added weight. Savi used the machete to trim the branches so they would fit tightly next to one another. Then she finished the makeshift ark by binding everything together firmly with freshly cut pieces of rope.

The girls dragged the raft to the river's edge with earnest determination. After they had pulled the craft across the beach, the girls returned to the enclosure and woke up the boys.

Following a quick breakfast of water and the last of the berries, Savi explained her plan to them. Rico was too weak to eat or argue with Savi. Conner tried to hide it, but his arm hurt worse than it did the day before, and it was bleeding again. Any ideas Savi had that would get them across the river were okay with him.

Carefully, the girls helped Rico and Conner to their feet. And just before leaving, Savi made sure everyone drank some extra water as a final precaution.

Suddenly they were startled by the terrifying sounds of a bear roaring in the distance. Moments later, it let out another loud and frightening growl. Everyone could only guess, but they were sure the beast was less than a quarter mile away. The hair-raising ferocity of the noise left little doubt what they were hearing.

Chapter Thirty-One

Judging by the horrific sounds they heard in the distance, Vexel was close and getting closer. Quickly and carefully, Savi and Jade helped Rico and Conner exit the cave. The maneuver took significant effort because both of them were moving slowly and still in great pain. But despite their undeniable discomfort and tortured groans, there was no time to waste.

The journey from the enclosure to the river's edge was too overwhelming a task for Rico.

"Savi, I can't!" He moaned and fell to the ground after taking only a few steps. "My leg won't support me. There's no way I can make it. You've got to leave me here and get to the river. Vexel is close, and the dam is going to open at any minute. Now go!"

Instantly, Savi exploded. "You get your butt up now! I'm not kidding!" She screamed with a fury he had not seen before. "I told you: I'm not leaving you!" Without a moment's hesitation, she grabbed his arm and pulled him up to one knee with a violent jerk.

"Savi, we've got to go!" Conner yelled. "Vexel is right behind us."

"I know, but I'm not leaving Rico."

"What are we supposed to do? Stand here and die?"

"No! You and Jade get to the river. Drag the raft up the shore as far as you can. Otherwise, when we launch it, the current will pull it downstream before we can get to the other side. Now go, hurry!" she commanded. "We'll be right behind you."

"We can't leave them," Jade started to say to Conner.

Savi interrupted her in mid-sentence. "You do what I said, and do it now! Or we're all going to die out here. Got it?"

Reluctantly Jade sobbed as she turned her back on Savi and Rico. She held Conner steady by his uninjured arm, and the two of them hobbled into the woods toward the river to find the raft. The short trek was slow because he was struggling with intense pain. To make things worse, Conner scraped against a branch while they were moving through a particularly dense area, and his arm started to bleed freely again. With Vexel in pursuit, there was no time to stop and deal with his injury. Jade had to keep Conner moving, which meant assisting him with every step. She guided him through the bush-laden uneven terrain with a determination to get to the beach and complete the task Savi had assigned her.

"Slow down," he pleaded. "I can't move that fast. My arm feels like it's on fire."

"We can't slow down. We've got to keep going," Jade replied between heavy breaths. "We've got to get to the beach and drag the raft up the shore."

"No way I can pull anything," he objected. "Not with this arm."

"Quit whining! You've got to help me, or we're finished. We've got to get across the river, and the float is the only way. You and Rico could never swim that far with your injuries."

A short time later, Jade and Conner heard the sound of the rippling water. Then they broke out of the tree line and saw the river. Instantly Jade spotted the raft about twenty yards down the shore where she and Savi had left it. All of a sudden, Conner staggered forward and fell to the sand. Jade tried desperately to lift him up, but he refused to budge. Frustrated, she ran to the raft and attempted to drag it on her own. But as hard as she pulled, the craft only slid a few yards. Conner lay face down on the shore exhausted and anguishing over his wounds. Jade let go of the raft and rushed back to him.

"Conner! Get up and help me. I can't do this by myself."

"No way. My arm is bleeding, and I'm exhausted."

"I know that. But your legs aren't broken," Jade shouted.

Unwilling to take no for an answer, she grabbed him by his uninjured arm and, with all her strength, pulled him up to a knee. "Come on, and help me. We've got to get the raft up the shore now!"

Though Savi and Rico were far behind Jade and Conner, they were slowly making their way toward the river. Rico lacked the strength to use his spear as a cane any longer, so after it had dropped to the ground for the third time, Savi left the spear where it fell. Now Rico was leaning hard against her petite frame, and she found herself having almost to carry him. His severe injury and difficulty in walking made the journey extremely slow for both of them.

"We're almost there. You can do this," Savi encouraged him. "Just hold on to me and use your good leg."

"I'm trying," he grimaced. "But please, I've got to stop for a minute," he begged.

"Not a chance! We've got to keep going. Look at me," Savi yelled. "The river is right there through the trees. Listen! Can you hear it? It's less than a hundred feet away."

Rico leaned hard against her and then stopped. "I can't do it. Just let go of me, please Savi."

"Listen, I can't carry you and argue at the same time," she shouted. "Now shut up and walk, or I'll drag you. Got it?"

"Okay! Okay! I'll try." Rico took in a deep breath, and then Savi helped him up to his feet. He put his arm around her shoulder and steadied himself.

Then she shoved him forward and again they were moving toward the sound of the water.

Finally, after several minutes and many agonizing steps, they were only a stone's throw away from the river. Rico collapsed.

Savi shook him as he lay on the ground, but he wouldn't move. She bent down and grabbed him with both hands by the collar.

"Rico, you've got to get up. Look! The river is right here."

"It's over, Savi," he said resolutely with his head down and both eyes closed. "I can't take another step."

"Oh, yes you will!" she screamed. Suddenly she reached down, grabbed Rico's injured calf, and squeezed it hard. Instantly, he let out a piercing shriek as loud as Savi had ever heard. He glared at her with rage and unleashed a flurry of obscenities.

"Now, you get up right now, or I'll kick your leg the next time," she threatened while pulling him up by his vest onto his knees.

"I hate you!" he shouted.

"I hate you, too!" she shot back. "Now get your butt up! Do you understand me?"

Somehow, Savi managed to get Rico back on his feet and, despite his fierce protests, she got him hobbling forward. Again she wrapped her arm tightly around his waist. Livid, he tried to push her away, but he lacked the strength to do so. Grudgingly, he leaned on her, and they traveled at a snail's pace the last fifty feet to the river.

Savi realized Rico was furious with her, but for now she didn't care. Finally, after several more minutes of almost having to drag Rico, the weary duo reached the shore. They toppled to the ground with Savi utterly exhausted and Rico bloody and in severe misery.

Meanwhile, Jade had managed to convince Conner to help her drag the raft nearly two hundred feet up the river's bank.

Now the two of them lay on the sand wearied from pulling the float so far.

All at once, Vexel let out another bone-chilling roar. Conner and Jade quickly sat up. Then noticing that Savi was sprawled out and needed her help to move Rico, Jade bounced up and hurried down the shore. After hearing Vexel, Savi had stood. The two girls lifted Rico up and put one of his arms around each of their necks. Terrified that Vexel was closing in on them, they carried Rico up the riverbank toward the raft. The short jaunt up the beach was agonizing for Rico, and his painful cries echoed over the water.

After several minutes of tough work, the girls finally got Rico to the raft. Concerned that Vexel would break out of the woods at any second, the girls dragged the raft from the shore halfway into the water. Carefully, they sat Rico on the wooden float and helped him lie down on his back. His groans were awful to hear as Savi and Jade situated him on the raft.

Now the craft sat dangerously low in the water because of the added weight. Fortunately, it stayed afloat just enough to keep Rico's head slightly above the water.

Suddenly another terrifying roar sounded in the nearby woods. This time it appeared to be no more than a stone's throw away. Then out of nowhere, the verse Savi had read from her Bible the night before flashed through her mind. In an instant, it became clear to her what she needed to do. The only way to protect her friends was to distract Vexel and, if necessary, sacrifice her life to save theirs. If she could entice the beast to come after her, the others might have time to get away.

"Jade, you and Conner get Rico across the river," Savi ordered. "You'll have to kick hard, or you won't make it to the other shore. Remember, the current will be trying to pull you down the river. Conner, use your good arm and hold on to the extra line of rope I tied between the logs, but you've got to hurry! Vexel's on us, and the dam will open at any minute!" Then with all of her might Savi shoved the raft away from the shore.

"Now kick! And don't stop for anything!"

Jade and Conner did what Savi told them and started using their legs to propel the craft toward the other shore. After a couple of minutes, Jade looked back and began to panic when she realized that Savi had disappeared.

"Savi!" Jade screamed. "Where are you?"

Without Savi, Jade and Conner weren't sure what to do next except to keep kicking.

"We can't leave her there alone!" Rico protested. "We've got to go back."

"We can't go back, or we'll all die!" Conner shouted. "Savi said she'd be right behind us. We've got to get to the other shore. That's what she told us to do."

"He's right," Jade said. "She told us to get you across the river."

"I don't care what she said," Rico yelled angrily. "We've got to turn back and get her." Then he rolled over on his shoulder and looked toward the shore they had just left, almost tipping over the raft.

"Lay down, Rico, or you'll drown!" Conner shouted. "You can't swim with your leg, and neither of us can carry you across."

Suddenly they heard a terrible roar behind them. Rico, Jade, and Conner looked back and saw Vexel thrashing about near the water's edge. The hideous beast was terrifying and stood taller than a one-story building on his hind legs.

Vexel's burned face was frightful looking, and there was scarcely a trace of fur left on his head or neck. His enormous frame revealed scarred patches from top to bottom.

The enraged bear snarled viciously at the teens while Jade and Conner kicked frantically to propel the craft farther away from the shore. The repulsive creature roared in protest as he stared out at the helpless trio only fifty feet away. For a few seconds, his cold, and hungry gaze stayed fixed on the defenseless threesome. All of a sudden, he started to walk into the water.

"Oh my God, he's coming after us!" Jade screamed. "Conner, kick harder!"

"Savi!" Rico screamed. "She'll die if that thing finds her. We can't leave her!"

Jade and Conner chose not to respond to Rico's pleas. Instead they continued to expend all their energy propelling the raft toward the opposite shore.

When Vexel entered the water, Jade and Conner's fear and adrenaline skyrocketed. Now they knew for sure that there was no turning back to get Savi. The only option before them was to get across the river as quickly as possible.

Meanwhile Savi removed the plastic bag that Luke had given her from the back pocket of her vest. She knew there was a good chance if Vexel saw the others first, he'd probably go after them. Determined to save their lives, Savi ran up the shore and climbed on a rocky incline. The spot looked out over the river and was about twenty feet high above the water. While moving up the slope, Savi dropped pieces of the deer's organs that Luke had cut up and given to her. She hoped that the stinky animal guts would lure the beast from the river and, most importantly, away from her friends.

Suddenly Savi appeared on top of the ledge overlooking the water screaming and waving.

"Hey! I'm up here!"

By this time, Vexel was up to his chest in the water, but when he heard Savi's voice, he stopped and turned. Instantly, the beast looked one way and then the other, searching for the source of the noise.

"Here I am!" Savi shouted. "Up here!" She jumped up and down waving.

Immediately Vexel's head swung to the right and his eyes locked on Savi. She was fully visible standing on a rock ledge only a few hundred feet away from him.

"Hey!" She screamed and taunted him to lure him away from her friends. "Hey! Come and get me!"

Vexel turned and looked at the raft now nearing the middle of the river. Then he shifted his focus back on Savi. Again she waved her arms wildly, jumped up and down, and shouted as loudly as she could.

All at once, Vexel retreated from the river and violently shook the water off his enormous body. Then, in a frightening pose, he stood on his hind legs and let out a fierce roar. The beast turned away from the shore and disappeared into the woods, heading in Savi's direction.

"Savi, run!" Rico shouted. "He's coming after you!"

But instead of running, Savi stood and waited by the rock's ledge to ensure that Vexel did not return to the water and go after her friends again.

"Savi!" Rico wailed.

Resolved, she waited and stared out into the water as her friends floated further away. Then gazing at the raft one last time, she spoke in a gentle whisper, "I don't hate you, Rico . . ."

She heard rocks tumbling behind her and knew Vexel was coming up the hill. Then his dreadful head appeared over a pile of rocks at the back of the ledge. He paused as his eyes locked on the helpless prey standing near the edge less than fifty feet away. All at once, he let out a deafening roar and then charged her.

"Savi!" Rico screamed in one last desperate plea.

Chapter Thirty-Two

Seeing the size and ferocity of the beast charging Savi petrified her and made the hair on the back of her neck stand straight up. Now that she had distracted Vexel away from her friends, she quickly moved to the tip of the rock ledge and pushed off with a powerful thrust. Flying through the air and dropping twenty feet into the river was frightening and painful. The collision with the water stunned her, but only momentarily.

Savi's hard push off the ledge helped her to enter the water at a 45-degree angle. This shallow entry prevented her from smashing into several big rocks hidden just a few yards below the surface. Since she was a little girl, Savi had always been a good swimmer, but just how good was about to be tested. Once she recovered from the powerful impact, she started to swim with all her might. After swimming hard for about a minute, she looked back to see where Vexel was. The furious beast was standing on the ledge, shaking his head violently and roaring in protest. Then unexpectedly, the creature turned and hurried away from the overlook. Within a few seconds, he had disappeared into the nearby woods. Savi flipped over and floated on her back a few moments to rest. She stared at the shore hoping the creature had given up and moved on elsewhere. Suddenly, to her surprise, Vexel emerged from the tree line at full speed and charged toward the river and Savi.

Instantly Savi flipped over and started swimming for her life.

"Savi! He's coming!" Rico shouted. "Swim faster!"

By this time, the craft was over halfway across the river and well above the targeted landing spot on the other shore.

Unfortunately, Jade was the only one left with the leg strength to propel the craft. Conner's legs had given out completely. His wounds had sapped his strength and limited his ability to help. Now Conner was struggling just to hold on, while Jade worked tirelessly to get the float to shore.

"Conner!" Jade cried out. "Where's Savi?"

"She's in the water and swimming toward us," he groaned.

"I don't know if I can keep going! My legs are almost gone," Jade muttered between breaths.

"Take a break, but just for a minute or the current will take us too far down river," Conner told her. "I'll try to help you get us to shore."

Kicking and pushing the log raft was slow and tedious. But little by little, Jade and Conner managed to propel the craft closer to the other side and ultimately to safety. Jade held tightly onto Rico's ankle to prevent him from rolling off the partially submerged raft. While her tired legs just kept pumping, her focus was riveted on the beach now less than a hundred yards away.

In the meantime, Vexel had burst into the water and was paddling in Savi's direction. Her energy was now nearly depleted from having carried Rico, as well as the hard swim. Increasingly, she began to falter.

Conner glanced back and saw Savi grappling in the water with Vexel in hot pursuit. But he knew if he yelled, she was too far away and wouldn't hear him.

Savi did not need a warning. She knew the relentless beast was behind her and steadily closing the gap between them. She tried to dig deeper and continued to swim, but her energy was waning. Lifting her head, she spotted the sandbar that Luke had pointed out from the summit the day before. Realizing she couldn't swim much further without a break, she turned to make her way toward the sandy island. Before she knew it, she had reached the sandbar. The touch of the sand gave her a renewed sense of hope. All she needed was a few minutes to catch her breath and regain some strength. Now she was halfway across the river and about an eighth of a mile from the other shore.

Savi crawled on all fours up the sandy mound until the water was below her ankles. Once her fingers hit a dry patch of sand, she collapsed, her face half-buried. For the next couple minutes, she laid still fighting for air and hoping to recover quickly.

Still in relentless pursuit, Vexel's hideous looking face bobbed up and down in the water as he paddled slowly but determinedly toward her. After a couple of minutes, Savi had gathered enough strength to lift herself up again. Instantly she turned and locked eyes with the beast heading straight toward her. Panic shot through her when she saw that Vexel was probably less than a hundred feet away.

Unexpectedly a loud warning siren blared out. The harsh sound reminded her of home and the noise of a tornado warning. All at once she realized it was the warning siren that Luke had told them about, indicating the dam would open within twenty minutes. The siren sounded a second time, and then an eerie silence descended over the river.

Startled by the unusually high-pitched sound, Vexel stopped paddling for a moment and looked around confusedly. After the siren had quieted, he refocused his attention on his prey and again started moving steadily toward her. Savi looked over her shoulder and saw that the raft with Rico, Jade, and Conner was rapidly approaching the beach on the other side. Lying on the sandbar thoroughly exhausted, she doubted she could muster the energy to swim the remaining distance. Then she glanced the other way and saw Vexel's ferocious and scarred face only twenty-five feet away. In one last-ditch effort to save herself, she struggled to her feet, stumbled off the sandbar, and went back into the water. With every ounce of strength remaining, Savi swam toward her friends.

She knew what she was trying to do, but her arms and legs were beyond tired.

"Savi, swim faster!" Rico shouted with all his remaining strength. "He's catching you!"

No longer able to swim freestyle, Savi flipped over on her back. Floating helplessly, she attempted to do a half-hearted backstroke but sadly lacked the power to do so. Despite her best efforts, Vexel inched closer and closer by the minute. Savi now realized she was only moments away from being overtaken by the relentless monster. Attempting to muster all her remaining strength, she willed her legs to kick, but they no longer would.

Floating on her back, Savi raised her head and saw Vexel approaching. A sense of panic and fear overwhelmed her like she had never known. The beast's heavy breathing together with the sounds of his vicious snarls now began to fill her ears.

Oddly a keen sense of peace descended upon Savi, and she realized that after everything they had been through, she was about to die. Defenseless and devoid of strength, she floated helplessly on her back and waited to be overtaken by the beast. Then she closed her eyes and said a short prayer. Knowing that Vexel was only a few feet away, she looked up at the cloudless blue morning sky one last time. Without the strength, desire, or energy to scream, she lay motionless in the water. Savi never imagined her life would end in such a violent way and hoped the pain would not last long. Then she whispered a final prayer, "Please God, let me die quickly!"

All of Vexel's unrelenting effort had finally paid off. He was now only a few feet from his defenseless prey. Savi floated, calm and still, not wanting to see the awful face of the creature that was about to end her young life. Then piercing pain shot through her leg as Vexel's claw hooked her ankle. She instinctively cried out, recoiled, and kicked one last time in an attempt to free herself from the claw.

Boom! Boom! The crack of two rifle shots rang out over the river. The distinct sound came from the lookout point where Savi had jumped into the river earlier.

Immediately, Vexel released his grip on Savi's lower leg.

Stunned and in severe pain, at first she wasn't sure what was happening. She feared by the feel of her leg that it was bleeding badly. While gasping for air, she lifted her ankle just above the water to survey the damage. She was bleeding from a deep gash above her ankle. Savi could hear Vexel howling in agony and was thrilled to see he was paddling away from her. He appeared to be making his way back toward the sandbar.

In the meantime, Luke had dropped his rifle and stripped off his gear. Diving into the water, he started swimming toward Savi as fast as he could. Luke knew Savi was in danger of drowning and laboring to keep her head above the water.

Despite her painful injuries, the valiant teen continued to bob up and down on her back in a desperate effort to stay afloat. Vexel, now back on the sandbar, wailed in distress from the dual gunshots that had penetrated his body. As Luke swam past the sandbar, he noticed Vexel was bleeding heavily from both his shoulder and backside. Hearing him pass the small sandy island, Vexel turned his head toward Luke and then growled viciously at him.

All of a sudden, the siren sounded again, this time indicating only ten minutes until the dam opened, making the river impassable.

"Savi, hold on!" Luke yelled. "I'm coming!"

Not sure if she was hearing Luke's voice or was just imagining it, she cried out, "Please help me!"

"I'm almost there!" She heard a voice shout back.

"Luke?" she whispered, just as she started to take in water, sink, and lose consciousness.

"Savi!" He screamed seeing she was beginning to go down.

Moments later, Luke reached her. Savi was still partially floating, but her head was now under water. Luke quickly slipped his arm under hers in a lifeguard rescue. This elevated her head above the water line. By now, she had quit breathing. So he flipped her around till she faced him, placed her head on his shoulder, and wrapped his arms around her midsection. Then he squeezed her firmly against himself a few times vigorously.

Instantly, water spewed out of Savi's mouth followed by a desperate gasp for air. Holding her close, he turned her limp body carefully around and was shocked by how pale her face looked.

"Missy, I'm here. Just breathe. I've got you now."

"Luke," she whispered appreciatively and then flopped her head onto his shoulder.

Luke was tired and needed to rest awhile, but he knew the clock was ticking, and that the dam could open at any moment.

Savi's ankle was still bleeding badly, which further complicated an already challenging situation. To make things even worse, she could hardly hold up her head, and he feared she would swallow water again. Thinking quickly, he grasped her firmly and turned her. Again he put his arm across her chest in a lifeguard hold. Then, without a moment's hesitation, he started hauling her through the water toward the shore where the raft with her friends had already landed.

Luke was exhausted from the hard swim to reach Savi and from the added effort of having to tow her. Despite his weariness, he pressed on knowing he was on the clock. It was plain to everyone that any second the dam would open. If it did unlock before the two of them reached the shore, they would be swept down the river and, without life jackets, would surely drown.

"Luke, hurry!" Rico shouted from the shoreline. "The dam is ready to open."

"Go faster!" Jade screamed in a panicked voice.

Luke heard the yelling and glanced over his shoulder. To his relief, only a hundred feet remained between him and Savi and the safety of the shore. Suddenly, the siren rang out again, signaling the final one-minute warning before the dam opened.

Upon hearing the alert, Jade and Conner helped Rico up and escorted him away from the river's edge to a safer place on the beach. They quickly propped him up against a pine tree and left him there. Rico anxiously watched as Jade and Conner returned to the riverbank. Luke was now only a few feet away from the beach.

When Luke turned and saw Jade and Conner standing by the water, he yelled at them to get away from the shore.

"Move back! Or you'll be swept down the river!"

Jade and Conner listened to Luke and scampered away from the riverbank. In a last ditch effort to get to shore, Luke expended every bit of his strength. He kicked his legs and feet furiously and used the cupped palm of his free hand to pull the water toward him. All of a sudden, a series of three short blasts sounded, followed by a longer one, indicating the dam was opening. Then everyone heard a roaring sound and saw a mass of white water cascading from upriver toward them.

Despite his warning to stay back, Jade and Conner now realized if Luke and Savi were going to survive, they needed help. Risking their lives, they dashed down to the river's edge and grabbed Savi by the arms and dragged her limp and bleeding body up the beach and away from the rising current. Meanwhile, Luke crawled on his hands and knees away from the shore fighting to stay ahead of the rapidly rising water. The will to survive and an unexplainable surge of energy powered him away from the rising tide, up the shore, and out of danger. When he sensed he was at a safe distance from the current, he flipped over on his back in a desperate attempt to get air.

Savi's leg and ankle were bleeding badly and needed immediate attention. Though weak, her breathing was steadily improving. Unfortunately, there were no medical supplies to treat her. So instead of bandages, they used Conner's shirtsleeve to wrap around Savi's ankle to stop or at least slow down the bleeding.

"Savi, we made it," Jade said, tears streaming down her face. "You saved our lives."

Savi looked up and smiled, but she was still too weak to saying anything.

Rico, still hurting himself, carefully slid over to Savi and squeezed her hand tenderly. Then, he kissed her gently on the forehead. Rico's unexpected kiss brought a blush of color back to Savi's unusually pale face.

"You risked your life to save us," Rico whispered appreciatively. "You could have died out there. Savi, I—"

"Look!" Conner shouted interrupting what Rico was about to say to Savi.

"Vexel is finished! He's about to be swept down the river!" Conner directed everyone's attention to the sandbar where the wounded bear was struggling against the rising water.

Vexel stood on his hind legs and roared ferociously in their direction. In a few seconds, the sandbar disappeared, and moments later, Vexel was swept downriver by the powerful current. The last they saw of him, he was flying down the river and paddling frantically. A short time later, to everyone's relief, he flew around a curve in the channel and disappeared.

"Do you think he'll drown?" Jade asked.

"I hope so," Luke said, speaking for the first time since reaching shore.

"The current is so powerful I don't see how he can survive," Jade asserted.

"Well, I'm not gonna believe he's dead until I see it with my own eyes," Luke replied.

Suddenly they heard the unmistakable thump, thump, thump of propeller blades cutting through the air. Looking up, they noticed the black silhouette of a helicopter against the cobalt blue sky. It appeared to be the kind of chopper that delivered packages and supplies to Camp Arrowhead on occasion. The longer they stared at it, the closer it came toward them.

When the helicopter flew over the shore area, Jade began jumping up and down and waving her arms frantically. At first, the helicopter pilot flew over them as if he hadn't seen them yet. Then, he quickly banked the chopper hard to the right and circled back around, affirming that he had indeed spotted the survivors.

Within minutes, the chopper descended and hovered around forty feet above the beach. It was now so close that the wind from its blades stirred up dust and debris from the shore. Moments later, the side door of the aircraft slid open, and a man with a bullhorn yelled out.

"We see you! Don't move! We know you have injuries! We are dropping a medical kit! Help is on the way!"

Chapter Thirty-Three

It was finally over. No one could believe they had survived. It seemed almost dreamlike as they watched the rescue helicopter hover above them.

For a second time, the bullhorn sounded from the chopper. It cautioned the survivors again that a crewmember was going to drop a medical kit onto the beach. The container slammed into the sand and bounced a couple of times before settling down about fifty feet away from the group. Jade scurried over and retrieved the kit; she unlatched it and quickly pulled out all the supplies she would need to treat everyone's injuries.

Savi's ankle was still bleeding though Conner's shirt did aid in slowing down the blood flow from the gashes. And even though she was obviously still hurting, all of them were relieved her breathing had returned to normal again. With each passing minute, Savi was looking more and more like herself.

Everyone appreciated Jade's helpfulness in tending to their injuries. She cleaned and disinfected Savi's wounds thoroughly and then bandaged them carefully.

Quietly, Luke, Rico, and Conner watched as Jade tended to Savi's needs. They observed her with admiration and marveled at how poised and skilled she had become in dealing with severe injuries. It was fascinating to see how much she had grown in that sense in such a short time. Rico joked with Conner and said he was going to nickname her, "Nurse."

In addition to the medical kit, the crewman dropped several bottles of water and a few packets of trail mix, a combination of dried fruits and nuts. Jade and Conner retrieved the water and welcome snacks, and everyone ate and drank happily except Savi. When Jade offered her some water, she declined it politely. She was only interested in the trail mix.

"I think I've had enough water for one day," she said, smiling at Jade.

Jade grinned back. Then she bent over and gave Savi a friendly kiss on the forehead.

"God spared you, Savi. I know it was Him," Jade said with tears welling in her eyes. "Luke helped, but only God could have saved you like that."

"You won't hear me arguing with you."

For the next several minutes, everyone was quiet. They appeared to be reflecting on the ordeal. Overcome with a sense of gratitude they patiently waited on the beach for the help they had been promised to arrive.

Fifteen minutes later . . .

Rico, Conner, and Luke sat leaning against some small trees nearby while Savi was still recovering and was propped up against a rock. Jade had just finished attending to Rico's injuries and now sat quietly beside him.

"Luke, you saved my life," Savi said with genuine thankfulness. "I had given up. I thought I was dead."

"Missy, after everything you've been through, I couldn't let that happen, could I?" he said with a smile. "Savi, the world needs more people like you. God must still have some mighty big plans for your life. It just wasn't your time to go home."

Savi reached out and held Luke's hand tenderly. She took a few seconds and studied each of her companions' faces. Then with a sense of purpose, she reached down in front of her and took the next few moments to select four different palm sized stones. As she carefully examined the rocks in her hands, tears began to well up in her eyes. Before long they were running down her face. With her head bowed Savi sat for a few moments in silence. No one was quite sure what she was doing. Finally, she looked up.

"I'd like to say a few things to each of you," she said.

First, she turned to Luke and handed him an oval shaped red-colored rock.

"This stone is a symbol of our friendship and how I'll always be thankful for what you did for us. Without you, none of us would be here right now, especially me. I hope you know, no matter how long I live, I will never forget you. I will always think of you as a close friend."

Luke, took the stone appreciatively, nodded, and smiled down at the young girl he had just rescued. No words were spoken or needed to be. A mutual admiration was apparent to everyone observing the exchange.

Next Savi turned to Conner and handed him a light gray rock she had selected just for him.

"I hope this rock will always remind you that you don't have to try to be anyone else but you. You are a caring person who is funny and brave. And now you have a couple of fresh scars to prove it," she said smiling.

Conner felt a lump grow in his throat, and an embarrassed look flashed across his face. At the moment, all he could think to say was a simple, "Thanks."

Then Savi turned to Jade and handed a small light brown speckled colored rock to her.

"Jade, despite everything you've gone through in the past, I want you always to remember how special you are. And it's not just your beauty that makes you exceptional, it's your heart. Over the course of this trip, you learned to be strong and courageous. I must say, it took you a while, but you got there."
Everyone including Jade smiled.

"We all know, in the end, you played a major role in saving Rico and Conner's lives."

Both Rico and Conner shook their heads in agreement while Jade sat and relished Savi's encouragement.

Finally, Savi looked at the last dark-colored stone she held as if it were a precious gem. Unexpectedly, a fresh stream of tears started to flow. Embarrassed by her tears, she slowly lifted her wet face and gazed into Rico's dark brown eyes. When she did, her face glowed and revealed something inside her that touched Rico deeply. She glanced down at the dark-colored stone and handed it to him.

"You are a tough but tender warrior and remind me so much of my dad. He never quits, and neither did you, even through the most difficult of circumstances."

"I would have given up if it wasn't for you," he said sincerely. "I'd be dead right now, but you forced me to keep going."

"And you kept me going, too," Jade added. "Even when I was freaking out and wanted to give up, you never let me."

"Thanks for saying that, but I still feel terrible that I slapped you," Savi recalled with regret.

Then Savi looked back at Rico.

"Someday, God willing, I'm gonna get married, and I want my husband to be a lot like you. Too bad you already have a girlfriend," she said with a blush and a glance at Jade.

For the next few minutes, everyone sat in silence and thought about the things Savi had said.

Then Luke bent down and picked up a smooth white stone. He held it for a moment, and then, to everyone's surprise, he touched the rock to his lips, kissed it gently, and handed it to Savi.

"Savi, since I was a little boy my momma taught me to live my life so that when I get to heaven, I will hear seven words."

"What do you mean?" Savi asked curiously. "What seven words?"

He paused a moment and studied her kind but tired face. Then he looked into her eyes. "She meant the seven words that I'm about to say to you, missy." Luke handed her the white stone and said, "Well done, my good and faithful servant."

Deeply humbled, Savi bowed her head and started to weep.

The delicate moment was interrupted by sounds in the distance of the helicopter approaching again. Meanwhile, several vehicles came zooming down the access road toward them. The first truck skidded to stop, and a man sprang out of the front seat and started to run straight toward them. Immediately, they could see he had a big bandage wrapped around his forehead. Although no one was sure who he was, he did look strangely familiar the closer he got to them.

Jade was the first to recognize him. Without saying a word, she sprang to her feet and hurried over to meet him. Puzzled, the others looked on in stunned silence. When the two of them reached each other, Jade practically leaped into the man's arms.

"Oh, my God, Doug! You're alive!"

Though they had just met days earlier, the two of them hugged like old friends reunited. After a short time of conversing with Jade, Doug gave her a fatherly kiss on her forehead, and the two of them made their way over to Savi, Rico, Conner, and Luke.

"I can't believe you guys are alive!" Doug exclaimed. "We all thought you had drowned. Finding you alive is a miracle!"

"You have no idea how much of a miracle," Savi sighed.

Jade took another look at Doug and slapped her wrist, just to make sure that she wasn't dreaming.

"We thought you had drowned, Doug!" Conner told him. "How did you survive the rapids after you fell out of the raft?"

Doug ran his fingers through his hair. "As soon as I hit the cold water, I woke up. Once I got my bearings and started to realize what was happening, I rolled over on my back and pointed my feet down river. I rode the rapids about a quarter mile until it slowed, then I swam to shore. A short time later, another raft came downstream and rescued me. As soon as the bus got to the pickup point, I used the radio to report the accident. Rescue teams have been searching for you guys ever since."

"We saw aerial rescue teams in the distance a few times and tried to signal them, but they never saw us," Savi said with an air of frustration.

"And who might this be?" Doug asked no one in particular.

"Oh, I'm sorry. I forgot to introduce you guys." Rico perked up. "Doug, this is Luke. He found us in the wilderness, thank God, and rescued us from a pack of wolves. We couldn't have survived without him," Jade contended.

Just then, a medical team arrived and began working on Savi, Rico, and Conner. Jade also had some bruises and cuts on her arms and legs, but besides that, she was in reasonably good condition, especially when considering what she had endured the last couple days.

During their examinations, the sound of another helicopter filled the air. This one was a rescue helicopter designed to transport up to six injured passengers.

Within twenty minutes, the rescue team had carefully secured everyone into the craft and quickly returned them to Camp Arrowhead where a temporary triage center had been set up for the survivors.

Rico was the first into surgery, followed by Savi, and then Conner.

Within a couple of hours, they were all lying side by side in a large recovery area with Luke, Jade, and Doug by their bedsides.

Chapter Thirty-Four

Leaders of the rescue team notified family members that the campers had been rescued and were undergoing a variety of non-life-threatening medical procedures. Anxious yet relieved parents quickly made their way to Camp Arrowhead from the nearby town of Evergreen. Several of the survivors' relatives had spent the past week there waiting for news from the search teams.

Conner's family was first to arrive at Camp Arrowhead, then Rico's dad, and Savi's parents. Welcome hugs and unbounded joy was visible everywhere at the tearful reunion, except when it came to Jade. After all the introductions, it was obvious her parents were missing. She tried to hide her disappointment and tears but soon lost the battle when she noticed everyone else being welcomed back so warmly and enthusiastically.

Suddenly a huge commotion erupted down the hall. Everyone could hear a hysterical woman yelling loudly.

"What do think is happening?" Savi asked Jade, lifting her head and looking in the direction of the uproar.

At first, Jade seemed to ignore Savi's question. Instead of answering her, she took a moment to compose herself and listen carefully to the woman making all the commotion in the corridor. Then she looked back at Savi, shook her head, and rolled her eyes. "I'm guessing my mom just got here."

Jade's suspicion about who was creating the uproar was confirmed immediately. Right on cue, Jade's mom burst into the room with a distraught look on her face. Her hands were waving wildly in the air and the smell of strong perfume assaulted the shocked onlookers.

"Where is she?" she shouted, looking around in a panic. "I don't see my girl!"

"Mom, I'm over here," Jade answered with her inside voice.

"Oh, my baby! We thought we'd lost you." Then she bent down and hugged her daughter tightly.

"Where's Dad?"

"Oh, he's away on business. He told me to send his love."

Jade received the hug gracefully, but couldn't ignore the conflicted feelings swirling around inside her. For too long she had buried her feelings toward her mother. But, in that moment, she realized she could no longer pretend. Those days were over.

Unexpectedly, Jade pulled away and held her mother at arm's length. Looking at her squarely in the eyes, she spoke in a solemn and deliberate tone. "When we get home, we need to talk," she told her.

Instantly, a look of concern shot across her mom's face.

"What's going on? Is there something wrong with you?" she asked anxiously.

"Oh no, that's not it at all. I'm doing fine. It's not me we need to talk about, it's about the way you've been treating me!"

Instantly, her mom's face flushed red, and her anger began to flare. She knew what Jade meant. Her harsh and abusive treatment of her daughter was no longer an unspoken secret. Shocked and embarrassed, she quickly suppressed her rage and decided it was best to hold her tongue.

Just then the medical team entered the room and insisted the family visits come to an end. Everyone was quick to agree that the survivors all needed to get some much-needed rest.

Savi, Rico, Jade, and Conner said goodbye to their parents but asked for a few extra minutes of privacy to say their goodbyes to each other.

Though it took a little time to clear the room, reluctantly the parents finally departed, leaving the teens and Luke alone and together again.

After the families had gone, Conner was the first to speak.

"I'm going to miss you guys a lot," he confessed with an air of genuine sadness. "I really want to stay in touch. After what we've been through, you're more than just my friends."

Rico looked at Conner, shook his head, and smiled.

"I can't believe I'm saying this to you, Hot Dog, but I want to stay in touch with you, too."

"I'll never forget any of you," Jade promised. "This was the worst and best experience of my life. Savi, don't forget to call me as soon as you get home, okay?"

"Sure. I was already planning on it," Savi acknowledged.

"Thanks for everything, including the slap," Jade said with a smile and tears starting to roll down her cheeks. "I'll miss you all so much."

"You're always welcome to come to San Antonio for a visit," Rico offered.

"Same goes for San Francisco," Jade replied.

"And Chicago," added Conner.

"If you ever want to experience some Southern hospitality? Come and see me in Oxford, Mississippi," Savi drawled.

"Well, I guess its time to say goodbye again," Luke, said. "I'm headed back down to the river to make sure that Vexel is dead. You all keep in touch. Here's my address. I told you before that we live deep in the woods and far away from town. You'll probably laugh . . . we don't even have a phone or computer at the cabin. But occasionally I go into town and check my email. We also have a post office box, if any of you still write cards or letters. I'll get you that address."

"I'll email you for sure," Savi promised. "You can count on hearing from me in the next couple of weeks."

The others also agreed to do the same.

First, Luke shook hands with Rico and Conner.

"You guys should be proud of yourselves. You did great out there considering what happened on that river."

Then he moved over to Jade and hugged her. When he finished, he held her hands, leaned back, and looked at her with admiration. "You're quite a girl, Jade. You stepped up in a big way at the end and helped save these guys. I wouldn't have thought you had it in you," he said with a wink. "I mean, you being a city girl and all."

Jade's eyes filled with tears again as she looked at Luke. Lost for words, she hugged him again, convinced it was for the last time.

"Thanks for everything," she finally whispered, squeezing his hand as he started to walk away.

Finally, Luke stepped over to Savi's bedside, bent down, and kissed her gently on the forehead.

"Well, missy, as I told you before, God must have some big plans for your life. You should have died out there more than a few times." Suddenly, tears welled up in Luke's eyes. "I need you to know my life is better because I met you, missy. And I haven't said that to very many people."

Savi and Jade could not hold back their tears. As Luke was about to leave the two girls wept openly. Even Rico and Conner were misty-eyed. Then Luke walked out of the room and disappeared around a corner.

"Do you think we'll ever see him again?" Jade asked.

"I can't say for sure," Savi replied. "But something inside tells me that we just might see him again."

The next morning . . .

By mid-morning, the parents had gathered the remaining gear from each of the teens' cabins and once again assembled at the triage center. Conner's parents were the first to talk to the doctor on duty and sign his discharge papers. After securing permission for him to leave, they helped him gather his belongings and get ready to depart for home. One by one the other parents did the same thing and eventually made their way to the circle drive to load up their cars and head out. After a heartwrenching and tearful goodbye to his friends, Conner slowly walked away with his mom to find his dad who was patiently waiting for him in the car. Savi, Rico, and Jade watched with sadness as their friend was driven away. Together they waved enthusiastically until the vehicle was out of sight.

Mrs. Chang pulled up in her rental car and tooted the horn twice to alert Jade she was ready to go. Jade rolled her eyes and motioned to her mother emphatically that she needed a minute. Savi gave Jade a big hug and said her farewells. Jade hugged her back and made her promise she'd stay in touch. When they had finished, Savi discreetly wandered away knowing that Rico and Jade needed some space. Savi watched intently as Rico walked Jade to the car where her mother was waiting impatiently. Not wanting to hear another honk, Jade hugged Rico quickly and tightly and talked about staying in touch and visiting one another someday soon. The two of them stood by the car and Savi watched as Rico wiped streaming tears from Jade's cheeks. They hugged for the last time, and then Jade got into the car and reluctantly shut the door. No sooner had Jade closed the door when her mom sped away with a fury that left another trail of dust similar to the one she had when she dropped Jade off at Camp Arrowhead the first time. Rico quickly retreated to avoid being engulfed by the dust storm and made his way back to Savi.

"That must have been hard to do," Savi offered.

"Goodbyes are always rough," Rico sighed.

"I wish we didn't have to say it to each other," Savi lowered her head.

"So how about we don't say it," Rico suggested.

"Yeah, let's not!" Savi looked up with tears and smiled.

Savi's parents and Rico's dad shook hands. After hearing tales of the adventure, the parents' were so thankful their loved ones had survived the harrowing ordeal. Mr. Cruz was especially thankful to Savi as Rico had shared with him about Savi's tough love that got him across the river despite his wanting to give up. Following a few more minutes of conversation, Rico's dad shook hands warmly with Savi's parents and then they went off to get their cars. For a few moments, Savi and Rico were alone. They stared at each other, but as agreed, no farewells were exchanged.

Finally, Rico grabbed Savi's hand. "Thanks again for saving my life," he said while looking tenderly into her eyes. "It's going to be so weird not seeing you every day."

Savi tried to fight back her tears but could not. "I'm going to miss you, too," she said as she smiled, which only made her tears flow even more. As they hugged, they both heard their parents' cars roll up in the driveway behind them.

"I'll call you in a couple days," said Rico.

"I'll count on it," Savi replied as cheerfully as she could.

Mr. Cruz waited patiently as Rico and Savi hugged one last time. Rico took Savi's chin in his hand and then kissed her forehead, causing Savi to blush.

Rico got in the air-conditioned car and slowly closed the door. Then he placed his hand on the window with his palm out. Savi stepped forward and put her hand on the other side of the glass over his. They both smiled and nodded. The car slowly pulled away. Savi raised her arm. Rico signaled back through the rear window.

Before the vehicle disappeared, Rico stuck his arm out the window and waved one last time. Blinded by her tears, Savi whispered, "I don't hate you, Rico." Then as quickly as he had come into her life, he was gone.

Instinctively, Savi reached into her vest pocket and pulled out her compass. As she held it in her hand, a host of memories flooded into her mind. Then with a sense of resolve, she pointed the compass toward the last spot she saw Rico wave at her and said softly, "Lord, you helped us find our way back, now help me find my way forward. And in case that means running into Rico again, I'm just fine with that!"

Now grinning, Savi opened the car door and sat down. Within moments the car headed for the airport. It seemed the adventure was finally ending, or was it just beginning?

THE END OF BOOK ONE

88886251R00146

Made in the USA
Middletown, DE
12 September 2018